"*The Heart Stone*, appropriately titled and powerfully written, is indeed a 'heart-grabber' from first page to last. Author Sherry Kyle pens her story with emotion and insight, bringing her characters to life and enabling readers to care about what happens to them. More than just a good story, *The Heart Stone* challenges us to consider the hard places in our own heart—and to turn them over to the One who stands waiting to heal and restore."
—Kathi Macias, author of *The Moses Quilt* and *Last Chance for Justice*

"Love—and Sherry Kyle's new book *The Heart Stone*—is for hearts of all ages. It's a heartwarming story that testifies to the enduring power of faith, hope, and love."
—Kathy Harris, author of *The Road to Mercy*

"*The Heart Stone* is a gem of a book, with a lot of heart and a hint of mystery. Parents and grandparents will love how Sherry Kyle weaves two unlikely love stories together in a realistic yet redemptive way. Oh, and little Jacob often threatens to steal the show. Great pacing, with warm, unforgettable characters."
—Linda S. Clare, *The Fence My Father Built*

Other books by Sherry Kyle

Delivered With Love

THE HEART STONE

Sherry Kyle

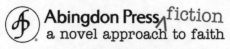
Abingdon Press fiction
a novel approach to faith

Nashville, Tennessee

The Heart Stone
Copyright © 2013 by Sherry Kyle

ISBN: 978-14267-3351-2

Published by Abingdon Press, P.O. Box 801, Nashville, TN 37202
www.abingdonpress.com

Library of Congress Cataloging-in-Publication Data has been
requested.

Printed in the United States of America

1 2 3 4 5 6 7 8 9 10 / 18 17 16 15 14 13

For Doug,
My hero, my love,
and my best friend

Acknowledgments

My heartfelt thanks and appreciation go out to my loving family. Doug, Carson, Brittany, Noah, and Grace—it's all because of your love, support, and encouragement that this book is a reality. Thank you to my parents, Roy and Billie Hoffman for always being there for me and cheering me on.

I am grateful for my critique group: Karen O'Connor, Miralee Ferrell, and Kimberly Johnson. Thanks, gals, for all your grammar changes, comments, and smiley faces. This book is better because of you.

I'm blessed to have such wonderful friends and cheerleaders—Marcia, Barbara, Suzy, Michelle, Kelly, Kira Lee, Sylvia, and Karen. You're the best!

To the American Christian Fiction Writers, the Christian Authors Network, as well as the many mentors of the Mount Hermon Christian Writers Conference, who have provided me with a wealth of wisdom, knowledge, and support. Thank you.

Thank you to my agent, Etta Wilson, for believing in me. Even though I didn't want you to retire, I'm grateful Rachel Kent chose to represent me. What a blessing!

A big thank you to Ramona Richards, my editor at Abingdon Press, as well as Julie Dowd and the sales team, for bringing this story to life. I'm so grateful I get to work with you.

Thank you, Misty Taggert, from Trailer to the Stars, for making such a wonderful book trailer. I can't believe I was so fortunate to win a book promotion package.

And most important, thank you to my Heavenly Father who shows me each and every day how much He loves me. Your grace knows no bounds.

1

Fresno, California

Jessi, it's Andrew . . . Andrew Lawson."

At the sound of his voice, Jessica MacAllister's knees went limp and her palms grew moist. She sat down on the wooden stool near the kitchen counter and leaned her head on her hand, her elbow resting against the cold tile. Why was he calling? She hadn't heard from him since he signed the papers relinquishing his rights to Jacob six years before.

"Jessi, you there?"

She fought the urge to hang up the phone. "I'm here."

"I want to see him."

Her heart beat a strange rhythm. She had prayed this day would never come. "Andrew, I—I—I don't know," she stuttered. As a speech pathologist, she prided herself on her communication skills, but this man could trip her up regardless of her training.

"We can meet at a park. I'll sit at a distance and watch." The desperation in his voice was palpable.

Jessica's jaw clenched and her stomach churned. How could she trust that he wouldn't rush up to Jacob and tell him that he was his biological father? Or worse, what if he wasn't sober? His behavior when he was drunk could be . . . No.

She wouldn't let a man who had no part in Jacob's upbringing suddenly waltz into his life—especially someone who had shown her the ways of the world. But Andrew wasn't entirely to blame. She'd given in.

"No. No, that won't work." Jessica ran her hand through her shoulder-length hair.

"How about a restaurant? I'll eat at a separate table. I only want to see our son."

Our son. Jacob was not *their* son. He was hers and hers only. Andrew wasn't there for her when she was pregnant or gave birth. He'd never been there. Why the sudden interest now?

When Jessica woke this morning, she planned to spend the whole afternoon with Jacob—alone. What right did Andrew have to show up in her life after she'd assumed he was long gone? He'd abandoned her when she needed him most. The wound hurt deep and it would take a lot more than a casual demand.

A fire burned in her belly. "The answer is no—"

"Mommy, who you talking to?" Jacob padded into the kitchen, clad in his dinosaur pajamas. He rubbed the sleep from his eyes.

"Is that my boy?" Andrew's voice rose.

Jessica stared at her innocent son. Her hand shook and a lump lodged in her throat. She couldn't tell Jacob who was calling, and she couldn't tell Andrew the small voice he heard was indeed his son's.

"Come on, Jessi, work with me here—"

A firm resolve flowed through her veins. She wouldn't allow Andrew to worm his way into her son's life. Not now, not ever. "I've got to go." She pressed the off button and hung up the receiver.

"Hungry, buddy?" On shaky legs, she swung around the counter. She hoped Jacob didn't notice how rattled she felt. "How about some pancakes?"

"With chocolate chips?" He hopped on a stool and grinned, showing the gap that once held a baby tooth.

Several months ago, she'd made his favorite pancakes for his birthday. And now, after receiving the unexpected phone call from his birthfather, she'd give Jacob anything he wanted. "Sure." She smiled back.

"Can we go see Uncle George today?" Jacob pleaded.

"Thought you wanted to spend the day with me." A twinge of jealousy twisted her insides.

She chided herself, and then grabbed a mixing bowl from the cabinet. Uncle George had been through a difficult patch lately. If they could spend an hour or two visiting, it would make a world of difference to the older man.

"I've never seen someone without a leg." Jacob's eyes grew big and round.

Jessica cringed—neither had she. Why hadn't she taken the time to visit her uncle before now? The answer made her pulse race. Fear. The smell of hospitals and rehabilitation centers turned her stomach. Glancing down at her hand, the heart-shaped stone glistened and caught the light filtering through the window. Uncle George had given her the diamond ring when he found out she was pregnant with Jacob to fend off any unwanted advances—or unwanted questions. He had said, "It's hard enough being a single parent."

"Can we, Mom?" Jacob's voice interrupted her thoughts.

The phone rang. She recognized the number from moments ago. *Andrew.*

The phone rang twice more.

Jessica continued to gather the utensils and ingredients for the pancakes. Maybe if she ignored him, he'd go away.

"Can I answer it?" Jacob reached for the phone.

"NO!" She stopped him, and then clicked the off button of the answering machine before it could pick up.

"Who keeps calling?" Melissa, her roommate of a couple years, strode into the room. Her short blonde hair stuck out here and there, and her pink jersey T-shirt hung almost to her knees over navy sweat pants.

Jessica shot her a "don't ask" look, and then gestured to her little boy. "Jacob and I are going to Santa Cruz today to see Uncle George."

"Yeah!" Jacob hopped off the stool and thrust his arms in the air. He ran around the table like a speeding train pumping his small fists.

"Whoa, buddy." Jessica caught him, wrapping her arms around his chest. "Jacob, listen. I need to talk with Melissa. Why don't you watch cartoons and I'll call you when the pancakes are ready." Jessica rubbed the top of his head, his soft, brown hair slipping between her fingers.

"Okay." He ran toward the couch. On his way, he reached down and grabbed his favorite dump truck from the floor, and then huddled in the corner cushion of the sofa.

Jessica flipped on the television, then motioned for her roommate to join her in her bedroom.

"What's up?" Melissa planted her hands on her hips. "You're acting strange."

"It's Jacob's birthfather. I spoke with him this morning." Jessica paced the room. She grabbed her purple terrycloth robe and slipped it over her shoulders. "I hung up on him. And now he's calling again."

"What does he want?" Melissa sat on the edge of Jessica's unmade bed and covered her legs with the striped comforter.

"To see Jacob." Jessica leaned against the wall, slid down, and landed with a thud on the hardwood floor.

"Has he ever been part of Jacob's life?"

"No, and I won't let him start now. When he found out I was pregnant, he made it clear he didn't want anything to do with the baby or me. He even blamed me for sleeping around, saying the baby wasn't his." Jessica hugged her legs with both arms. "I wish I'd never gone to Mexico on that college trip. But I did." She sighed. "My roommates and I wanted to celebrate. I knew better."

"Celebrate what?"

"Graduation from Fresno State." Jessica bit her lower lip. "We were seniors looking for a good time. That's where I met Andrew." She stared at the floor, wishing the memories away.

"Don't be too hard on yourself. You have a beautiful little boy." Melissa stood and meandered over to where Jessica sat. Holding out both hands, she pulled her up. "From now on, I'll answer the phone. I think Jacob's waiting for those pancakes." Her roommate was never one to mope and she wouldn't allow Jessica to either.

She cinched the belt of her robe. "Please don't tell Jacob who called."

"Never in a million years." Melissa led her back to the kitchen. "So, when do you leave for Santa Cruz?"

"Right after breakfast."

"It's spring break. Why don't you take the whole week? I'll ward off any unwanted callers."

With Jacob having time off from school, Jessica *had* cancelled all her clients. Her speech pathology business, *Speak Easy*, would take a hit financially but she'd promised Jacob to spend time with him. Santa Cruz sounded great. Still . . . .

"But tomorrow is Easter and we planned a big dinner. I can't leave you alone." Jessica poured a cup of coffee and handed it to Melissa. "I bought more vanilla creamer. It's in the side door of the refrigerator."

"Don't worry about me." Melissa's eyes danced. "A guy from work hinted he had no place to go."

"Oh, I get it." Jessica grinned. "Don't let us get in your way."

"It's not like that, and you know it." Melissa returned the tease. "I was going to ask you today if he could join us, but since you're leaving town, I didn't want you to worry." She grabbed the creamer and poured a hefty portion into her coffee.

"If it makes you feel any better, I'm glad you'll have company."

"Where will you stay in Santa Cruz?"

"My uncle has a trailer. I'm sure we can crash there." Jessica cracked two eggs into a bowl and beat them before adding the flour, baking powder, sugar, and milk to the bowl. "He's going to be surprised to see us. I've been hesitating—didn't want to scare Jacob. He's never seen someone without a leg."

Melissa took a swig of her coffee. "Jacob didn't look scared to me. Are you sure you're not the one who's nervous?" She winked.

Jessica placed a small bowl of butter in the microwave. "Okay, you got me there. I admit I'm scared. I can't imagine my uncle, someone I've leaned on for strength my whole life, needing assistance. I'm glad the nurses at Pacific Coast Manor are available around the clock." She stirred the batter gently, leaving small clumps of dry ingredients. "I almost forgot the chocolate chips."

"In the pancake batter? It's not anyone's birthday." Melissa opened the cabinet above the dishwasher and handed the bag to Jessica. "You really are worried about that phone call."

Jessica nodded and let out a breath.

Melissa sidled up to her and spoke in hushed tones. "Remember, it's not the end of the world. So, he wants to see his son. Are you sure that would be a bad thing?"

Jessica scrunched up her nose and looked directly at her roommate. "I'm positive." She placed a frying pan on the stove and turned the heat to medium low before she added a handful of chocolate chips to the mix.

Melissa dropped a pat of butter into the pan. "Okay, if you're sure, then I'm with you on this."

"Thank you."

"But promise me you'll take this week to really think it through. Jacob needs a man in his life. And you haven't brought one around since he was born." Melissa sprinkled a few flecks of water into the pan. The drops sizzled.

"You forget. We're going to visit my *uncle*. He's the best role model I could ask for. No other man is needed." Jessica poured circles of batter onto the hot griddle.

"If you say so."

"Jacob, can you please turn off the television," Jessica called. "It's time for pancakes."

———

"Buckle up." Jessica glanced over her shoulder at her six-year-old. He sat in his booster seat between several suitcases, clutching his stuffed teddy bear.

"How long 'til we get there?" Jacob clicked the seat belt.

"About three hours, give or take."

She couldn't get out of her apartment fast enough. Considering she hadn't heard from Andrew in years, he'd suddenly become persistent. He must have done plenty of searching to locate her unlisted phone number. She'd been careful to keep her whereabouts a secret.

Melissa stood by the curb waving as Jessica turned the key.

"Jacob, wave goodbye."

"Why can't Melissa come?" Jacob leaned toward the door and moved his hand back and forth.

"Because she has a special guest coming for Easter dinner tomorrow." Jessica grinned.

No one should be alone on a holiday, including Uncle George. It had been at least two years since the last time they'd been together, and she hadn't been with him much before that either, although they'd always stayed in touch. His ministry to the people in the Philippines had spanned decades. She knew he'd hoped to live out his days there, but his high fever and toe infection brought him back home to the States. No amount of antibiotics could cure the gangrene that set in or the hearing loss in his right ear. His left leg was amputated below the knee, and he was fitted for a hearing aid. And now, according to the nurses, he was becoming more and more withdrawn as the days wore on. Jessica could hear it in his voice every time she called. The last thing she wanted to do was add to his troubles by telling him about her problems. But still, he'd always been there for her in the past.

After weaving through town to load her car with gas, she turned onto CA-180W toward CA-99 and drove her Honda Civic with the air conditioner on full blast. She flipped on the radio and sang along.

"Mommy."

Jessica looked into her rearview mirror. "Yes?"

"I need to go potty." He bit his lower lip.

Jessica let out a sigh and stared back at the road. "Didn't I tell you to go before we left?"

"I forgot."

"I'll look for a rest stop. You may need to wait until we get to Madera."

"How long is that?"

"Twenty miles." Jessica glanced at him once more. Her son's brows were furrowed, his lips pinched, and his arms were tightly wrapped around his stuffed animal. The life of a six-year-old was hard. She stifled a grin. If worse came to worst, she'd pull over to the side of the road.

"When we gonna get there?" Jacob whined.

This was going to be a long trip.

2

Santa Cruz, California

Jessica held Jacob's hand as they stood in the hallway outside Uncle George's room at Pacific Coast Manor. A knot formed in her stomach. The nurses had kept Jessica updated on his status these past couple months with phone calls. He wasn't happy. Most were amazed at her uncle's recovery despite his negative attitude. The last time Jessica spoke with the physician, he said the time had come for Uncle George to be released. They'd done all they could for him. Now it was up to Uncle George whether or not he'd use the prosthetic leg.

"What are we waiting for?" Jacob tugged on Jessica's arm.

A queasy sensation made its way up her throat. Skilled nursing facilities made her nauseous. She eyed Jacob.

He smiled up at her, apparently more relaxed than she. "Come on, Mom. I can't wait any longer."

Leave it to her son to push her forward and give her courage. Jessica grinned. "You're right. Uncle George needs someone like you around to lift his spirits."

"Can we go in *now*?" Jacob once again pulled her arm.

"Yes." Jessica took one step toward the door to the room when her son bolted in. "Jacob, wait!" She scurried to catch up with him.

The sight of her aging uncle sent ripples of grief washing over her. Why hadn't she visited him before now? Besides the one hundred and sixty miles that separated them, the answer was obvious. Work. It had always been her excuse—work and raising Jacob. Being a single parent took its toll. Now she realized how much time had passed since she'd seen him last. Uncle George's skin looked pasty, he'd grown a beard, and he'd lost weight. He sat in a wheelchair, his pant leg tucked under his left knee and thigh revealing the hard fact that he was dealing with the loss of his calf and foot. His prosthetic limb leaned haphazardly in the corner of the small room.

"Uncle George, it's me, Jacob!" Her son wrapped his arms around the man's neck like a monkey hugging a tree.

The man coughed. "You're choking me, boy—" His brows knit together as he unwrapped Jacob's arms to catch his breath.

Jessica cleared her throat. "Jacob, remember what I told you. Slow down, okay?"

"Oh, yeah." Jacob stepped back and stared at George's stump. His nose wrinkled. "Does it hurt real bad?"

"Jacob!" Jessica scolded. "Sorry about that, Uncle George." She approached and laid a hand on his shoulder. "It's good to see you."

George grunted.

"Tomorrow is Easter." Jacob sat on the edge of the twin bed. "I'm going to get lots of candy, right, Mom?" He turned his face toward Uncle George, not waiting for her reply. "Maybe you can have some, too. Candy always makes me happy."

Bless Jacob for trying to put a smile on her uncle's face. The nurses were right. The man had turned bitter, different from the vibrant missionary who could light up a room and win people to Christ. Now, he sat in his wheelchair with a scowl on his face, his hands nervously clutching the armrests.

Better get right to the point of the visit. She wanted to help George transition back to normal life, or at least his *new* life. Jessica sat beside Jacob on the bed and directed her words at her uncle. "The doctor told me you're ready to go home."

"Sold my mobile home a few months ago." Uncle George barked. "Don't know where I'll go."

The shocking news jarred her. Her uncle had owned a trailer by the beach for as long as she'd known him. Why would he sell? Didn't he think he was going to get better?

George rubbed the back of his neck. "I'd rather stay here."

"I understand," said Jessica. "The nurses take good care of you and you've become comfortable here, but it's time to move on. Jacob and I will help you all we can."

Uncle George had always been there for her, especially when she was dealing with an unwanted pregnancy and low self-esteem, and now it was time for her to reciprocate.

"What's the use?" He wheeled himself toward the window and looked out.

Maybe he'd enjoy moving to Fresno. The moment the thought came to mind she knew it would never happen. There were only two places her uncle would live—near the beach in Santa Cruz, or on the eastern shores of Manila Bay in the Philippines where he'd been on and off for the past forty-something years.

Jessica joined him near the window and rested her hand on top of his. Trees lined the U-shaped building and sculpted bushes dotted the main quad area. She must help him see that he could take care of himself on his own. "You know I love you and want the best for you. Just because you've lost part of your leg doesn't mean you can't lead a productive life. I will be here to help you." Her words echoed her uncle's sentiments after she told him of her pregnancy. If only he'd remember, but he could be as stubborn as she. It took the entire nine months for Jessica to see God's plan in her situation.

"This is different." George turned his head.

Jessica glanced at Jacob. He was slumped on the bed, distracted by the remote used to move the bed up and down. She wouldn't scold him. In fact, she was glad he was preoccupied. She didn't want him to hear the tough words she might have to say to get through to her uncle.

"How is it different?" she challenged.

"You were just starting out. I'm at the tail end." He flicked his hand in the air.

"Uncle George, you're in your sixties." Jessica pulled up the small chair in the corner of the room and sat down next to him. "There's still plenty of time for you to reach out to others like you've always done. If not in Manila, then here."

"I don't have a home to go to . . ."

"Yes, that's a problem. But one we can handle together." Jessica looked around the room for a newspaper. "We'll start looking. Jacob and I have all afternoon." She glanced at her watch. "I'll talk with the supervisor and see if you can stay a few more days, and then I'll book a hotel for Jacob and me." At that moment, Jessica was glad she put her nerves aside and came to Santa Cruz. If she'd known her uncle had sold his trailer, she would've come the moment she heard he needed to leave the facility.

George sighed. "I know you're wondering . . ."

"About?" Jessica prodded.

"I sold the mobile home to help out a friend who needed money. Didn't think I was ever getting out of here so it didn't matter."

Jessica folded her arms across her chest. Her uncle would give away the shirt off his back. "And where is this friend now?"

She reined in her feelings, hoping her voice didn't betray her feelings.

George's shoulders sagged. "Don't know. Haven't heard from him since the money was deposited into his account." What else had her uncle given away? She hoped he had some left to support himself.

"How much rent can you afford?" Her tone rose a few notches.

"Like I said, I want to live here." He rubbed his temples.

The only way Jessica was going to get to the bottom of this was to talk with the supervisor. She wouldn't be able to find her uncle a place to rent until she knew more details about his care and financial situation.

"Uncle George, do you mind keeping an eye on Jacob? I promise I won't be gone long." She stood and headed toward the door.

"Where are you going?" He called after her, his tone gruff.

"Mom?" Jacob squeaked. His brows puckered and his lips compressed in a thin line.

"It'll be good for the two of you to hang out together." Jessica blew a kiss to her son, recalling her roommate's concern that Jacob needed to spend time with a man. "I'll be right back."

She hurried down the hall looking for the supervisor's office. She doubted her uncle would be forced to leave with no place to go, but the skilled nursing facility probably had a list of people waiting for beds.

A warm voice called to her. "May I help you?"

"Yes. I'm looking for Holly Branson." Jessica couldn't help but notice the redhead's kind hazel eyes.

"That's me." Holly clutched a clipboard to her chest.

"I'm Jessica MacAllister, George MacAllister's niece."

"Nice to meet you." The two women shook hands.

"Do you have a few minutes?"

"Sure," said Holly. "Follow me. We can talk in my office." She led Jessica down the hall to a small room with a desk, filing cabinet, and a few straight-back chairs. A vase filled with multicolored flowers graced the windowsill and a photograph of Holly and her beautiful family sat on the corner of Holly's desk. Her son looked to be the same age as Jacob. And her daughter, a few years younger, held her dad's hand. A slight ache gnawed at her chest. What would it be like for Jacob to live in a two-parent home?

Holly sat in the chair behind her desk and gestured toward the seat across from her. "What can I do for you?"

Jessica took a deep breath. "As you know, it's time for my uncle to leave Pacific Coast Manor. Frankly, he has no place to go. A couple months back he sold his mobile home. Didn't think he'd ever get well. And now, he's made it quite clear he'd rather stay here."

Holly shook her head. "Your uncle is not eligible for skilled nursing. And it wouldn't be good for him to remain stagnant." She shuffled through her file cabinet, drew out a piece of paper and handed it to Jessica. *Instructions for Amputees*. "He knows what he must do to take care of his leg. I have a feeling you'd be surprised at his change of outlook if he would get beyond these walls."

"Do you know his financial state?" Jessica felt uneasy asking this question, but she needed to know if she hoped to find him a place to live.

Holly averted her eyes and pressed her lips together. "His insurance will end at the end of the month. I've offered to help him apply for Medicare . . ."

"My uncle has nothing—no home, no insurance?" The question, spoken in a hushed tone, was meant more for her own ears. Her only hope was that he was collecting Social Security. Jessica covered her mouth with a hand as reality set in. Her cell phone rang. She pulled it out of her purse grateful for the distraction. *Melissa.* "Do you mind?"

Holly smiled. "Not at all."

Jessica flipped open her cell phone. "Hey, Melissa. What's up?"

"Wanted to make sure you arrived in Santa Cruz in one piece." Melissa's cheery voice was a welcome sound.

"Yes, we made it." Jessica stood and moved toward the window and the vase of wildflowers.

"How's Uncle George?"

"Ornery." Jessica wasn't in the mood to give out more information, especially in front of the supervisor. "Is your guest coming tomorrow?"

"Yes. At noon." Jessica could hear the lilt in Melissa's voice.

"I'm happy for you." She yearned to be home to celebrate Easter with her spunky roommate. Now was not the time to break down. "Say, I need to get going. Can I call you later?"

"One more thing . . ." Melissa's tone turned serious. "Andrew called again. I forgot to look at Caller ID and answered it. He sounds like a really nice guy. You sure I can't give him your cell phone number?"

That's all Jessica needed right now. She left Fresno to avoid Andrew's calls. She couldn't deal with him wanting to see her son *and* tend to her uncle's needs. In her mind, the topic had closed years ago when Andrew signed the relinquishment papers. "Please, Melissa. If you're my friend, don't give him my number. I've gotta run. Talk to you soon." Jessica clicked her cell phone shut and sat back down. "Now, where were we?" She pasted a hesitant smile on her face.

Holly tapped a pen against her chin. "I'll give you a couple days to figure out where your uncle will live. For now, enjoy the Easter holiday."

Jessica stood. "Thank you for giving us some time. I'll do my best to find him a place."

"No problem. Everyone deserves a break now and then." Holly smiled. "Will you be spending Easter with George?"

The idea of sitting in her uncle's room on a holiday instead of going to church, sitting around a dinner table, hiding eggs and filling up on way too much chocolate, caused her shoulders to sag. If she felt like this, how would Jacob be able to deal with it? The image of sand and waves crashing on the shore gave her an idea.

"Do you think I could take George out? By the ocean?" Jessica raised her brows.

"You're welcome to try," Holly encouraged. "It would be his first outing and possibly give him a new outlook on life."

"Thank you. I think I will." Jessica smiled as hope filled her. If Uncle George saw the ocean again and smelled the salty air he'd be renewed, she knew it. Jessica shook Holly's hand and left her office.

When she returned to her uncle's room, George was in the same position by the window, but where was Jacob?

3

Evelyn Sweeney ran her hand down the sleeve of her husband's favorite shirt. She gathered the fabric to her face and rubbed it against her cheek. The soft flannel and slight musky smell brought an ache to her throat. Had it been a year? She'd never imagined she'd be alone in her sixties. Her husband's sudden death and her new life as a widow had changed her whole world.

Tears cascaded down her cheeks as she folded the shirt and tucked it among the others in the brown box. She hadn't been willing to part with his clothes until now, the pain of getting up every day finally subsiding. Time to put an end to that chapter in her life and start a new one. She was an independent woman. Always had been. And she'd make a life for herself even now.

Evelyn marked the box for Goodwill and stacked it with the others. She'd always remember Edward and their forty years of marriage. She reached down and picked up his slippers and a pair of loafers that were neatly arranged on his side of the closet. After placing them in a box, she gathered her husband's ties that hung color-coded on a rack. A lump formed in her throat. Edward's organized ways had at one time driven her crazy, but over the years she grew to appreciate them.

Looking at the empty space, Evelyn let out a heavy breath. "Goodbye, my love."

She closed the closet door and walked to her bedroom window. The view of Golden Gate Bridge from her two-bedroom condo gave her a sense of normalcy. She'd lived four decades in San Francisco, though Santa Cruz had once been her home.

Santa Cruz. She sucked in a breath, guilty for where her mind was taking her.

Edward hadn't been her only love. Before she met and married her husband, there had been someone else. She'd thought about him occasionally over the years, wondered what had happened to him. But her love for Edward had kept the idle wondering just that. Evelyn turned away from the window and moved to her small kitchen. She loaded the dishwasher, and swept the hardwood floor.

It had been forty-three years since she first laid eyes on her teenage love. The memory of that day flooded back like a wave crashing against the shore.

Patricia, her best friend from high school, had dragged her by the arm toward Twin Lakes Beach the second she stepped out of her Ford Galaxy the summer of 1969. "There you are. I thought you'd never come. Ronald brought his friend. He said you two were sure to hit it off."

Evelyn took uneasy steps toward the two figures she saw in the distance by the glow of the sunset and small bonfire at their feet.

"Ron said he's quite the adventurous sort and loads of fun." Patricia lengthened her steps.

Adventurous, huh? Evelyn pressed her lips together. She was known for her shyness. What was her friend trying to do to her? Bring her out of her quiet existence?

"Oh, Evelyn, would you pick up the pace? It's been days since I've seen Ron."

With the gap now closed, Evelyn stood near Ron's friend. Heat rushed up her neck at the sight of the handsome guy standing next to her. His shirt hugged his broad chest and he smelled of musk mixed with smoke from the burning logs.

Ronald swung an arm around Patty's shoulders. "George, this is Evelyn. You know, the gal I mentioned to you on the way here. She's a friend of Patricia's."

Evelyn felt like sinking into the sand. She couldn't think of a thing to say.

"Nice to meet you." George took hold of her right hand and pumped it a few times. "Don't worry," he whispered, "I don't bite."

"Nice to meet you, too." Evelyn giggled. She was as nervous as a girl on prom night. Later after roasting hot dogs, George led her down the beach with a flashlight, grabbed her hand to escape the rush of water when the tide rose, and shared his lemon-lime soda. That night had been one of the best of her young life—the first of many with George.

Now, after all these years, how could it be that her heart ached to see him again? Was it part of her grieving process for Edward? Leaning down, she scooped up the pile of debris from the floor and tossed it into the garbage can. She should throw away her memories as well, and leave them in the past where they belonged.

The clock chimed the top of the hour interrupting her thoughts. Just as well. The members of her new book club would arrive any minute. And she still needed to brew the tea.

Evelyn closed the door behind the last of her guests. Her mind had strayed more than once during the discussion of *Redeeming Love* by Francine Rivers. The hour she spent with the women was something she looked forward to all week. Then why couldn't she concentrate?

George MacAllister.

Thoughts of her first love flitted through her mind. Evelyn picked up a couple of empty teacups and brought them to the sink. She returned to her small family room, straightened the pillows on her sofa and picked up the remaining dirty cups and napkins.

The last she'd heard about George, he'd left California and was making a life for himself in the Philippines. It had been a long time. More years than she wanted to admit. For all she knew he could be married with children and grandchildren. But why couldn't she stop thinking of him? She must be lonely for Edward.

Evelyn sauntered to the kitchen and glanced at her calendar. *3 p.m. Babysit for Amy.* She had forty-five minutes to finish setting her condo in order and drive to her daughter's house. If Amy timed it right, three-month-old Isabella would be taking her afternoon nap so she could shop for a new Easter dress.

After washing and drying the teacups, Evelyn shrugged into her windbreaker and made her way to her one-car garage. She locked the door to her condo, then climbed into her sedan and drove the twenty-five minutes to Daly City where Amy and her husband owned a 1953 two-story home.

"Thank you, Mom," Amy said the minute she answered the door. "You don't know how much I need to get out of the house." She helped Evelyn take off her jacket and hung it on the coat rack.

"Where's Bella?" The nickname for her granddaughter rolled off her tongue.

"Asleep. And let's hope she stays that way for a couple of hours. She's been colicky and hasn't been sleeping well."

"Poor baby." Evelyn followed Amy to the kitchen.

"There's a bottle in the fridge in case she gets hungry and an extra pacifier on the counter." Amy hurried around the family room collecting her purse, jacket, and car keys. "Are you sure you don't mind? I know you must be busy preparing for Easter."

"I don't mind at all. Any chance I can see Bella is great with me." She didn't dare tell Amy that the menu for the Easter dinner had yet to be decided. In years past, she'd have the meal items purchased and the eggs decorated by now. One year she made a cake in the shape of a cross. But that was when Edward was alive and her life had a schedule. A rhythm. Predictability. Now she felt out of sorts.

Amy slipped her feet into her sandals near the front door. "Before I forget, what time do you want us tomorrow?"

Evelyn thought for a minute. "One o'clock?"

"Perfect. We'll come right after church." Amy gave her mom a quick hug. "Do you need anything? I could stop by the store on my way home today. It would be nice to go up and down the aisles by myself." She sighed, clutched her purse to her chest, and looked off into the distance.

Evelyn laughed at Amy's theatrics. A few moments alone would be a treat for any new mother. Her mind worked swiftly. "How about some dinner rolls and a cherry pie?" She rattled off the two items that took the longest to make by hand—something she did every Easter, but this year would be different.

"Oh Mom, there's nothing like homemade. You make the best rolls and your pie is one-of-a kind."

Evelyn decided to be forthright. "I won't have the time. I plan to attend the service in the morning, too."

"Okay." Amy's brows arched.

Evelyn was grateful her daughter kept silent about the store-bought treats. Maybe she was surprised to hear that she planned to go back to church, something she hadn't done since the death of her husband.

"Well, I better run." Amy checked her watch. "The clock is ticking. Isabella's been asleep for twenty minutes now."

"Can't wait to see your new dress. Have fun and don't worry. Bella's in good hands." Evelyn waved Amy out the door.

At the click of the lock, guilt squeezed Evelyn's chest. She didn't know if she was truly ready to go back to church and see everyone. True, the book club she started had helped her fellowship with other women, but the congregation at San Francisco Community Church was different altogether. The people were kind and caring, but Evelyn felt self-conscious for being away so long. Her anger at God for taking her husband right before he retired continued to gnaw a hole in her heart. In any case, Easter was a good day to blend with the crowd.

Once in the kitchen, Evelyn grabbed a sheet of paper and a pen. With the rolls and pie taken care of, she could concentrate on the other items she needed to purchase. Honey-baked ham, French-style green beans, mashed potatoes, and a fruit salad, all food she could make after the early service. She smiled as she wrote them down.

This last-minute menu planning wasn't half bad. Over the last couple weeks, she was turning into someone she didn't recognize. It had started when she'd sold Edward's favorite chair on Craigslist. She'd never liked it. Then she cleaned out the garage, only keeping a few mementos that reminded her of special times. She completed the job today when she removed his clothes from the closet. Maybe she'd tried to please Edward all these years by being organized like him. Or did she suddenly want to be carefree because of a certain man that stole her heart years ago?

The sound of Bella's cries forced her back to reality. "Coming, sweetheart."

What would Amy say if I told her I needed a vacation? The question lingered in Evelyn's mind as she rocked Bella back to sleep. She'd never taken a vacation on her own. Edward had always been with her. She didn't need to go far, only to Santa Cruz. The rugged cliffs overlooking Steamer Lane where surfers had been riding the waves for years held special memories. Standing from the rocking chair, Evelyn gently laid Bella in her crib. Grasping the soft pink blanket, she covered her granddaughter and tiptoed from the room.

Evelyn ambled down the hall, the decision made. Yes, she would take a vacation this week back to Santa Cruz. Maybe then she could put George out of her mind.

4

Nick Fuller stepped into his newly built home with a sigh, his forty-eight-hour shift as a firefighter over until after the Easter holiday. He set down his duffle bag and ambled to the kitchen for a glass of water. From the window, he could see the old two-bedroom structure where he'd lived for the past year and a half. He couldn't wait to tear it down and use the lumber for firewood.

The cabin had been nothing but trouble since the day he purchased it along with the three acres in the Santa Cruz Mountains. He knew his carpentry skills would come in handy when he built his new home on the flat piece of land flanking the small home. If he knew beforehand how time consuming the permit process would be, he might have thought twice.

The light on his answering machine blinked and he pressed the button.

"Hey, it's Aaron. Holly reminded me to call you about the Easter shindig tomorrow. Said if I didn't, you'd forget. But I know how much you love my wife's cooking." Nick heard the smile in Aaron's voice. "See you at church."

Nick shook his head and grinned. Leave it to his buddy to make sure he didn't sit in front of the tube with a frozen dinner on a holiday. No. He wouldn't forget. Actually, he couldn't wait to hang out with Aaron and his family. His best friend's two children made him laugh with their silly antics. He looked forward to hiding Easter eggs and buying candy for the youngsters.

It made him want a family of his own.

As the only child of career-oriented parents, he planned to do things differently from how he was raised. Instead of allowing his kids to hide in their rooms for hours entertaining themselves, he hoped to be involved—play ball or board games, help with their homework, and do projects together. He had his own life as a firefighter, but he'd be there for his children when he was home. Of course, he needed a wife first and the prospect of that happening any time in the near future seemed slim. The church he attended was filled with women of the more mature variety.

Nick picked up the phone and dialed Aaron's number. On the third ring, his friend's voice came on the line.

"Nick, good to hear from you. You off for a while?"

"The next four days."

"Ah, the easy life. Wish I only worked ten days a month." Aaron teased.

"Hey, what can I say? It worked out that I have time off during the Easter holiday."

"Ryan and Sarah can't wait till you come over. They expect plenty of candy and attention, nothing unusual. You spoil them, man."

"I don't have any children of my own to indulge." Nick sat down on the couch and swung his feet up on the coffee table. "I figure I can load them up on sugar, then go home and let you deal with the effects." He laughed.

"Holly and I would love to tiptoe on out of here like we did last summer. You're good for one night, right?" Aaron's voice sounded hopeful. "There's a bed and breakfast down the road—"

"Whoa, buddy. Hold on a minute." Nick ran his hand through his hair. "I love your kids and all, but I've got plans."

"What type of plans?"

"Tearing down the shack."

"You're finally getting rid of the old dwelling, huh?"

"Can't do it fast enough. I'm starting this afternoon."

"Why not rent it?" asked Aaron.

"Because I wouldn't want the tenants to suffer the way I did for so long." Nick joked. "The place isn't insulated and the pipes must be from the dark ages the way they moan and rattle." He peered out the kitchen window. "No, I think it's best to tear it down. Plus, I could use the land to build a two-story garage. Who knows, maybe then I can rent the upper half. For now, I can't wait to demolish the place."

"Makes sense to me."

"I'll watch your kids some other time. Tell Holly I'll be there tomorrow. Can I bring some sparkling cider? Dinner rolls?"

"Sure, sounds good. I'll let Holly know. Say, have you thought about inviting someone? You know you're free to bring a guest."

Nick knew exactly where this conversation was headed. His friend had tried to set him up one time too many. "Oh, no. Aaron, you didn't."

"Not this time."

"Thank goodness." Nick let out a breath. "Don't get me wrong. I appreciate the gesture, but I'd like this holiday to be relaxing. With no pressure."

"It's going to be you, me, Holly and the kids."

"Great. See you at church?"

"We'll be there."

Nick hit the off button on his phone, and set it on the coffee table. He looked forward to tomorrow, a kick back day with people who knew him well. Sinking deeper into the sofa cushions, he grabbed the remote and turned on the television. The midday news was on. He was about to change the channel when a photo of a wanted man flashed across the screen.

Nick bolted upright, his stomach tightening into a hard knot.

Moments later, unable to watch anymore, Nick charged out of the house, desperate to walk off his shock and anger. Redwood trees surrounded Nick's property, dwarfing the small structure. He strode around the perimeter of his yard, and paced back and forth.

How could it be that his childhood friend was charged with killing his girlfriend? This was someone he trusted with his dog when his family had gone on vacation. According to the news anchor on television, the woman died of an overdose and his childhood playmate was accused of being an accessory to her murder. Murder? How was an overdose murder?

Nick balled his fists as a wave of nausea swept through him. He sat down on a nearby redwood stump, rested his elbows on his thighs, and hung his head low as he attempted to catch his breath. Witnessing his friend's face plastered on the screen felt raw, painful. Almost like seeing his own. *Breathe.* He sat straight and willed his pulse to slow down.

Unable to calm himself, he stood, snatched a short fir log from the ground, and placed it on the stump. Might as well release his aggressions and have a pile of wood to show for it. He grabbed his axe by the shed, looped it around in one swift movement to smack the log in two. The newscaster said A.J. was last seen in Central California. A phone number flashed across the screen. Nick had no idea his friend had a problem with drugs or alcohol. He let out a breath.

The axe met the next piece of wood with a loud whack, splintering it in half. Nick had sworn off social drinking years ago, back when he helped with the youth group at church. Even now, an occasional glass of wine with his dinner was a rare occurrence, though there wasn't anything wrong with it as far as he was concerned.

After twenty minutes, the task was complete. Too bad the weather didn't call for a fire. The heater in the cabin had broken this past winter. He could've used the logs when he was putting the final touches on the new house. Grabbing an armful, Nick strode to the small home and placed the wood against the sidewall. His motions felt odd, like his body knew something his mind had a hard time taking in. Was A.J. planning on hiding here? Nick had made sure all his friends knew he'd bought this place. Would A.J. use that knowledge to come here? Why else would he be in Central California?

Moisture formed on his hands. He wiped them on the side of his jeans and felt the blisters that had quickly appeared. He knew better than to swing an axe without gloves. He also knew better than to hide a man wanted by the law. *Please, A.J., don't put me in that predicament.* But even as he pleaded mentally, Nick knew if A.J. showed up on his doorstep, he'd help his friend, no matter what.

Lord, he thought, *help me out here. Most of all, help A.J.*

5

Uncle George, where's Jacob?" Jessica's voice sounded strained.

George shrugged a shoulder. "He took off right after you left."

"And you didn't call someone to go after him?" Jessica peeked into the bathroom and then bent down and looked under the bed.

"You're kidding, right?" George glanced at her. "I can't keep up with a six-year-old. But don't worry. I'm sure he hasn't gone far. The nurses keep a close eye on everyone. I have yet to evade them."

"But they expect you to be here. You're their patient. Jacob could slip by without anyone noticing." Jessica's voice shook. "I'm going to the reception area. Maybe someone has seen him. If I don't find him, I'm calling the police."

Jessica didn't wait for a response. With her heart in her throat, she ran down the hall, turned a corner, and followed the corridor to the entrance. She was about to talk with the secretary sitting at the front desk, when she spotted Jacob's orange shirt. He sat Indian style on the floor next to a coffee table, playing cards with two other children, a boy about Jacob's age, and a little girl a couple of years younger.

Jessica ran to him. "Jacob Ethan MacAllister, you scared me half to death." She leaned down, hugged him tight, then held him by the shoulders with firm fingers.

Puppy-dog eyes stared back at her. "Uncle George scares me." His lip quivered.

"I'm sorry, honey." Jessica wrapped her arms once again around her son. "I shouldn't have left you alone with him, not with his sour attitude. I promise you, when he's back to his usual self you'll like spending time with him. He really is a good man. Right now he's having a hard time accepting what happened to him."

The two children who sat opposite Jacob didn't say a word. "I think I scared your new friends." Jessica joined the kids on the floor. She looked at the boy first. "My name is Jessica. What's yours?"

"I'm Ryan. And this is Sarah. Our mom works here."

A striking man with dark hair approached. "I was gone for only a moment and you're telling our family secrets." He winked at the boy.

Where had Jessica seen him and the children before? The picture in the supervisor's office. This must be Holly's family.

Jessica stood. "I found Jacob playing a game of cards with your children."

"Pacific Coast Manor isn't a child's favorite place." He extended a hand. "I'm Aaron Branson, Holly's husband."

"Nice to meet you." Jessica shook the man's hand. "Your wife has been more than accommodating to my uncle. She's an angel."

Aaron chuckled. "I've been told that a time or two. Holly has a heart of gold and a hard time telling people 'no,' but don't let her fool you. She's a tiger when it comes to dealing with insurance companies. She can be quite intimidating on the phone."

Holly rounded the corner. "Did I hear my name?"

"Honey! Only saying what a wonderful supervisor you are." Aaron sidled up to his wife and wrapped an arm around her waist. "Are you ready to get out of here?"

Holly expelled a breath. "Sure am."

"Thanks again for giving me some time to find my uncle appropriate housing," said Jessica. Aaron's mouth twitched and one of his brows lifted. Jessica pictured Holly as a tiger with sharp claws and stifled a giggle.

"You're welcome." Holly smiled. She turned toward her children. "Come on, kids, let's go home and decorate Easter eggs."

Jacob's shoulders sagged and the sides of his mouth turned down.

Why had she forgotten to bring his Easter basket from home? It was filled with all his favorite candy—chocolate eggs, jellybeans, and marshmallow treats shaped into little chicks. And now he wouldn't have any candy on Easter unless she went to the store tonight. But how would she go shopping without Jacob knowing?

She couldn't ask her uncle to watch him. He needed a sitter himself—or at least someone to encourage him to keep up with his hygiene instead of wallowing in self-pity. It hadn't been that long ago she was in the same state. She knew what her uncle needed, and she'd provide for him like he had for her. Jacob would have to understand, a tall order for a young child. *Lord, help me.*

"Mom, can Jacob come too?" Ryan's eyes pleaded. "He's six like me."

Holly bit her lower lip. "I'm sure Jacob wants to be with his mom and uncle."

"No, he doesn't. He told me." Ryan rubbed his nose. "He said his uncle is a grouchy old man."

"Ryan." Holly's tone indicated he'd said the wrong thing.

Jessica never imagined Uncle George would be described in such a way. Caring. Giving. Kind. Those were the words that came to mind before he was ill.

"Sorry, buddy. It won't work today." Aaron braved the awkwardness that permeated the room. "But if Jacob wants to come to our house tomorrow to find the eggs, he's more than welcome." Aaron turned toward Jessica. "We'd love to have you and your son later in the afternoon, if you're available." He leaned in and whispered, "There's always more than enough candy to go around."

Was this the answer to the quick prayer she'd sent up moments ago? "We'd love to come—if that's all right with you." Jessica directed her comment to Holly.

"Yes, please." Holly dug in her purse, pulled out a piece of paper, and scribbled an address. "But, if you're having a good time with your uncle, please don't feel obligated."

Jessica doubted that would be the case. Today after ten minutes in George's presence she was ready to leave. In his defense, he'd had a life-altering illness, and Jessica was sure she'd be just as ornery—or worse.

"Thank you." She gladly received the Bransons' address, leaned down and smiled at Jacob. "Won't this be fun?"

Aaron passed a look to his wife. "Indeed."

Jessica had no idea what he meant by that, but she didn't want to think too long and hard about it. Jacob would have some candy on Easter. Not that sugary treats were the true meaning of the holiday.

"Excuse me, Miss?" An elderly nurse tapped Jessica on the shoulder. "Your uncle is asking for you."

Jessica strode into her uncle's room. "You called for me?" Jacob waited in the hall.

"Wanted to make sure you found the boy." Uncle George scratched his gray beard.

So he did care about Jacob. How could she have questioned his intentions?

"Yes, he was in the lobby playing cards with the supervisor's children."

"Where is he now?"

"Right outside your door." Jessica pointed.

George arched a brow. "Did I scare him away?"

"Well, he, um . . . ." She hesitated.

"This blasted limb." He sighed in frustration.

She would have a tough time explaining to him that it wasn't his residual limb that had frightened her six-year-old, but his attitude. "No, Uncle George you have it all wrong."

"I do, do I?" He wheeled himself closer to her.

Did she dare tell him the truth? "If you'd soften your voice, and smile once in a while, Jacob might warm up to you." Jessica's tone was gentle.

"Bah." Uncle George waved a hand in the air and turned away.

This was not going well.

Jessica approached him and laid a hand on his arm. "Tomorrow is Easter. I'd like to take you to church."

He sat still, his mouth clamped shut.

She pressed further. "Then we can go to West Cliff Drive and stroll along the path. I'll push you in your wheelchair."

The view of the ocean against the cliffs would brighten anyone's mood.

He glanced her way. "They're serving ham tomorrow. I want to be back for lunch. No time for church." His voice held a hard edge.

At least he was open to getting beyond these four walls. That was a step in the right direction. But his words and his body posture told her that he was far from being the uncle she remembered. He'd gone to church every Sunday rain or shine for as long as she could recall.

Being in nature would have to fulfill her need to be in God's presence. "I'll be here in the morning, around nine." Jessica patted his arm. "I'm sure you'll enjoy the fresh air and seeing the ocean again. It'll lift your spirits."

George grunted.

Jessica squeezed her uncle's shoulder, then moved toward the door and her son waiting on the other side.

"Promise you'll bring me back if I get strange looks?" Her uncle's question tore at her heart.

So that was it. He was afraid of strangers staring at him. Since when was her uncle concerned with what other people thought?

An idea occurred to her. "You could always wear your prosthetic leg." She grinned. "Time to book a hotel for the night. Bye now." She slipped out the door before her uncle had a chance to protest.

After signing in, Jessica wheeled the suitcases down the hall to room #37, Jacob close on her heels. The Best Western on 41st Street was near her uncle at Pacific Coast Manor. The price of the room was more than she wanted to pay, but she had other things on her mind, like staying away from Andrew's unwanted calls and finding housing for her uncle.

Jacob jumped up and down on one of the queen-sized beds. "Yippee. Look at me! Can we stay here all week?"

"At least until we find a place for Uncle George." Jessica hiked the luggage onto the other bed. She unzipped the larger one and retrieved her makeup bag. A little freshening up was in order.

Jessica's cell phone rang in her purse. She picked up on the fourth ring.

"Jessi, please don't hang up on me."

Andrew. Why didn't she look at the number? Her mouth went dry. "I've said all there is to say."

"I know this seems out of the blue." He sighed, obviously aware of the awkwardness of the situation. "I haven't been there for you . . . or Jacob."

At the mention of her son's name, she turned around and glanced at Jacob. He continued to jump up and down on the bed, something that wasn't allowed at home. In that instant, she didn't care. Jessica tucked a strand of hair behind one ear and played with her hoop earring. Jacob hadn't asked or talked about wanting a dad in a long time.

She took a few steps toward the window, her voice low. "No, you haven't. But that's okay because I've done fine without you."

"Hear me out."

"You have one minute." Jessica glanced at her watch. "Starting now."

"I don't have much time."

Jessica rolled her eyes. "Like I said, one minute."

"No, you don't understand. I really don't have much time—"

"Are you sick?" An unexpected niggling of empathy grabbed at her gut.

"If you listen, I'll tell you what I can."

She granted him a moment of silence.

"It's imperative that I see Jacob now. Otherwise, it might be years . . ." His voice trailed off.

He said he only wanted to see Jacob. But what was next? Visitations? Weekends? After her parents divorced, she was shipped back and forth from one house to another, her parents consistently fighting for custody and arguing about how she should be raised. Jessica had felt torn. Broken. Like it was somehow her fault they divorced in the first place. When she turned eighteen, she left the craziness behind, grateful to be on her own. Even now she rarely saw them. It was a hard life, one she didn't want to repeat with Jacob. If Andrew got a glimpse of Jacob, would he want partial custody, or heaven forbid, try to take him from her for good? No, she couldn't risk it—especially with a man she couldn't trust with her son. She had to protect Jacob at all costs.

"That doesn't explain anything." Jessica pulled back the curtain and looked out. The pool beckoned her. She slid the window open and the smell of chlorine wafted into the room.

"Mommy, can we go swimming?" Jacob came up from behind and tugged on her shirtsleeve.

She leaned down and covered the cell phone's mouthpiece with the palm of her hand. "Good thing I brought your bathing suit," she whispered. "Why don't you get changed while I unpack?"

"Yippee!" Jacob jumped up and pumped his fist. With suit in hand, he ran into the bathroom.

"Unpack?" Andrew questioned. "You're not in Fresno, are you?"

"Why do you ask that?" Jessica's stomach churned. She hadn't meant for him to hear.

"From what I remember, you have an uncle who lives on the coast."

Jessica said the only thing that came to mind. "Time's up." She clicked the off button, and dropped her phone on the bed. Next time he wouldn't catch her off guard.

6

Jessica woke the next morning to the sound of her cell phone. Why wouldn't Andrew leave her alone?

"Mommy, is it time to get up?" Jacob's warm body snuggled next to her. Every night, he started out in his own bed but wound up in hers by morning. She didn't have the heart to force him back to his bed, especially now that Andrew had intruded on her world.

"Yeah, baby. It's morning." Jessica planted a gentle kiss on the boy's cheek.

"Where's that music coming from?"

"My phone. It's reminding us it's time to wake up."

Jacob sat, arched his back, and stretched. "Your phone tells time?"

Her son was a smart boy. She put on a brave face and didn't let on how threatened she felt by the person on the other end of the line. "Look, it's close to seven. Let's get dressed and grab a bite to eat before we see Uncle George."

Jacob dove under the covers.

"Come on, sweetie." Jessica reached under the sheets and found her son's shoulder. She tickled his armpit. "Uncle George isn't that bad."

Jacob giggled, then sobered. "I don't want to see him. He's grouchy."

Jessica flipped the covers onto the floor and sat on the bed. "Come here." She patted the spot next to her.

Jacob crawled over and rested his head on her arm. She ran her hand through his hair. "I know Uncle George isn't happy right now, but we need to help him find a new place to live."

"Why can't he stay where he is?" Jacob's voice was soft.

"You sound exactly like Uncle George." Jessica let out a breath. "The truth is he's not sick anymore. He's sad."

"Like I was when I broke my favorite truck?"

"Exactly." Jessica hugged Jacob. "The doctor said it's time for him to move into his own place. Come on. I saw a McDonald's yesterday as we drove down the street."

"Really? We never go there." Jacob's eyes lit up. "I bet I can beat you getting dressed." He scurried off the bed.

Jessica laughed. "I bet you will."

Her phone rang again and her body tensed. "Go to the bathroom and wash your face first, okay?"

"Okay, Mom." Jacob ambled to the small room, and closed the door behind him.

Jessica dashed to her purse, pulled the offensive noisemaker out, and brought it to her ear. "Please, leave us alone," she said through gritted teeth. "You have no right to call me—"

"Jessi? It's me." Melissa's voice surprised her.

Jessica bit her lip. "I forgot to look at the screen and thought you were Andrew." Her voice wobbled.

"That's who I'm calling about. He showed up at our door this morning, and I didn't know what to do."

A sickening feeling washed over her. How dare he? What if they'd been home?

Melissa cut into her thoughts. "I hate to say this, but I can see why you were so enamored by him. Wow, he's gorgeous in a movie star sort of way."

Her roommate was not helping. Jessica rolled her eyes. "Please, don't tell me you told him where we are!" Her voice rose.

"I'm not stupid. Give me some credit." Melissa huffed.

Jessica heard the toilet flush. Jacob would come out of the bathroom any minute. "How long did he stay?"

"Not long. After he learned you weren't home he begged me to tell him where he could find you. When I refused, he seemed beside himself."

Jacob came out of the bathroom. "Mom, what do you want me to wear? It's Easter, right?"

Jessica held up her index finger. "I'll be there in a minute. I'm talking with Melissa."

"Can I say hi?" Jacob dashed to her side.

Better to appease him than let on how jittery she felt. She handed him the phone.

"Hi, Melissa." Jacob grinned. "Mom's taking me to McDonald's for breakfast, and then later we're going to Ryan's house to find Easter eggs."

It wasn't lost on her that Jacob didn't say anything about Uncle George.

"Uh-huh. I will." Jacob nodded, then handed the phone back to her. "Melissa told me to eat a lot of chocolate." He grinned.

"I'm not surprised." Jessica rubbed his head. "Why don't you turn on cartoons while I finish talking? I'll get out your Easter clothes when I'm through." She gestured to the remote sitting on the nightstand between the beds. While Jacob did as she asked, she moved to the bathroom for more privacy.

"Oh, and one more thing," said Melissa. "He might have seen the letter from Pacific Coast Manor on the counter. Please don't be mad at me. I didn't say anything about you going to see your Uncle George. And I didn't give him your cell number." Melissa hesitated. "I think . . ."

"What?" Jessica closed the door. "Did he see the pictures of Jacob in the hallway?" Tears pricked her eyes.

"No." Melissa's voice was firm. "At least I don't think so. I steered him away from the hall and bedrooms. We stayed mostly in the kitchen . . . I think he saw your cell phone on the list we keep for Jacob's sitters. And there's that one picture of Jacob. It was kinda scary how it seemed his only goal was to find you—"

"And Jacob." Jessica sat on the side of the tub, her shoulders sagging under the weight of Andrew's intrusion into her life.

"But he doesn't know where you are. And from now on, I'll make sure my mouth is sealed."

"Thank you."

After saying their goodbyes, Jessica set her phone on the counter and lay her head in her hands. She might as well plan on staying away from Fresno forever. After all, how could she go back home when Andrew knew where they lived?

―◦◦◦―

"Evelyn, good to see you, dear." Carol, her friend of twenty plus years, patted her arm as the women walked up the church aisle together.

"Thank you. It's nice to see you, too," said Evelyn.

It felt good to be back fellowshipping with the people who had been nothing but kind to her the past twelve months.

"Wasn't the service lovely?" asked Carol. "And the Easter songs . . . the choir sounded like a host of angels."

Evelyn gave her friend a tentative smile. She hated to admit that something stirred her soul when the pastor spoke about Christ ascending into heaven and the hope of eternal life.

But she wasn't ready to face her anger. She'd given her whole life to supporting her husband and God took him away when they'd planned to travel the world and enjoy one another's company—something they'd talked about for years when the pressures of her husband's work kept him busy and preoccupied.

The trip to Santa Cruz once again crossed Evelyn's mind. Did she dare make a commitment to go? She'd wanted to mention it to Amy before leaving her house yesterday, but she'd chickened out. Her stomach fluttered with a mixture of hope and apprehension.

"If you don't mind me saying so, you seem lost in your own thoughts. Is there anything I can do for you?" Carol squeezed her hand.

Time to make a decision. Evelyn stopped mid-aisle and turned to face Carol. "Yes, there is something you can do for me. I'm going on a vacation and need someone to water my plants and gather my mail. Are you up for it?"

"I didn't know you were planning a trip. Are you traveling alone?" Carol's brows shot up and her eyes widened.

"Yes," Evelyn answered, sounding more confident than she felt. "I'm not going far, only down the coast a ways."

"I'm glad to hear you're doing something for yourself. I've been worried. It's not like you to stay away from church so long. You practically ran the homeless food drive every month. Don't get me wrong, others have stepped up in your absence, but we've missed you."

A small pang hit Evelyn in the chest. She'd thought about the different ministries she'd let go of since the day she'd found Edward cold and lifeless in their bed, but she didn't have the energy to tackle them alone. "Thanks for saying so. It means a lot to me." She shifted her stance. "Back to my plants and mail. Can you do that for me or should I hire the teenager in the condo next door?"

Carol smiled. "Don't think about it another minute. I'll stop by your place every afternoon."

"Thank you."

The sanctuary emptied and the two women found themselves alone. The rows of pews lined the room as if they were rows of soldiers at attention. Evelyn remembered a day when they'd beckoned her each week. Now the thought of coming to church every Sunday gave her little comfort.

"Mind me asking where you're headed?" Carol asked.

"Truth is, I'd like to go back to Santa Cruz where I grew up." Her friend didn't need to know that her mind had strayed to George MacAllister and their long-ago love. She'd thought about George more than once over the years, and their sweet time together. She loved Edward with all her heart, but all love is special. Today reminded her, again, how short life had been.

"A death can make us nostalgic for the past." Carol nodded. "I know life must be difficult without Edward. He was a good man. But remember, *you're* still living. Enjoy your time away, then come back to us refreshed—and then when you're ready, jump back into ministry. We need you here." By the tenderness in her friend's eyes she knew Carol meant well, but Evelyn didn't know if she'd ever be ready to serve God again. He was the one who took Edward from her too soon.

"Thank you for caring—and for taking care of my mail and plants while I'm gone. I'll phone you later when I know my itinerary." Evelyn reached out and pulled Carol into a tight hug. After a moment, she stepped back and pushed her unruly bangs away from her eyes. She'd need a haircut before she took off on vacation. Maybe she'd buy a new outfit or two. "Now I better get going. Amy and her family are coming over for Easter dinner and I have to put the ham in the oven."

Her vacation might be the best thing she'd do for herself all year. Of course, Carol would say it was coming back to church.

7

The breeze from the opened window tousled Jessica's hair. She tucked a wayward strand behind her ear, and glanced at her son in her rearview mirror. A smile tugged at the corners of Jessica's mouth when Jacob shrieked at the sound of the waves crashing against the rocks.

"Did you hear that Uncle George?" Jacob's voice rose to a high-pitched squeal.

Leaning an elbow on the window frame, Jessica came to a stop on Swift Street and turned left on West Cliff Drive. She stole a glimpse of her uncle sitting beside her. His face remained stoic, as it had when she visited him at Pacific Coast Manor. How could he not enjoy the slow drive with the gust of ocean air and the pounding of the surf? He must be more depressed than she'd thought. Either that or he had turned down his hearing aid. She'd give him the benefit of the doubt.

If her uncle wouldn't answer Jacob, than she would. "Yes, Jacob. Aren't the waves amazing?" She looked up at him again in her rearview mirror.

He wiggled in his booster. "Can we get out of the car?"

Uncle George hadn't wanted to, but she couldn't keep Jacob locked in his seat for too long. He was, after all, a six-year-old boy with more energy than she knew what to do with.

"We will, sweetie. Hold on till we get to the lighthouse. Maybe we can watch the surfers at Steamer Lane."

"Yippee!" Jacob called from the back.

Uncle George shifted in his seat.

Had he heard me?

A young man jogged past on the bike path that wound its way along the cliffs. Two women pushed strollers and walked in the opposite direction. A surfboard sat on top of the car in front of her and the driver was moving slowly, probably checking out the waves. In Jessica's mind, West Cliff Drive was one of the most beautiful places in the world and it appeared others thought so as well.

She switched on her blinker and turned right into a parking space in front of the lighthouse.

Uncle George cleared his throat. "You go on with the boy. I'll wait here."

She'd been discouraged to see that he'd opted out of using his prosthetic leg this morning. Jessica's brows furrowed. "I'll help you into your wheelchair."

"Go on. It's too much trouble—"

"It's no trouble at all." She exited the car before he had a chance to argue and moved around to the back.

Jacob scrambled out of his booster seat and stood beside her.

Jessica opened the trunk, hoisted the wheelchair out, and set it down on the pavement. "Do you want your baseball hat? It's windy." She pointed to the cap sitting in the trunk.

Jacob reached in, grabbed it, and set it on his head. "Can we go to Ryan's house after this?" His eyes pleaded. She couldn't blame him. Beautiful ocean or not, keeping company with her grouchy uncle didn't compare to the candy or company he'd have later.

Jessica set up the wheelchair. "We'll go to Ryan's house after we have lunch with Uncle George." She grabbed the blanket from the trunk. After she and Jacob had taken a dip in the hotel pool yesterday, they'd gone to the store and picked up a bag of plastic eggs and filled them with assorted candy. At first she'd wanted to keep the treats a secret from Jacob, but he seemed to enjoy helping her surprise Ryan and Sarah.

Jacob kicked a stone by his foot. "I don't think Uncle George wants to be here—"

"You might be right, but he hasn't seen the ocean for a long time. It used to be one of his favorite places. Let's try to cheer him up, okay?"

Jacob crossed his arms and turned his head away from her.

She touched her son's shoulder. "If you don't do it for Uncle George, than do it for me. Please?"

He let out a loud breath. "All right."

"Good boy!" Jessica winked, and then pushed the wheel-chair close to the passenger door. She opened it wide and tugged on the brakes. "Okay, Uncle George. We're ready."

He didn't budge.

"Step out with your right foot and I'll help you slide into the chair," she encouraged.

He still wouldn't move.

"Uncle George, it's Easter. There aren't many people around and the fresh air will do you good. I promise I'll bring you back home after we take a stroll."

George heaved his shoulders and let out a low growl. He muttered under his breath as he swung his right leg out of the car. With his hand resting on the dashboard and his other firmly gripping the armrest, he pushed himself out of the car, turned on his heel, and plopped into the wheelchair.

He was strong and didn't need her help at all.

Jessica shut the car door, flipped down the footrests on his chair, and spread the blanket on his lap. It hung down to George's right ankle.

"Here, you can wear my hat if you'd like." Jacob handed George his cap.

George tried to pull the hat down on his head, but it was several sizes too small.

Jacob giggled.

A hint of a smile crossed George's face, but it quickly disappeared. He handed the cap back to Jacob and motioned for Jessica to move him forward. "You can put me over there and take the boy for a walk." He pointed to the guardrail overlooking the ocean below. "I'd like to be alone."

Alone? Why would her uncle choose to be by himself when his family was with him for the holiday?

It was a small feat that he'd agreed to go on this outing in the first place, and she wouldn't contradict him. But with his mental state, she wouldn't go far.

"All right, Uncle George." She pulled back on the brakes and pushed him up onto the pavement that wove around the lighthouse.

When she was pregnant with Jacob, she'd heard Uncle George speak of a special memory he'd had at this exact spot, but didn't remember the details. Maybe her uncle wanted to remember a time when he had his leg intact, the thought tugged at her heart. Once settled, she locked the wheelchair and grabbed Jacob's hand. "Let's go watch the surfers."

They walked toward an older woman who stood a short distance away. She pumped her fists and hollered. "Way to go, Eddie!"

Jacob wrapped his arms over the guardrail and peered over the edge as the surfer carved the wave. "Who you cheering for?"

"My grandson, Eddie." The woman smiled. "He was named after Eddie Aikau. Ever heard of him?"

Jacob shook his head.

"He was famous for surfing the big Hawaiian waves. He died in 1978, but his memory lives on." While the lady continued to talk, Jessica kept an eye on her uncle. Why couldn't he enjoy being outside? The weather was a mild seventy degrees and the view of the Santa Cruz Beach Boardwalk and the ocean were spectacular. Something else must be bothering him. Admittedly the man had a lot going on, but couldn't he put it aside for a short time? *She* was doing her best not to think about Andrew.

After twenty minutes, Jessica was itching to get back to George. From her vantage point, he appeared to be sleeping the way his shoulders stooped and his head dipped to the side. As much as he'd like to be alone, Jessica doubted it was a good idea. She tapped Jacob on the arm. "Time to go."

"Bye." Jacob raced down the path.

Jessica hurried to keep up. Once they drew near she laid a hand on George's shoulder. He stiffened under her touch, and she pulled back and dropped her hand by her side.

"Why'd you have to scare me like that?" he barked.

Like Jacob, she suddenly couldn't wait to get away from her uncle. She'd have a much better Easter at the Branson home watching Jacob hunt for colored eggs.

When Uncle George wanted to leave, she'd gladly bring him back to the skilled nursing facility—his home for now.

With a bottle of sparkling cider tucked under one arm and a bag of dinner rolls and Easter candy in the other, Nick rang the doorbell of the modest two-story home in Carbonera Estates.

Ryan and Sarah's excited voices exploded on the other side of the door. He grinned. Felt good to be loved. The kids had accepted him as part of the family even though no bloodlines connected them.

The door opened and Holly greeted him with a smile.

"Uncle Nick!" Sarah rushed past her mom and wrapped her small arms around his waist.

Ryan joined his sister on the porch and tried to peek inside the bag.

"Let Uncle Nick inside. We don't need to bombard him at the door." Holly laughed and tugged at her daughter's arm, prying her away. "Dinner is almost ready. I see you brought something to drink. Look, kids. Nick has sparkling apple cider."

Ryan grinned up at him. "What else did you bring?"

"What do you think, buddy?" Nick handed the bottle to Holly.

Sarah clapped her hands and jumped up and down. "Candy!"

"Dinner rolls, of course." Nick teased and stepped inside.

Ryan pointed to the bag. "There's something else in there."

The corners of Nick's lips turned up. "Like what?"

"Last year you brought us jelly beans—"

"And chocolate," added Sarah.

"Okay, kids. Leave Nick alone. We're not having candy until Jacob arrives."

"Who's Jacob?" Nick set the bag on the kitchen counter.

"My new friend," said Ryan. "I met him yesterday when we picked Mom up from work."

"Kids, go outside and tell your dad Uncle Nick's here."

"Okay," said Ryan. He and Sarah raced to the back door.

Once out of earshot, Holly continued. "Jacob's mom is in town to help her uncle move out of the nursing home. He had his lower leg amputated a while back and is now able to use his prosthetic, when he's not being stubborn. I gave Jessica a few more days to find him a place with it being a holiday weekend."

"That's nice of you."

"Yeah, well, I hope I don't get in trouble with management."

Aaron came inside the house through the back door and wrapped Nick in a bear hug. "You're here. Glad you made it. Didn't see you in church this morning."

He didn't want to tell Aaron the real reason he missed the service. The image of his childhood friend plastered across the television screen kept him awake most of the night and by the time he was able to go back to sleep, the sun had already peeked through his bedroom window. Needless to say, he'd showered and dressed a half hour ago. Nick clapped Aaron's shoulder. "Can you believe I overslept?"

"It happens." Aaron leaned against the counter. "By the way, we're doing something a little different this year. I'm barbequing beef ribs in the backyard."

Nick licked his lips. "Sounds great."

"Would you like something to drink? I've got soda, juice, bottled water?" Holly opened the refrigerator and leaned in, waiting for his reply.

"A soda, preferably with caffeine if I'm going to keep up with your two youngsters."

"Good choice." Holly pulled one from the side door. "Want it from the can or on ice?"

He was a bachelor and never dirtied a cup if he didn't have to. Nick took it from her outstretched hand. "Straight from the can is fine by me."

Holly grinned. "A man after my own heart."

"Hey, I'm the only man for you, so you'd better keep your eyes focused here." Aaron joked and pulled his wife to his chest.

"Honey, it's only an expression—"

"You two. Think I'm going to be sick." Nick rolled his eyes. Truth was, he was jealous. *Very jealous.* High time he found someone to share life with, preferably a woman who wanted a couple of kids. He popped open the lid and took a long swig of his soda.

Faint whispers from the pair drew his attention.

"I'll talk to him," Aaron's hushed voice cut into the silence.

Nick decided to let it go. If Aaron needed to speak to him about something, he'd do it before he went home. And that's exactly what he planned on doing right after the kids searched for the candy. He wouldn't be persuaded to stay the night so the lovebirds could sneak out and have a night on the town. No. His goal the next few days was to take down the small shanty that nearly drove him crazy when he built his home.

Ryan burst into the house. "Dad, can I help you barbeque?"

"That's what Nick is for." Aaron faked a punch to Nick's middle. "But, I'll toss you the football." Father and son headed out the back door.

Nick directed his words at Holly. "I brought candy for the kids. If you think there's too much, you can give some to Ryan's friend. Jacob is it?"

"Yes. That would be nice. I'm sure his mom would appreciate it." Holly peered inside the bag and pulled out the dinner rolls. She grabbed a basket and spread a cloth over the top.

"What about Jacob's dad?" The innocent question rolled off his tongue. "Is he coming, too?"

"No, only Jessica and her son. From what I understand, there's no man in the picture."

Nick had been set up one too many times. He knew Aaron meant well, but he'd prefer to find his own girlfriend. "I get it. Did Aaron have anything to do with inviting Jessica and Jacob over today?"

Holly situated the rolls in the basket. "Actually, it was Ryan's idea."

Now that he knew Aaron didn't set him up on a blind date, he could relax.

Sarah rushed into the house. "Uncle Nick, Dad needs you. Something about trying a rib to see if it's done."

"Duty calls." Nick beamed.

"Sarah and I will finish up in here." Holly handed her daughter the basket.

On his way to the backyard, a strange thought crossed his mind. It sure would be nice to meet someone special—even if she already had a child.

8

Evelyn wrung her hands and looked out the family room window at the street below watching for Amy, Daniel, and Isabella. No sign of them yet. The smell of baked ham filled her condo and she turned toward her bright yellow kitchen.

The dining room table was set with a floral tablecloth, and her best white china. Once the trio arrived, she'd light the thick white candle that served as the centerpiece. Everything looked beautiful.

Her thoughts turned to the empty suitcase sitting on the floor of her bedroom and the reservation she'd made on her computer when she first came home from church. Two whole weeks in Santa Cruz. The three-bedroom vacation rental was a bit extravagant, but she couldn't resist the ocean view. The money wasn't an issue and she hadn't treated herself since Edward died, so she had no reason to feel guilty. Plus, maybe Amy and her family could come for a night or two to ease her conscience.

Daniel's Ford Explorer pulled into her driveway and her heartbeat quickened. She felt as though she were a teenager telling her parents of her upcoming vacation instead of the grown adult she was. Running her hands down the sides of her skirt, she collected herself, and moved to the dining room table to light the candle.

The doorbell rang.

She shouldn't be nervous. Her daughter wasn't controlling or critical. She steadied her breath, tucked her hair behind her ear, and answered the door.

"Hi Mom." Amy stepped inside the condo and greeted her with a hug. The robin's egg blue knee-length dress Amy wore was sleeveless and had an empire waist, perfect for her curvy body. "Smells good in here."

"It's the ham." Evelyn stated the obvious. "Daniel, come in. How's my girl?" She cocked her head to look at Bella lying snugly on her son-in-law's shoulder.

"Sleeping. There's something about the car that knocks her right out."

"You can lay her down in my room. I have the portable crib set up." The minute the words were out of her mouth she wanted to take them back. Daniel would see her suitcase and would know something was up.

"All right. Thanks for always being prepared." Daniel winked at Amy, then headed toward the back of the house where her bedroom was located.

"On second thought, why don't you lay her on the couch." Evelyn's words came out in a rush. "We'll set up a couple of chairs so she won't fall off. I'm not ready for my granddaughter to be in a different room quite yet."

Daniel quirked a brow. "O-kay."

She was being silly and she knew it. Might as well come right out with her plans and face whatever her daughter and Daniel had to say. Maybe they'd be excited for her and happy she was ready to move on with her life.

"Here, I'll put a blanket down." Amy pulled a pink flannel out of her diaper bag and spread it on the corner cushion of the sofa.

"On second thought, she might be more comfortable in the crib." Daniel hugged his daughter close and took a step toward the back room.

Evelyn bit her bottom lip. "Whatever you think is best."

"Mom doesn't have a baby monitor and I'd rather be able to hear her if she cries." Amy gestured her husband back to the couch.

Fortunately for her, her daughter was an overprotective first-time parent. Amy's anxiety worked in Evelyn's favor. She released the breath she was holding.

"You do have a point there." Daniel approached the chenille couch, laid Isabella down, and pushed a couple of dining room chairs against the side.

"I almost forgot the cherry pie in the car." Amy grabbed her keys from her purse. "I hope you don't mind, but I decided not to buy dinner rolls. I figured with everything else, there'd be plenty of food."

"No problem." Guilt nagged at Evelyn. Daniel loved her homemade rolls and usually couldn't wait to take home the leftovers. She'd have to do some baking when she returned home from Santa Cruz.

Daniel opened his palm. "Here, honey, I'll get the pie. Why don't you relax while Bella's asleep?"

Amy gave the keys to Daniel. "Thank you." Once Daniel was out the door, she dropped into the nearest chair.

"The dress you bought yesterday flatters your figure nicely," said Evelyn.

"You think so? After trying on dresses yesterday, I realized I have a way to go to lose the extra baby fat."

"It takes a while," Evelyn said encouragingly.

"Daniel's been sweet. I've tried to exercise, but he knows how tired I am." Amy set her feet on the ottoman and sunk down lower in the chair. "Isabella has her days and nights mixed up and I haven't gotten much sleep." She yawned.

"That little dickens." Evelyn stood behind the couch and looked down on Isabella's cherub-like face. Her mouth worked the pacifier. "She's dreaming of you."

Amy rolled her eyes. "I'm about to give her bottles. I feel like a feeding factory."

"She'll be a toddler before you know it. Enjoy these days while she's small."

Daniel walked through the doorway producing a frozen cherry pie. "We better get this in the oven soon. According to the box, it takes over an hour to bake."

Evelyn took the pie from Daniel and moved toward the kitchen through the open floor plan, which allowed her to mingle with her guests while she cooked. She set it on the counter next to the stove and leaned down to check the ham.

"Did you ask her?" Daniel's hushed voice floated across the room.

"Not yet," said Amy, her voice as soft.

"Looks like the ham is done. I'll finish up in here and then we'll eat." Evelyn slipped on a pair of oven mitts and pulled the meat out of the oven. She turned the temperature up to 350° and made slits on the top of the pie. Her mind whirled about what her daughter needed to ask her and hoped it didn't conflict with her vacation plans. At this point, nothing would stop her from taking time out for herself, something she hadn't done in a long time.

"Do you need some help?" Amy called from across the room as she yawned. Evelyn peeked at her daughter from the kitchen. Her eyes were half closed. Evelyn didn't have the heart to ask her to mash the potatoes.

"No, honey. You stay there. I'll finish up here." She turned off the heat under the French-style green beans and removed the fruit salad from the refrigerator.

It wasn't long before slow, rhythmic snores tumbled from Amy's lips.

Daniel joined Evelyn in the kitchen. "Do you mind if I look something up on your computer?"

She eyed her son-in-law. "What's going on?"

"I'm worried about Amy. She's not getting enough sleep and she's been moody. On top of that she's been having crying spells and seems anxious most of the time. I've tried to convince her to see a doctor, but so far she won't listen to me. A friend of mine told me his wife had something called postpartum depression—"

"And you thought Amy might have it, too?" Evelyn leaned a hip against the counter to brace herself.

"That's what I wanted to find out. Do you mind?" Daniel's voice pleaded. *Poor man.* On top of a new baby, he had to deal with a tired, unstable wife.

"Go right ahead. You know where I keep my laptop."

"Thanks. I sure would like to know how to help her."

"I'll call you when dinner is ready." Evelyn patted his shoulder.

As she mashed the potatoes, a surge of motherly protection wrapped itself around her heart. She remembered the days when she held Amy in her arms as she rocked her colicky baby to sleep. Could it be twenty-seven years ago already? Her mind drifted to a long ago Easter when Edward cut the ham and she tended to her newborn.

Evelyn jumped when she felt someone touch her shoulder. She turned off the mixer and peered over her shoulder.

"Sorry to scare you, Mom." Amy yawned again. "Want me to put the food on the table?"

"Did I wake you? I'm sorry, honey. I know how tired you are."

"It's okay. Bella should be waking up soon and I wanted to at least eat a little before she does." Amy grabbed the fruit salad.

Once everything was on the table, Daniel said a blessing, his words of Christ's resurrection touching Evelyn's heart. Her anger toward God hadn't changed what she believed deep down. She'd never forget what Christ did on her behalf and knew she'd see Edward again in heaven.

Not two bites into the meal, Daniel asked, "Where're you going, Mom?"

Her laptop. "What do you mean?" She stalled, her hands growing moist.

Bella's cries pierced the air. Amy jumped up and rushed to her daughter's side.

"Your suitcase is next to your dresser. I thought you might be going somewhere." Daniel shoved a bite of ham into his mouth. His jaws worked the piece of meat.

The time had come to tell them her plans. Evelyn straightened in her chair. "I'm going on vacation—"

"What? You're leaving?" Amy's voice rose. She cuddled Bella to her chest. "Daniel and I were hoping you could babysit in the afternoons so I could run errands, or at least take a shower. We'd pay you, of course."

Daniel's shoulders slumped.

"I'll only be gone a couple of weeks." Evelyn consoled. "And when I come back, I'll help you."

"You promise?"

"I'll do my best." Evelyn scooted out from under the table and came up beside Amy and squeezed her hand. "You're a good mother. And don't you forget it."

In that moment, she didn't know if she'd made the right choice—a vacation over helping her daughter. How selfish could she be?

9

Jessica clung to the small piece of paper with the Bransons' address as she drove into the entrance of Carbonera Estates. Nicely built homes with greenbelt views dotted the landscape. What would it be like to live in a neighborhood like this? A sudden surge of jealousy reared its ugly head. She tamped it down and narrowed her eyes as she tried to read the names of the street signs.

"Are we almost there?" Jacob asked for the third time since leaving her uncle at Pacific Coast Manor.

They'd invited him to come along, but thankfully he refused saying he'd rather take a nap. "Yeah, sweetie. We're looking for Esmeralda Drive. It starts with the letter E."

"Like this?" Jacob held up three fingers and tipped his hand to the side.

Jessica loved playing this game with her son. "Exactly. Can you help me find it?"

A few minutes later, she saw the correct street. She slowed down and glanced up in her rearview mirror.

"There it is, Mommy." Jacob pointed out the window.

"You're right." She turned left. "Now can you help me find number 624?"

A nervous flutter danced in her belly. What did she really know about this family beside the fact they had two children and Holly was the supervisor at the skilled nursing facility? She hoped the conversation with Holly and her husband would flow and wouldn't be awkward. All that really mattered was that Jacob would be happy and be able to play with someone his own age. She glanced in both directions trying to locate the house.

"I found it!" Jacob directed her to the two-story home on the left.

Jessica pulled to the curb in front of the sage green house with white trim. Wood shutters graced the windows and mature shrubs and flowers in bright colors lined the walk. A Jeep Cherokee sat in the driveway. She hesitated once the car was in park.

Jacob bounded outside and pulled open her door. "Hurry, Mom." His energy was infectious—and so was his grin.

"I'm coming." Jessica unclasped her seatbelt and grabbed the paper bag of candy-filled Easter eggs that she and Jacob filled the night before. She followed her son to the front door.

Jacob's eyes widened. "Can I ring the bell?"

"Go ahead. But only once."

Jacob did as he was told.

They stood together on the stoop waiting for Aaron or Holly to answer. Jessica couldn't help but notice the beautiful front door. The intricate stained glass design must have cost a fortune. She thought about her drab apartment in Fresno. Would she ever be able to go back home without fearing Andrew might show up?

"Mom, can I ring it again? They're not answering." Jacob's face pinched.

"One more time, but that's all, okay?" Jessica shifted the bag to the other hand.

Jacob nodded, and pressed the bell.

She hoped they didn't forget she and Jacob were coming.

Laughter floated from somewhere in the back of the house. "On a beautiful day like today they must be in the backyard. Let's go see." Jessica forced a smile and gestured for Jacob to follow her around the side of the house. The sound of children playing grew louder.

"Now what do we do, Mom?" Jacob tucked his hands into his pants pockets and shrugged his shoulders, a sure sign he was uncomfortable.

"Leave it to me." Jessica tapped the tip of his nose.

Truth be known, she'd rather hightail it out of there, but she wouldn't disappoint Jacob. She pulled on the string attached to the gate. It opened and she took a few steps forward. She couldn't see the backyard from her vantage point, only the side of the garage. Jacob hung on to her shirt with both hands and followed behind. "Hello?" Jessica called out.

"They're here!" A child's voice responded, then Ryan appeared from around the corner of the house.

Jacob let go of her shirt and stepped forward. "Hi, Ryan. How come you didn't answer the door? Me and my mom waited forever." The excitement on his face contradicted his words.

"I didn't hear you." Ryan shrugged nonchalantly. "We're almost done eating, then we're going to hunt for Easter eggs. Uncle Nick is here, too. You're going to like him. He always brings lots of candy."

Jessica pictured Uncle Nick to be like George, an older man with a beard to match. Suddenly she got the feeling they were crashing a family get-together. "Any other relatives here?"

"Nope." Ryan shook his head. "Only Uncle Nick. And he's not really our uncle even though we call him that."

Aaron came into view. "There you go again." He raised a hand. "Telling more family secrets."

"It's not really a secret, is it Dad?" Ryan looked up at his father.

"Don't let Uncle Nick hear you say that. He'll be sad for days." Aaron teased.

Ryan ignored his father's playful comeback and tugged on Jacob's arm. "Come on. Let's play football until they're ready to hide the eggs."

"Are you sure we're not interrupting?" Jessica asked once the boys ran around the corner.

"Positive. I'm glad Holly invited the two of you. We always have more candy than we know what to do with. Nick spoils the kids."

"You mean you won't be needing these?" She opened her sack far enough for him to take a peek inside.

Aaron moaned, then laughed. "Maybe we should invite the whole neighborhood. There're enough eggs to go around."

"On the bright side, the kids will be entertained for hours trying to locate them all."

Aaron made a move toward the backyard. "I hope you haven't eaten yet, I barbequed ribs."

The ham dinner with Uncle George had gone better than their trip to the ocean. Jessica was thankful for that. "We already ate with my uncle, but thanks for the offer."

"I hope you saved room for dessert. Holly baked a carrot cake."

"Dessert sounds wonderful." Jessica's nerves rattled a bit. As nice as Aaron was, the fact remained Holly was the supervisor where her uncle lived. She hoped Jacob wouldn't say anything to embarrass her like moments ago when greeting Ryan.

As they rounded the house, she nearly ran into a male figure. The top of her head came up to his broad shoulders and she couldn't help but notice his manly scent. Stepping back, she looked up into his handsome, clean-shaven face. A dimple creased his cheek when he shot her a grin and his mesmerizing blue eyes stared back at her. Her face flushed.

Nick definitely looked nothing like her uncle.

———

"Dessert is ready. Whoa—" Nick startled, stopping before he plowed into the brunette. He let his eyes linger on the woman's pretty face.

"Perfect timing." Aaron chimed in. "Nick, I'd like you to meet Jessica . . . I'm sorry, I didn't catch your last name."

"MacAllister."

Nick held out his hand and Jessica shook it. He noted her green eyes—flecks of gold around the pupils and dark blue outlining the rims. Stunning. "Nice to meet you. I'm Nick Fuller, Aaron's long-time friend."

Jessica nodded, apparently lost for words.

"She brought along some Easter eggs." Aaron filled the gap.

"Great." Nick rocked back on his heel. Was that all he could say? This was getting embarrassing.

Aaron jumped in. "I'll take your bag and Nick can show you around the place. I'll keep an eye on the kids."

Jessica handed the paper sack to Aaron. "Thanks."

Nick found his voice. "Knowing Holly, she'd want you to come through the front door. She's in the kitchen making coffee. Follow me." He opened the gate and let Jessica pass through.

"She's been nice to my uncle," said Jessica. "He's being discharged from Pacific Coast Manor, but has nowhere to go. Because of the holiday, Holly is giving us a few more days to find him a place."

"Sounds like something Holly would do." Nick walked by his Jeep Cherokee sitting in the driveway and led Jessica to the front door. "How long are you going to be in town?" He hoped he didn't sound too forward.

"As long as it takes to get my uncle situated. You never know. Jacob and I might end up here." Her tone took on a strained quality. "Life's complicated back home."

He'd like to know more, but they'd just met. He didn't want to frighten her with probing questions. Once inside, Nick couldn't help but notice the way Jessica took in her surroundings, one detail at a time. She ran her hand over the edge of the sofa and stopped to glance at a painting.

The Branson home was tastefully decorated and definitely had a woman's touch. He owned a secondhand sofa and coffee table and ate most of his meals in front of the television. He'd like to hang some pictures, but the thought of taking time out of his busy schedule and putting holes in the newly constructed walls had stopped him. "Nice house, huh?"

"Beautiful." Jessica's voice sounded wistful. "Maybe someday."

The thought took his mind in a new direction. Maybe someday he'd have a wife to decorate his new home. For now, he'd be content with bare walls and old furniture until he had someone to share life with. "Where's home?"

Jessica hesitated and gave him a wary glance.

Nick held up a hand. "Sorry. Didn't mean to get too personal."

She shrugged a shoulder, then folded her arms. "Fresno." By her stance, he'd put her on the defensive.

"Ah. Too bad." He purposefully used a playful tone.

Her mouth dropped and her eyes widened. "What do you mean by that?" She placed a hand on her hip, her voice a mixture of annoyance and flirtation.

"The way I see it, you're too far from the beach. How do you stand to live in the middle of nowhere?" He attempted to keep a straight face.

"I'll have you know there are plenty of reasons why I like Fresno."

"Name one." Nick challenged.

"I grew up there."

"That was too easy. Name another."

"Jacob goes to a good school. And my job is there."

"But why would someone move there? What's the draw?"

Once again Jessica hesitated.

"Got you stumped?" He teased.

"No, I'm thinking." Jessica tapped her chin.

He couldn't help but notice her slender neck and the strands of hair that escaped her ponytail. She was cute all right. "I can list a host of reasons why I live in Santa Cruz."

"I'm sure you can." Her tone was sarcastic.

Had he gone too far? He'd only meant to tease her a little.

Jessica's eyes lit up. "China Peak! Some know the mountain resort as Sierra Summit. It's only 65 miles northeast of Fresno and is a great place to ski or snowboard. Oh, and Fresno has something else Santa Cruz doesn't have."

He had to admit he liked her enthusiasm. "And what's that?"

"Affordable housing. I don't know where I'll be able to find a place for my uncle with his meager earnings."

She got him there. Santa Cruz was known for being one of the most expensive places to live in California. "Why not move him to Fresno?" His tone turned serious.

"I've thought about that, but he's only lived in two places— here and the Philippines—and I don't think he'd like the idea. Besides, with Jacob and my roommate, there's no space in my apartment. I'd rather get him settled here."

Holly walked into the living room holding two plates, each with a fork and a slice of carrot cake. "There you are. Aaron told me Nick was showing you around. After we eat dessert, we can hide the eggs. The kids are begging us to hurry. Can you imagine they refused my dessert?"

"I hope Jacob wasn't rude." Jessica worked her lower lip.

"No, not at all." Holly shook her head. "If I was a child, I'd wait for Easter candy, too."

"They're crazy if you ask me." Nick took the plates from Holly and handed one to Jessica. "No one makes a better carrot cake than you."

"Thank you, Nick." She gave his shoulder a sisterly pat. "I've got coffee and napkins on the table out back. Help yourselves. I'll be right out."

Nick led the way.

10

The last time Jessica was taken in by a handsome face, she ended up making choices she'd later regret. Not this time. She wouldn't allow herself to be attracted to Nick. She'd only planned to be in Santa Cruz long enough to see to her uncle's housing needs. But now that Andrew knew where she lived, she might change her mind. It was either stay away from Fresno, or get up the courage to face him.

Andrew hadn't called since yesterday. In all likelihood, he'd probably moved on and hadn't given Jacob another thought. It wouldn't surprise her. The phone calls ended when he found out she was pregnant. Her tense shoulders relaxed. She'd enjoy the afternoon hanging out with the kids and *old* Uncle Nick. The conjured image made her smile.

Jacob, Ryan, and Sarah scrambled around the yard hunting for Easter eggs while Jessica leaned back in the patio chair, surprised at how comfortable she felt in her surroundings.

"Cold. Colder. Colder." Aaron called out to his four-year-old daughter. He pointed to a nearby bush. Sarah raced over and pulled the bright yellow plastic egg out of the shrub.

"No fair," Ryan hollered from the other side of the yard. "You're helping her!"

"You've got twice as many eggs as your sister. Share the love." Aaron turned toward the adults at the table. "Siblings. What are we going to do with those two?"

"Aw, they're just kids." Nick took a swig of his coffee, his third cup since dessert.

"Please, excuse me." Holly stood from her place at the table and charged into the house.

Once the door shut behind her, Nick leaned toward Aaron. "What's going on with Holly?"

"What do you mean?" Aaron's face paled.

Nick set his arm on the table. "Holly is spending more time in the house this afternoon than outside with us. Did we do something to upset her?"

"No. No." Aaron shook his head, his voice unconvincing.

"There's something you're not saying." Nick probed.

"Why don't I give the kids some pointers?" Jessica stood and walked away, giving the men a chance to have a private conversation.

"We're not doing well in the female department. Now we've run them both off." Aaron said to her retreating back.

Jessica crossed the yard to where the children were searching and settled near the fence. From her line of vision she could see the men talking and confiding in one another.

Suddenly, she missed Melissa. They'd planned their Easter dinner a few weeks ago by cutting out new recipes from magazines. Kielbasa and potato bake, apricot brown sugar ham, and asparagus Florentine would be the main meal with strawberry shortcake for dessert. They'd purchased all the ingredients a couple of days ago. Now her roommate and a guy she'd never met were eating the dinner without her and Jacob.

"Mom, look! I found two more!" Jacob held up his hands, showing her both the blue and green eggs.

"Good job, sweetie." Jessica smiled. Her son was enjoying every minute of the egg hunt. "Look in that direction." She pointed to the gazebo covering the hot tub.

All three children darted toward the spa, laughing and pushing each other like they'd known each other their whole lives. She was happy for Jacob and liked that he was spending time with kids his own age.

Nick crossed the yard to her side. "How's it going?"

"By my calculation, they've almost found them all. Where'd Aaron go?"

"Inside to pack." Nick tucked his hands in his pockets.

"Pack?" Jessica furrowed her brows.

"He and Holly are spending the night down the street at the Inn at Pasatiempo. I'm going to stay here and watch the kids."

"What's the occasion? Their anniversary?" She grinned.

"No. Nothing like that."

Nick's short response set alarm bells off in Jessica's head. Maybe the couple was having marital problems. She wouldn't be surprised. Over half of couples' relationships today ended in divorce. At that moment, she was glad to be single. Jessica held up a hand. "It's really none of my business. Once the kids find the eggs, Jacob and I will be going—"

"You're not going to leave me now when the kids are on a sugar high!" Nick nudged her arm with his elbow. The contact sent a jolt through her body.

"Well, I—"

"Please stay." Nick pleaded. "They're having fun."

"Uncle George isn't expecting us tonight. I guess we could stay for a little while—for the kids." She wanted to make her intentions perfectly clear.

"Right." Nick crossed his arms over his chest. "Maybe we can grab a pizza later."

"And rent the kids a movie."

The evening was shaping up to be a good time, much better than hanging out in a hotel worrying about Andrew's calls or her uncle's mental state.

"Do you think they'll ever get rid of all their energy?" asked Nick.

Jessica shook her head. "Doubtful."

Nick cocked his head. "Between you and me, a few months ago Aaron was laid off and Holly found out she's having another baby. They didn't plan on a third child."

"How scary. At least Holly has her job as supervisor."

"True, but they need both incomes to keep up with their mortgage payments."

Ryan walked toward them with Jacob and Sarah close on his heels. "Uncle Nick, we found all the eggs! Can we eat some candy now?"

"Ryan, you don't fool me. I saw you eating candy earlier," said Nick.

"Puh-lease, Uncle Nick." Sarah smiled sweetly.

He let out a breath. "All right, but only a couple of pieces."

Jessica nudged Nick's arm when the kids ran toward the table with their baskets. "I have a feeling that little girl has you wrapped around her finger."

"And what makes you say that?"

Jessica batted her eyelashes imitating Sarah from moments ago. "Puh-lease, Uncle Nick."

Holly stepped outside. Her eyes were red-rimmed. "Sorry for rushing out like this." She approached Nick and gave him a hug. "Thank you for watching the kids. Aaron and I need to get away."

"No problem. Make sure you send your husband my direction the rest of the week. I want to get rid of the eyesore in my backyard."

"You mean that darling little cottage?"

"That darling little cottage, as you put it, has been my nemesis for the past two years. I can't wait to get rid of it."

"Oh, you can't tear it down," said Holly. "I'm sure there's history in that little house."

Could this be the answer she was looking for? Jessica's eyes widened. "You have a vacant house on your property?"

"After this week it will be past tense," said Nick.

"I don't know why I didn't think of it before." Holly's face lit up. "Jessica's uncle needs a place to live. Your cottage would be perfect for his rehabilitation."

⁂

"Now wait a minute." Nick held up a hand, feeling trapped. "The cottage needs a ton of work before I'd let someone live in it, and even then I'd worry."

"How many bedrooms does it have?" Jessica's tone sounded hopeful.

"Two," said Nick. "But seriously, I don't think you'd want your uncle staying in an old house that creaks and rattles."

"I'm sorry if I spoke out of turn." Holly's expression indicated she knew she'd crossed the line. "I don't know what's gotten into me lately." Her eyes misted.

"Hey, don't worry about it. Now go on and have a good time." Nick turned Holly around by the shoulders and pointed her toward the back door.

She kissed Ryan's and Sarah's cheeks and gave them each a squeeze. "Dad and I will be home tomorrow after lunch. Uncle Nick is going to stay with you."

Nick enjoyed watching Holly openly showing affection to her children. Would the time ever come when he'd be a parent? He was quickly approaching thirty and he'd always imagined he'd be married by now.

"That's enough candy" Holly collected Ryan and Sarah's baskets. "I'll give you your Easter goodies tomorrow when Dad and I come home. Love you both." She scooted past Nick and Jessica and went inside the house.

"That goes for you, too, Jacob." Jessica took Holly's cue. She left through the side gate with Jacob's candy and returned a few minutes later.

The ringing sound of a cell phone filled the air. Jessica reached into her pocket and glanced at the number across the screen. The corners of her lips turned down. She tucked the phone back into her pocket.

Why didn't she answer? Interesting.

"Anyone want to go to the park?" Jessica cupped her mouth and called to the trio.

"Yay!" The kids rushed toward her.

Nick crossed the yard. "Great idea."

"I thought while the kids were playing, we could talk."

He didn't know what Jessica had in mind, but he hoped it had nothing to do with her uncle renting the old house on his property.

"Can I ride with Ryan and Sarah?" Jacob begged, tugging on his mom's arm.

"You can all ride with me." Nick placed his hand on Jacob's shoulder.

Jessica smiled. "Thank you. Does your Cherokee have three seatbelts in the back? I noticed it sitting in the driveway."

"Yes." Nick nodded. "Aaron said he'd put the kids' booster seats in the back and leave a key on the kitchen counter. I'll lock up the house."

Ryan and Jacob followed Jessica out the side gate.

Once in the kitchen, Nick turned to find Sarah on his heels. "Jessica's pretty."

"You think so, huh?" He grabbed the key and hooked it to his keychain.

She nodded. "Don't you?"

He'd have to be careful how he answered. Sarah more than likely would head straight outside and give Jessica an update. He patted the top of Sarah's head. "She's pretty. Like you."

Sarah brought her hands to her mouth and giggled.

"Come on, squirt. Let's not keep everyone waiting."

11

The kids piled into Nick's Jeep Cherokee tired and sweaty from all the swinging, climbing, and running they'd done at Harvey West Park. Nick had purposely avoided a one-on-one conversation with Jessica. More than once, he caught her eye and an undeniable chemistry sparked between them, but he played it off as two adults with the same mission—to keep the kids busy.

Nick started the engine. "Ready to go to Upper Crust? My treat."

"You don't have to do that." Jessica hooked her seat belt.

"You're right, I don't. But I'm hungry and I love Sicilian pizza. Consider it a thank you for helping me with the kids." Nick wanted to ask about Jacob's birthfather, but it wasn't the time or place. He wouldn't mention it in front of Jacob in case it was a sticky situation. Holly's words echoed in his mind. *From what I understand, there's no man in the picture.* The diamond she wore on her left hand suggested otherwise. Could it be an heirloom? Looked more like an antique, not that he was an authority on women's jewelry.

Nick pulled into traffic. "Do you work outside the home?"

"I'm a speech pathologist and have my own business—*Speak Easy*. But it's been anything but easy juggling work and being a single parent. It's not for the faint of heart." Her voice took on a melancholy tone. "But I couldn't imagine my life without Jacob. He keeps me going."

He was surprised how much it pleased him to know Jessica was single. She had courage, to be sure. "You're doing a great job with Jacob. He's a good kid. Aren't you Jacob?" He coasted to a stop when the light turned red and glanced in his rearview mirror. All three kids either had their eyes closed or were quietly looking out a window. "I think we wore them out."

Jessica looked over her shoulder. "We'd better not let Sarah sleep too long or she'll never go to bed tonight."

She sounded like the mom she was. Kind of made him feel like a family as they drove up Mission Street toward the pizza parlor. "It's not much farther."

"What's your line of work?"

"Firefighter. I've been with the same firehouse for eight years."

"That's a dangerous job."

"It can be, but I'm confident it's what I'm meant to do. I get a rush whenever I pull someone from a fire or put out a big blaze."

"So you like to be a hero." Jessica's voice held a teasing tone.

"Call me Superman." Nick grinned. "Able to leap tall buildings in a single bound."

"Let's not get carried away." Jessica laughed.

"I like Spiderman better," Jacob called from the back seat.

"What about Batman?" asked Ryan.

"Superman is the best by far. He's the man of steel." Nick flexed his bicep, hoping to impress the boys.

"Jacob, did you see that?" Ryan asked. "Nick has big muscles."

Jessica coughed and took a sip from her water bottle. "How did we get off topic?"

Nick liked seeing her cheeks turn pink. "You're the one who said I like to be a hero. Didn't she, boys?" He glanced in his rearview mirror attempting to solicit a response.

"You did, Mommy," said Jacob.

"I guess I did, but you have to admit I'm right." Jessica smiled. "You like it. Otherwise, you wouldn't be a fireman."

"Okay, that's fair." Nick agreed. "You could say I like saving people from disastrous situations." He switched on his turn signal and came to a stop, waiting for a clearing in the traffic.

"That's why you agreed to watch these two tonight." Jessica lowered her voice.

Nick stepped on the gas and pulled into Upper Crust's parking lot. "I'd do almost anything for my best friend."

"You could be my hero, too . . ."

He didn't know what Jessica meant by her words, but he had a sneaking suspicion it wasn't anything romantic. Dare he ask?

Jessica didn't give him a chance. "I'm hoping you'll reconsider letting my uncle rent your cabin. I'd really like to see it."

Could he consider fixing up the old house when all he wanted to do was tear it down? Nick expelled a breath and put the car in park. "Let's talk about it later, after we eat." He couldn't help it if he sounded irritated. That's exactly how he felt.

Jessica cringed at Nick's response. She hoped she didn't frustrate him. After all, he offered to buy them dinner even though she was far from hungry after the big lunch she had with her uncle.

She helped the boys out of the car while Nick scooped Sarah up in his arms. The tender way he held the little girl made her heart trip. He clearly liked kids—the opposite of Andrew. What would it be like to have a man in her life that genuinely cared about Jacob? She wished things were different.

Nick held Sarah in one arm and opened the back door of the pizza parlor for her and the boys with the other.

"Why the back door?" Jessica asked as they moved toward the front to place their order.

"It's a local thing." Nick smiled.

Her uncle needed a gentleman like Nick as his landlord. Nick's caring nature could see Uncle George through the tough times when she wasn't around and could possibly help him figure out why he turned bitter inside.

The kids decided on plain cheese pizza, while Nick ordered the works on his. Jessica opted for a salad.

After waiting fifteen minutes, a worker approached and placed their food on the table. The smell of pepperoni, melted cheese and freshly baked dough filled the air. Despite the enticing aroma, her stomach was in knots thinking about the upcoming conversation about her uncle renting the small cabin.

Halfway through the meal, Sarah spilled her soda on the table splashing Nick's pizza. He quickly moved the pizza pan and Jessica snatched some napkins and put them on the edge of the table before the liquid had a chance to go over the side.

"I'm sorry, Uncle Nick." Sarah's lip quivered.

"It was an accident. No harm done." He patted one of the slices with a napkin.

Jessica liked how Nick handled the situation. She didn't know if she would've responded the same way. As a full-time parent, she rarely had a break and sometimes her patience wore thin. It would be nice to share the load with someone—

someone as easy going as Nick. She pushed the thought aside and piled the soiled napkins on the empty side of the pizza tin.

Nick leaned over and whispered in her ear. "I like your idea of renting a movie for the kids. You up for it?"

"Definitely." She wasn't ready for the night to end when they had yet to discuss the cabin.

After the meal and a quick ride, they pulled into the Bransons' driveway with a movie in hand.

"Uncle Nick, can you make popcorn?" Ryan asked the minute they stepped inside the house.

"Are kids ever full?" Nick set his keys on the kitchen counter.

Jessica shook her head. "Never."

While Nick set up the movie, she put the popcorn in the microwave and rummaged through the cabinets for a bowl. It smelled like a movie theatre in no time. The kids settled on pillows on the floor, the bowl of buttered popcorn situated between them.

"Would you like some coffee?" Jessica fidgeted with the ring on her left finger. How could it be that after meeting him less than six hours ago, she already knew his preferred drink?

"Coffee sounds good, but I better have decaf or I'll be up all night." Nick touched her shoulder as he passed. "I'll meet you on the back porch."

It had been years since a man had touched her like that. She liked the contact. Maybe a little too much.

A few minutes later, she joined him by the patio table with two steaming mugs.

"Since we pulled into the parking lot at Upper Crust, I've been thinking about your question." He couldn't even voice what she'd asked.

Jessica had a feeling the answer was no. She sipped her coffee, the steam warming her face. She'd stay quiet to see what he had to say.

He ran a hand through his hair, then leaned forward resting his elbows on his thighs, his hands clutched tightly together in front of him. "It's only fair to let you see the place for yourself."

Jessica set her cup on the table. "Really?"

"Don't sound too excited. I have a feeling once you take a look, you'll reconsider."

"According to Holly, it's the perfect place for my uncle."

"She hasn't come to my property in quite some time. I don't think she remembers how bad it is."

"Thank you, Nick." Jessica laid a hand on his knee, then pulled back when his eyes met hers.

Nick grabbed his mug from the table and leaned back in his chair. "Don't thank me yet."

She prayed the cottage would meet her expectations.

12

Evelyn lugged her suitcases into the vacation beach house and shut the door with a sigh. The house had everything she could want including an ocean view and a jetted tub. The fact that she packed her own bathroom towels and linens seemed ludicrous now. But, it brought her comfort knowing she'd dry off with towels that had a familiar scent and sleep between her own cotton sheets.

Looking out the front window, two women walked side by side down the path that led from Natural Bridges Beach to the Lighthouse. Probably best friends taking an afternoon stroll. Evelyn couldn't wait to take a walk, but not before she unpacked her clothes and arranged her toiletries. She chalked it up to Edward's influence throughout the years. His organized ways had bordered on obsessive, but she decided early on in her marriage not to let it bother her.

She pulled her two suitcases, one in each hand, to the back of the house where the bedrooms were located. Each of the three rooms contained king-sized beds and was decorated with soft beach tones in tans, blues, and greens. She chose the far bedroom with the fireplace and full bath attached, set her luggage in the corner, and opened the window.

The first day of her vacation promised to be glorious with its blue sky and slight ocean breeze. The smell of the salty ocean air wafted through the window. She inhaled deeply as a memory from long ago flashed through her mind.

"I bet you can't run as fast as I can ride." She had sat atop George's candy apple red Phantom bike pedaling, the white-wall tires turning slowly while George MacAllister walked beside her.

He gave her a wry grin. "You know I won first place at every track meet my senior year of high school."

"Are you up for the challenge?" Evelyn wished she'd worn casual clothes instead of the skirt and blouse. She'd wanted to look her best for her first outing with George. Little did she know she'd be riding a bike or challenging him to a race.

"The last one to the lighthouse treats to a Marianne's ice cream." George upped his pace.

Evelyn looked ahead to the lighthouse. It was a good distance away. She couldn't be certain how far due to the winding, rocky coastline, but she had a feeling she could take him. "You're on."

George raised his hand. "On your mark, get set—"

Evelyn didn't wait for him to say go. She stood on the pedals and pumped hard before sitting down on the leather seat the moment she felt she had a comfortable lead.

Every once in a while, she'd glance over her shoulder. George's long legs made quick work of the ground under his feet. He'd catch up to her if she didn't pay attention.

A bead of sweat trickled down the nape of her neck, her ponytail swishing from side to side as she rode. As she approached the lighthouse, a small boy wiggled from his mother's grasp and darted out in front of her. She pressed hard on the front drum brake barely missing the child. The mother snatched up her son, hugging him tight, then set him down, reprimanding words sputtering from her lips. Evelyn took in the scene as George raced past.

"Hey!" She hopped back on the bike and fumbled for the pedals. He'd win now for sure.

As she rode behind George, she had to admit she admired the view. She giggled. George MacAllister was handsome to be sure. And he chose to spend the day with her. Another thought crossed her mind. No matter who won the race, they'd be spending more time together this afternoon at Marianne's. She'd win either way.

By the time she arrived at the lighthouse, George was sitting on the bench, his lean body stretched out. She parked the bike and sat next to him.

"Can't say I didn't warn you." George placed his hands behind his head, his scent of pine and spices mingling with the ocean air.

"You're light on your feet and as fast as lightening. Of course, you took advantage of what could've been a terrible situation. The boy came out of nowhere."

"Good reflexes." George laid an arm on the back of the bench. She wished he'd rest a hand on her shoulder.

"You won fair and square," said Evelyn. "Looks like I'm buying."

"I'd like vanilla, please." George winked. "Make it a double scoop."

She nudged him in the ribs with an elbow, and for a moment he'd cupped his hand around her shoulder, and gave a squeeze before releasing his grip.

Even after forty years, Evelyn could still feel the rush of excitement from George's touch and taste the creamy vanilla ice cream on her lips. Suddenly, she didn't want to unpack her bags. No, she'd take a walk to the lighthouse, then drive down Ocean Street to Marianne's for a scoop of vanilla ice cream. For old time's sake.

———

Jessica had exhausted every available apartment for rent that had wheelchair accessibility. None seemed to fit her uncle's needs or budget. Some places were unfit for an animal let alone a human. And from her visit with George this morning, his list of requirements seemed unobtainable. She stared at the newspaper in front of her, her car parked on the side of the road in one of Santa Cruz's nicer neighborhoods near West Cliff Drive.

"Mom, can I play with Ryan today?" Jacob broke into the silence. Poor kid. She'd dragged him from apartment to apartment.

"Nick invited us to his house. Maybe Ryan will be there."

"If he's not, can we invite him to go swimming at the hotel?"

"Let's take one thing at a time." Jessica set the paper down on the passenger's seat and glanced at her watch. Her stomach knotted. Time to check out the "old shanty" as Nick put it. As much as he appeared uneasy about the possibility of her uncle staying there, she was as eager to make it work. To know a fireman would look in on George when it came time for her to go home to Fresno made her feel better about leaving.

If she was brave enough to go home.

Andrew sent her a text message a short time ago. *I want to see him. The clock is ticking.* His words felt more like a threat than those of a loving father. She pushed all thoughts of Andrew out of her mind. She couldn't deal with him right now. Her uncle's housing situation was her first priority.

Jessica turned the key in the ignition and her car roared to life.

Please God, let Nick's place be the one.

⸺∞⸺

The dirt and gravel on Tie Gulch Road crunched under Jessica's tires, the narrow single lane encased by surrounding redwoods.

"Does Nick live in the forest?" Jacob's tone was a mixture of doubt and wonder.

"Looks like it, huh? There are a lot of trees." Jessica gripped the steering wheel, her hands suddenly moist from driving into unfamiliar territory. They went over a small wooden bridge and passed a house on the left. By the number on the side, it wasn't Nick's place. She kept going until she spotted his Jeep Cherokee parked in front of what looked like a newly built home. The two-story structure gleamed in the sunlight with its copper gutters and clean windows. Jessica grinned. It was beautiful.

"There's Nick's car," said Jacob. "But I don't think Ryan and his dad are here."

Until that moment, she didn't think twice about being alone with Nick without Ryan and Sarah as buffers. Truthfully, she wouldn't really be alone. Jacob was with her, but she didn't know how her son would act or how she would feel. She had tossed and turned last night in the hotel bed thinking about the handsome firefighter. She hadn't been this attracted to a man since Andrew. And look how that turned out. Truth was, she didn't know Nick well enough to judge what kind of guy he was, but from what she'd witnessed yesterday he had a different moral compass than Andrew. She redirected her attention to her son. "Remember to be on your best behavior—"

"I know, Mom." At six, he was already starting to act and sound like a boy twice his age.

"I'm sure you will, buddy." She kept her voice light as she pulled to a stop next to Nick's car.

The small cottage caught her eye. She wouldn't describe the building as an old shanty like Nick had done, but the place must have been at least fifty years old, maybe more. The wood looked splintered in a few places and the sparse windows were definitely single-paned. The shingled roof was also in dire need of replacing.

Nick appeared on his front porch with a mug in his hands. Her breath caught in her throat. His denim shirt hugged his shoulders and chest. Catching herself staring, she looked away, tossed her keys in her purse, and unbuckled her seat belt. She was here for one reason only—to find her uncle a place to live and help him move on with his life. By being on his own, she hoped he'd be able to get over being angry and bitter about his new existence as an amputee. Maybe in time he'd even go back as a missionary to the Philippines or find volunteer work in Santa Cruz.

The minute they were out of the car, an Australian Shepherd bounded at their feet. He jumped up on Jacob, knocked him down, and began licking the boy's face.

Jacob laughed and attempted to push the furry animal away. "Get him off me!"

"Rosco!" Nick called from his place on the front porch. "Come here, boy!" He came toward them. "Sorry about that. Usually he's well-behaved."

The irony of the situation wasn't lost on Jessica. Here she was afraid her son would do something to embarrass her. Of course, they'd only arrived. She reached down and helped Jacob to his feet, and dusted him off.

Nick grabbed the dog's collar with one hand while balancing the mug in the other. "Can I get you two something to drink?"

"Do you have soda?" Jacob smiled up at Nick. His eyes darted to Jessica for approval.

She was going to protest, but Nick took care of it. "I don't right now. But I have orange juice or milk." His tone lifted.

"Nah, I'm good." Jacob dug his hands in his pockets and kicked the dirt with the toe of his shoe.

Jessica shook her head. "Nothing for me, thanks."

"If you'll give me a minute, I'll put Rosco in the house and grab the key. I'm sure you're eager to see the place." Nick tilted his chin toward the cabin. He appeared at ease. Either he was confident she'd decline the place or he had changed his mind about tearing it down.

In her excitement, she'd neglected to ask how much he'd charge for rent. It might alter her plan. Jessica hugged her purse to her side.

Nick came toward them a minute later with jangling keys in hand. "I don't always lock it up, but I've started to recently."

"Look, Mom." Jacob pointed. "There's a tree swing! Can I try it?"

"If it's okay with Nick."

"Fine by me." Nick barely got the words out before Jacob bolted across the yard. "I built it for Ryan and Sarah when they come to visit. It's safe."

"Thanks for letting me know." Jessica walked beside Nick as they made their way to the cabin. "If you don't mind me asking, why do you feel the need to lock up the house now? Have there been burglaries close by?" Was this a ploy to make her change her mind about the house?

"No. Nothing like that." Nick didn't say anything more. He put the key in the lock and opened the door. "After you."

13

The door swung wide with a loud creak. Nick gritted his teeth. As much as he wanted to tear down the old house, a small part of him wanted Jessica to approve. Why, he didn't know. It would be a lot easier if she hated everything about it. But that would mean he'd probably never see her again.

"Here, let me open the curtains and turn on a light." Nick scooted past Jessica, her flowery scent hitting his senses despite the musty smell of the cabin. She looked prettier than the last time he saw her, if that was possible, with her hair down around her shoulders. He pulled the drapes back to let in the sun and opened a window to air out the room. For good measure, he flicked on the hanging light over the small dining table and four chairs.

Jessica pressed her lips together and glanced around the room. He couldn't read her blank expression.

He gestured to his right. "The kitchen is small. Only one or two people can be in it at the same time, but the stove works."

Jessica ran her hand over the edge of the tile counter, like she had done on Holly's sofa. Did he dare ask what she was thinking? Not yet. She hadn't even seen the bedrooms, if he could call them that. Neither room had a closet and the smaller of the two was barely big enough for a twin bed.

Jessica moved to the sitting area and sat on the olive green sofa he'd found at a garage sale. All the furniture in the cabin cost next to nothing, and looked it, too. "I like the wood–burning stove."

Suddenly his vision of a two-story garage, complete with poolroom or small apartment to rent flashed in his mind. Having Jessica's uncle stay here was definitely not in the cards a couple days ago. "It heats the room. Of course, it doesn't take much. One wayward spark would burn the place to the ground in no time."

"Spoken like a fireman." Jessica stood. "May I see the bedrooms?"

"Be my guest. There's a bathroom in between with a tub. No shower." Nick gestured to the opening between the family room and dining area. "You might want to check the hallway to see if it's wide enough for a wheelchair."

His attraction to Jessica was toying with his mind. One minute he wanted her to shake her head in disgust and leave, the next he hoped she'd move right in along with her uncle so he could get to know her better.

He let Jessica explore the remainder of the house by herself. When she disappeared from view, he moved to the window and looked out. Jacob sat on the tree swing, holding on to the rope with both hands and pumping his legs hard. His dark hair, the same shade as Jessica's, blew in the breeze as he swung back and forth.

Footsteps pattered behind him on the wood floor and he turned.

"How much to rent the place?"

Nick rubbed the back of his neck. "Honestly, I hadn't thought about it."

"When you come up with a price, will you let me know?"

Nick was about to respond, but Jessica kept right on talking.

"My uncle is going to be discharged and needs a place to live as soon as possible. If he can't afford it or you choose to tear it down, I'll have to find somewhere else. I guess he can stay with me at the hotel until I figure something out . . ." Her brows furrowed and she looked down. Her foot toyed with the edge of the rug. Made him wonder how long she'd planned to stay at the hotel. It would get expensive fast. His heart went out to her.

A shrill scream pierced the air.

Jessica bolted out of the cabin.

Jacob lay on the ground, clutching his wrist to his chest, his cries growing louder with each step she took. She dropped to her knees by his side. "Baby, are you okay?"

"Mommy, it hurts." He continued to hold tight to his left wrist.

"What happened?" Her voice hitched as she laid a hand on his shoulder.

Tears streamed down Jacob's face and his breath puffed in and out in short bursts. "I thought . . . I could jump . . . off the swing . . . and land . . . on my feet."

"Shh. It's okay. Mommy's here." She ran her fingers through his hair.

Nick rushed toward them with a towel and a bag of ice. He knelt down. "Mind if I check him out?"

"Please."

"Hey, buddy. I need to ask you a couple of questions, okay?"

Jacob nodded.

"It's best not to move. Do you have pain in your head, neck, or back?"

"No. Only right here." Jacob pointed to his wrist. "And it hurts real bad."

Jessica was grateful she didn't see blood anywhere.

"Can you feel this?" Nick touched the tips of Jacob's fingers.

"Uh-huh." Jacob hiccupped.

"Can you wiggle your fingers?"

"I think so, but it hurts." Jacob squeezed his eyes shut and tears slid down his cheeks.

Nick looked at Jessica. "We'll need to take him to the hospital after I splint his wrist. I think it's broken." He voiced her fear.

"But I don't want to go to the hospital!" Jacob wailed.

"Sweetie, they'll need to do an x-ray and if it's broken, the doctor will put it in a cast." Jessica ran her fingers down her son's cheek.

"Like when Matthew broke his arm?" Jacob's voice calmed a bit talking about his friend from school.

"Yes, like Matthew," Jessica soothed.

"Keep your hand on your chest and don't move." Nick placed the towel and bag of ice on Jacob's wrist. "I'll be right back."

Jessica was thankful she wasn't the only adult present. There were countless times she had been alone. At two, Jacob fell in the bathtub and chipped a baby tooth, and when he was four he cut his knee on a nail and wound up with a dozen stitches. A couple weeks ago, he strayed from her at the grocery store. She was about to call the police when a store clerk found him in the cereal aisle.

Nick returned with the splint and doctored Jacob's wrist, then offered to drive them to the hospital. He didn't have to, after all. They'd only met the day before. But Jessica didn't argue. She sat next to her son in the back seat and let him rest his head on her shoulder. She spotted Nick glancing at them in his rearview mirror a time or two and couldn't help the smile that tugged at her lips. He seemed to genuinely care.

Jacob groaned with every bump in the road and brought her back to reality. She was a single parent. And no matter what, she'd try to protect her little boy with every ounce of her being. Because she was all he had.

Her cell phone rang inside her purse.

Andrew.

The ER doctor came into the room and extended a hand. "Mr. and Mrs. MacAllister?"

Nick didn't correct him. Why bother with formalities? He only wanted to know if Jacob's wrist was broken. He shook the doctor's hand and watched Jessica do the same. She quickly moved back to Jacob's side at the examining table.

"I'm Doctor Litwiller." He turned his attention to Jacob. "I hear you had a fall today."

Jacob nodded. He appeared calm despite the pain. The medication the nurse gave him must be taking effect. "I tried to jump off a swing."

"Ah," said the doctor. "Probably not the best way to stop."

"No, it's not." Jacob agreed.

In a way, Nick felt guilty for Jacob's injury. He told Jessica the swing was safe. Of course, if Jacob hadn't jumped off they wouldn't be spending the afternoon in the ER.

"We'll need to take an x-ray of your hand and wrist to see if you have broken bones."

"Will it hurt?" asked Jacob.

The doctor shook his head. "No, it shouldn't."

Waiting for the x-ray results, Jessica's worried expression seemed to intensify when she checked her cell phone. Twice now, Nick had seen her ignore calls. Who kept calling and why didn't she want to pick it up? He brushed it off as none of his business.

A half hour later, Doctor Litwiller showed them the x-ray of the bones in Jacob's hand and wrist. He pointed to a small dark spot on the wrist bone near Jacob's thumb. "See this here? This is a distal radius fracture. The good news is that even though the bone is broken, it still remains in place."

"Will he need a cast?" Jessica asked.

"Yes," said the doctor. "It's the best way to make sure the bone heals properly."

A short time later, Jacob sported a cast and a sling as they walked out of Dominican Hospital. No one spoke the whole ride back. Once they arrived, Nick parked his Jeep in the usual spot in the driveway.

The open cabin door caught his attention. He forgot to shut it when they'd run out to check on Jacob. He realized now he never got Jessica's opinion, but if her inquiry about rent was any indication, she was interested. His thoughts went back and forth like a ping-pong ball. On the one hand, he didn't see the need to change his plans for someone he'd just met. But on the other, he didn't want Jessica and Jacob to walk out of his life, especially now with the painful memory of Jacob's fall.

"Thanks for driving us to the hospital." Jessica's words pulled him from his thoughts. She loaded Jacob into her Honda.

"It's the least I could do." Nick lowered his head.

"I hope you don't blame yourself for what happened to Jacob. He knows he shouldn't jump from a swing. I've warned him countless times not to do that."

"I don't, but I wish it hadn't happened."

"I understand." Jessica removed her keys from her purse. "I appreciate you letting me look at your cabin. It's definitely not in the best shape, but I can see what Holly's talking about. There's something serene about living among the trees. It would help my uncle get the perspective he needs, but I realize I'm asking you to change your plans."

How could he tell her goodbye? Maybe he could put off the inevitable. "Would you and Jacob like to stay for dinner?"

14

Dinner?" Jessica played with the keys in her hand. She was curious to know what Nick had in mind.

"We can set Jacob up in the family room. I'm sure the little guy is tired after what he's been through." Nick looked at the boy in the back seat of Jessica's car, hugging his stuffed teddy bear with his free arm.

"It's been quite a day." Jessica let out a breath.

"Well, you're in luck. As a fireman, we take turns cooking for the guys and I've learned a thing or two." He rested a hand against her small car. "I make a mean macaroni and cheese."

She folded her arms across her middle. "Homemade? Or from a box?"

"And what if it *is* from a box?"

"It'd be perfect." Jessica smiled. "Macaroni and cheese is the best comfort food around. It's Jacob's favorite."

"I can whip up a salad."

"Anything would be fine." Jessica rested a hand on Nick's arm, then quickly removed it. She had to stop touching him. She wouldn't want him to think she was buttering him up, or interested. "I appreciate it—"

"I'd enjoy the company."

"I've got to make a quick phone call." Jessica pulled her cell out of her purse. "Do you mind taking Jacob inside?"

Nick's expression told her he understood. "Don't mind at all. The reception isn't the best here. You might want to call from the house."

Jessica checked her phone. There were three bars. "I'm good."

He opened the car door and gestured to Jacob. "Come on, buddy. You're staying for dinner."

"Can Teddy come, too?" Jacob asked.

Usually Jessica didn't let Jacob's bear out of the car since he couldn't sleep at night without him. She didn't want to risk losing him, but tonight was different.

"Yes, Teddy can come." Jessica rubbed Jacob's hair. "Go on in the house with Nick, I'm going to make a phone call, okay?"

Jacob nodded. He followed Nick up the porch steps and into the house.

Truth be told, she needed to make two calls—one to Uncle George to let him know she wouldn't be stopping by until tomorrow morning, the other to Andrew. Her heartbeat quickened at the thought. He needed to understand she wasn't falling for his charade of pretending to be an interested father.

Jessica leaned back against her car and pressed her uncle's number.

On the third ring, a nurse picked up.

"This is Jessica MacAllister, George's niece. May I speak with him, please?"

"George is at physical therapy right now. Can I take a message?"

"Please let him know I'll pick him up in the morning around nine. He's being discharged."

"Will do. Is there a number where he can reach you?"

Jessica rattled off her cell phone number. "Tell him I think I've found him the perfect place." She hoped her words weren't premature.

"I'll do that. Bye now."

Jessica disconnected the call and glanced up at Nick's beautiful home. She could see him in the window. He raised his hand in a subtle wave.

She pointed to her phone signaling she had another call to make. A lump formed in her throat as she pressed Andrew's number.

She cut him off at hello. "Andrew, it's me."

"Tell me where you are and I'll come to you." His voice was low and gravelly, as though she'd awakened him.

"Hold on a minute. Who says I'm going to tell you where we are?"

"Jacob looks like me."

"You had no right going into my apartment."

"I've missed so much."

"Don't start talking like that. You knew exactly what you were doing when you signed those papers—"

"I was doped up. Had one too many drinks."

Precisely the reason she didn't want him part of Jacob's life.

"So now you want to step right into the loving father role?" How could she be sure he wasn't using now? She couldn't risk it.

"I'd like nothing better—"

"Well, you can forget it. Jacob and I are doing quite nicely without you." Her son's broken wrist came to mind. She could picture Andrew questioning what type of mother she was to allow such a thing to happen.

"I only want to see my boy."

"You've seen a picture—"

"It's not the same and you know it."

Truth laced his words, but she didn't want to give him the satisfaction. The bottom line was she didn't trust him.

Maybe she could stall a while until she thought of a different tactic to keep him away. "Let me think about it, okay?" She softened her voice. "Don't call me. I have your number."

"Don't take too long. I'm running out of time." He'd said that before, but it could be a ploy to butt into her and Jacob's life. She'd given in to Andrew in the past, but she wouldn't fall for his games this time.

"I'll take as long as I need." Jessica pressed the 'end call' button aware that she'd dug a hole in the gravel driveway with the toe of her shoe. She pushed the rocks back in place with the side of her foot and stamped it down, then chanced a glance at the window where she'd seen Nick earlier. No one was there. Right now, she'd give almost anything for protective arms to comfort her. And she knew the exact person she had in mind. She was losing it to think of Nick in that way.

Instead of acting on her impulse, she sat in her car and uttered a prayer.

⸺∙∞∙⸺

After setting Jacob up in the family room and turning on a kid-friendly movie, Nick had moved to the kitchen and looked out the window. Jessica was leaning on her car talking on her cell phone. Who was she calling? A boyfriend? Her roommate? Curiosity niggled at him.

"Nick? Do you have a blanket? I'm cold." Jacob called from his place on the couch.

"Sure do, buddy. Here let me get it for you." Nick reached into the coat closet and produced an afghan, the one his mom made for him several birthdays ago. "This will get you warm in no time." He opened it up and covered Jacob's legs and torso. "Is your arm hurting?"

"Only a little." Jacob looked up at him with tired eyes.

Poor guy. Maybe he'd fall asleep. "Enjoy the movie while I make dinner, okay?"

Jacob nodded. He rested his head back against the sofa and snuggled under the blanket.

Nick walked back to the kitchen and set a pot of water on the stove to boil. As much as he wanted to look out the window at Jessica again, he avoided standing too close and continued making the pasta and salad.

Twenty minutes later when the dinner was ready, Jessica still hadn't come inside and Jacob had fallen asleep. Nick sat on the corner of the couch and listened to the animated characters on the television screen. He'd watched this movie with Ryan and Sarah at least a dozen times and found himself mouthing the words to the catchy tune. He sat there for five more minutes, his eyes never far from the clock on the wall.

His stomach grumbled. He'd skipped lunch. Would it be rude to let Jessica know dinner was ready? Maybe it would hurry her phone conversation. He crossed the room to the front door and pulled it open. Jessica wasn't standing where he'd last seen her.

He hustled down the porch steps and looked across the yard. Was she in the cabin? Out of the corner of his eye, he spotted her in the front seat of her car. Her eyes were closed and her mouth was moving. Was she praying? He knocked gently on her window.

Jessica startled. A blush colored her cheeks. She stepped out of the car and tucked her phone in her purse. "I'm sorry. How long have I been out here?"

"Half hour or so. I hope everything's all right."

"It will be, I hope." Her short response indicated she didn't want to discuss it further. She shut her car door. "How's Jacob?"

"Sleeping. Hope you don't mind, but I put in a movie. It knocked him right out." Nick walked beside her toward his porch.

"I don't mind at all. He's probably exhausted. Hey, thanks for your help this afternoon. It was nice to have another adult with me at the hospital."

"Sure thing." Nick opened the front door and allowed Jessica to walk through.

"We'll have to give Jacob more pain medication before the last dose wears off." Once past the entryway, she moved toward her son lying on the couch. She smiled down on him and pulled up the afghan higher under his chin. Jessica's mouth twitched and a nervous expression flashed across her face.

"Jessica, Jacob's going to be okay. It was an accident." Nick wanted to make sure she remembered her words to him at the hospital.

"As a parent, you blame yourself even when you know you couldn't have prevented it."

"Like you said, you've told him countless times not to jump. Boys will be boys. We like adventure and sometimes push the limits."

Jessica pressed her lips in a hard line, and narrowed her eyes. Something was definitely bothering her. Maybe she was thinking about the cabin. He'd ease her mind on that front.

They settled by the table and Nick said a short prayer. He didn't know what Jessica believed, but it felt right to ask for a blessing in her presence.

A few bites into the meal, Nick couldn't wait any longer to reduce the tension in her features. "Your uncle can stay in the small house if he pays utilities and any supplies I might need to fix up the place."

Jessica set her fork down on the edge of her plate and rested her hand on top of his and gave a gentle squeeze. "Thank you, that's very generous."

Her fingers were soft and warm. He had the urge to cover them with his own, but he resisted. She quickly removed her hand and slid it under the table.

"The roof won't make it through another rainy winter. You might keep your eyes and ears open for another place." Nick forked up some macaroni and put it into his mouth.

"I'm grateful for any amount of time he can stay." Jessica's face lit up and she stabbed a bite of salad with gusto. "Thank you. It's a huge weight off my shoulders."

"Tell me about your uncle. I'd like to know exactly what I'm in for . . ."

15

Jessica could've hugged Nick on the spot. Between her struggles with finding her uncle a rental and Andrew's insistence he see Jacob, she felt completely spent—until Nick made an offer she couldn't refuse—the use of his cabin for utilities and supplies.

"My uncle is an amazing man. He's served as a missionary to the people in the Philippines for years. When he came home to Santa Cruz, he'd make sure I was doing okay." Jessica twisted the ring on her finger. "He's kind and generous, and has a loving heart."

Nick wiped his mouth on a napkin. "Sounds like an interesting man. I can't wait to meet him."

Jessica wrestled with whether or not she should come clean about who her uncle had become in recent months. He wasn't the same man she described. Now he was withdrawn, bitter, and—

"Mom? Mommy?" Jacob's sleepy voice called from the couch.

She bolted off her chair. "What, sweetie, I'm here. Does your arm hurt?"

Jacob nodded.

"Are you hungry?" asked Nick.

Jacob pushed the blanket off his lap. "Uh-huh."

Jessica ran her hand down her son's cheek and helped him off the couch. "Come to the table and I'll get you some macaroni and cheese."

Once Jacob was seated, she met Nick in the kitchen.

"Does he like applesauce? I can smash an ibuprofen in it." His words were soft, for her ears only. "I've seen Holly do it when giving medicine to her kids."

She appreciated his thoughtfulness. Jacob hated the taste of liquid medicine. "Good idea." She scooped some pasta onto a plate and handed it to Nick.

He added the painkiller to the small cup of applesauce, and placed the dinner in front of Jacob. "Here you go, buddy."

Jacob took small bites, mostly of the macaroni and cheese.

Jessica was glad his right arm wasn't affected. He would still be able to eat, write, and do many of the things he usually did. "Remember to eat your applesauce," she prodded.

The doorbell rang.

"Are you expecting company?" Jessica had taken a seat where her half-eaten dinner now grew cold.

"No. I'll go see who it is." Nick wiped his hands on a paper towel and strode to the front door.

"Uncle Nick, is Jacob still here?" Ryan's voice filtered into the dining room.

"Come on in," said Nick.

Jessica looked over her shoulder.

The entire Branson family filed in. Ryan carried a *Get Well* balloon and a wrapped package. "Here, this is for you."

"Thanks!" Jacob beamed. "Can you help me unwrap it?"

Ryan held on to the gift, while Jacob tore at the paper. "It's a football!"

"Dad said when your arm is better, he'll take us to the park," said Ryan. "You can come, too, Uncle Nick."

Jessica's gut twisted. Maybe her roommate was right. Jacob needed to spend time with a man in his life. "How did you know about Jacob's arm?"

"Nick sent me a text when you were at the hospital," said Aaron. "Ryan couldn't wait to see his cast."

"Me, too, Daddy!" Sarah wiggled her way next to Jacob.

Jessica could see Holly speaking with Nick in the kitchen.

"Can I be done, Mom?" Her son grabbed her attention.

"No, Jacob. Please finish your applesauce and take a few more bites of pasta. Your friends can wait a few minutes."

Aaron guided Ryan and Sarah away from Jacob. "Kids, Jacob needs to finish his dinner. Sorry, Jessica. We didn't mean to barge in while you were eating."

"We'd like to babysit the kids and give you two a break," said Holly. "I know they kept you busy last night while Aaron and I were away. It's the least we can do."

Jessica didn't know what to make of the situation. If she left with Nick, it would be like a date and he wasn't the one who asked her out. They were suddenly forced to spend time together. Alone.

"But Jacob's not feeling well," Jessica protested. Her son was the perfect excuse not to leave. Plus, as his mom she genuinely cared for his well-being. She stole a glance at Nick. It had been quite a day. Maybe he didn't want to go out with her either.

"You can go, Mom. I want to play with Ryan." Jacob downed his applesauce. At least she knew he had medicine in him.

"I'm up for it, if you are." Nick grabbed his jacket from the coat closet.

On second thought, Nick probably needed his space. He wasn't used to being around kids so much.

Jessica snatched her purse off the counter. "Where're we going?"

"You name it and I'll take you there," said Nick.

Yes, the man definitely needed to get away. And she needed a reprieve from all her worries. Looked like a night out would benefit them both.

Evelyn sank deeper into the water and inhaled the sweet jasmine scent of the lit candle she'd perched on the corner of the jetted tub. Ahh. This is exactly what she needed. She laid her head back, and closed her eyes. She couldn't remember the last time she'd taken a bath. Tonight's plan was to have a simple, relaxing evening. She'd get comfortable in her new cotton pajamas, curl up with a good book, and order take-out.

She ran her fingers through her wet hair. The stylist cut a good inch off the other day. The back was now slightly shorter than the front, her grey strands creating a perfect bob. She liked her hair that way and received compliments on a regular basis. Made her feel good.

The ringing of a phone interrupted her soak in the tub. Must be her daughter Amy. Or Carol her house sitter. Those were the only two people who knew she was here. She'd give them each a call when she finished.

Evelyn's mind went into overdrive. What if there was an emergency? She imagined her condo on fire. Or worse yet, what if something happened to her precious granddaughter?

That's it. Evelyn hoisted herself out of the tub, wrapped a towel around her midsection, and raced through the house to answer the phone.

"I'd almost given up," said Patty, her longtime friend.

"Patty, how did you know I was here?" Evelyn envisioned the two of them young and carefree. They'd double-dated plenty with Ronald and George.

"When you didn't answer your phone all day, I had to call Amy to find out where you were."

Pitiful. She definitely needed to get out more.

"You didn't tell me you were coming to Santa Cruz!" Patty's reprimanding tone lifted.

"I arrived a few hours ago."

"And . . ."

"I was going to call you first thing tomorrow morning."

"Uh-huh."

"Listen, I'm here for the next couple of weeks."

"All right." Patty laughed. "You're forgiven."

"Good. Can I call you back? I'm dripping all over the rug."

"As in you stepped out of the shower?"

"Bath," said Evelyn. "Yes, I know. I never relax long enough for a soak in the tub, but I'm on vacation."

"Call me back as soon as you dry off because I've got plans for us tonight."

Evelyn distinctly heard the playful tone in Patty's voice. "Tonight? Well, I've got plans of my own."

"Let me guess. It involves you, a book, and a quiet house. Tell me it's not so."

Once again, Evelyn was reminded of how boring her life sounded. Did she need to spice things up? She walked into the bathroom and combed her wet hair. "Okay, what do you have in mind?"

"That's the spirit!" Patty cheered.

Evelyn rolled her eyes. "You're not going to set me up with someone are you?" She joked.

"Who me?"

"Patricia Donovan! The last time led to heartbreak. Please, for the love of mercy, I don't want a blind date." Evelyn blew out the jasmine candle and pulled the plug in the tub.

"We're not kids anymore. Ronald's best friend is in town and so are you. It'd be one night of dinner and conversation. Nothing more. Plus, if you ask me, the man's a looker. I'm a happily married woman, but I've got eyes."

"Patty." Evelyn giggled. When was the last time she actually giggled? She moved to the bedroom closet and fingered her clothing options. It wouldn't hurt to spend a few hours in the presence of a man. It wasn't a date. Just old friends getting together.

Patty broke into her musings. "Are you up for it? Ron's paying—"

"He doesn't have to do that." Evelyn pulled her black pants out of the closet and paired them with a silk floral top. She carefully laid the items on her bed, the phone wedged between her ear and shoulder.

"Don't think anything of it. It's nice to have our best friends around."

Evelyn grabbed a pair of strappy sandals suddenly gaining energy for the night ahead. "Where do you want to meet? And what time?"

"Crow's Nest. Shall we say seven o'clock?"

If she remembered correctly, the waterfront restaurant had a beautiful view of the harbor. "I'll be there."

A nervous flutter gripped her stomach. The last time she'd seen Patricia and Ronald they'd come up to San Francisco to take in a Broadway show. They couldn't coax her to come with them. Since then, she'd promised herself she'd be more adventurous. She hoped Patty would acknowledge her new outlook on life.

"I'm proud of you. I know the past year hasn't been easy."

"Thank you. But I've turned a corner. I'm ready to live again and see what God has for me."

"Well I see a handsome man in your future."

"I don't know if I'd go *that far*. Let's take it one moment at a time. "Evelyn chuckled. "What did you say Ronald's friend's name was?"

"I didn't. But don't worry, a name's not everything."

"What do you mean by that?" Goosebumps covered Evelyn's body. She dropped her towel and slipped on her terry robe and cinched the belt.

"We'll introduce you at the Crow's Nest. See you soon."

Evelyn stared at the phone in her hands. The names of past friends flipped like a Rolodex in her mind. Who could it be?

16

Evelyn, dear. I'd like you to meet Horace Reddish." Patricia gestured to the man standing beside her husband Ronald.

It took everything inside Evelyn to keep her laughter at bay. She was sure the man had been teased his whole life for a name that sounded like a popular condiment. "Nice to meet you." She held out a hand.

"Pleased to meet you, as well." Horace shook her hand and smiled revealing a row of straight teeth no doubt whitened by a professional. His skin, tanned by either the sun or a salon, was bronzed to perfection. He reminded her of an actor with his good looks and silver hair.

"I thought we'd eat upstairs tonight." Ronald directed the foursome to the lower priced dining area of the Crow's Nest.

It suited Evelyn. She'd rather relax than have the pressure of a fine dining experience with friends she hadn't seen in quite some time and a man she'd only met five minutes before. By the grin on Horace's face, he appeared to be relieved as well.

They chose a table against the wall with a beautiful view of the harbor. Horace pulled out Evelyn's seat and then scooted her toward the table. What a gentleman. Patty sat across from her with Ronald at his wife's side.

"The salad bar here is amazing as is the clam chowder," said Ronald, wiggling his brows.

A young waitress approached the table, her black top and mini skirt revealing a twenty-something figure. She handed everyone a menu. "Can I get you folks something to drink?"

"We'll start with four waters." Ronald jumped in.

"Sure thing." The waitress nodded and turned on her heel.

In the past, Patty had told Evelyn how tight-fisted Ronald was with his money. She thought he might have loosened up a bit when Patty told her Ronald wanted to treat tonight. Just in case, she'd respect his offer and order one of the lower-priced dinners.

Horace perused the menu. He leaned toward Evelyn. "What catches your eye?"

Evelyn could smell mint on the man's breath and the out-doorsy scent of his aftershave. It had been a long time since she sat this close to a man. She liked it, which surprised her even more. "I thought I'd have the salad bar and a cup of soup. What about you?"

"Thought I'd try the fish tacos." Horace pointed to the menu.

"Good choice." Evelyn smiled. She glanced up at Patty and Ronald. The pair had silly grins on their faces. Oh no! They weren't trying to set her up with Horace, were they? From what Patty told her, the man lived in San Diego and was here on business. Certainly, her friend didn't think she'd start a long-distance relationship.

The waitress came back with four glasses of water and placed them on the table. "Are you ready to order or do you need more time?"

"I think we're set." Ronald jumped in once again. He ordered for everyone, remembering what he heard before the waitress arrived.

Evelyn grabbed hold of the straw in her cup and swirled the wedge of lemon in circles. Nothing was as refreshing as a glass of lemon water; however, she would've liked a cup of tea. But Ronald didn't allow them a choice. In fact, when it came time for dessert, she was sure Patty's husband would ask for the bill. Truth be told, she rarely had dessert at restaurants and had a feeling tonight would be no different. Maybe she'd come back on her own another night and order the crème brûlée. The thought made her smile.

In no time, the men struck up a conversation about gas prices and the stock market, while the women discussed grandbabies.

"Jayden is turning two in a few weeks and he definitely has entered the terrible two's. No is his favorite word, and he's driving my daughter-in-law crazy." Patty let out a sigh. "I can remember those days with all three of my children. What a tough season, but every mother goes through it."

Evelyn nodded, acknowledging the truth to Patty's words. "I hope Amy finds her stride. She's tired and moody, and begged me to help care for Bella right before I left. Daniel thinks she may have postpartum depression. I've heard some women need medication. I hope I did the right thing by coming to Santa Cruz." Evelyn promised herself she wouldn't focus on Amy's mood swings or pleas to help with Bella.

Her friend patted her hand. "You have every right to take a vacation. You've had a life-altering experience losing your husband. You deserve some time for yourself. And it's not like you'll be gone forever."

"But I worry—"

"For goodness' sakes, give it to the Lord and enjoy your trip. You'll be home in a couple of weeks and no doubt will be a doting grandmother in no time. Enjoy yourself. Relax.

And . . ." Patty winked and cocked her head in Horace's direction, "eat up the attention. It's good for you."

Evelyn had to admit it felt nice to be part of a foursome. She missed the days when she and Edward would go out with clients or church friends. She missed Edward. Most of all, she missed a companion, a partner, someone to share life with.

The waitress approached with three plates full of food and a cup of soup for Evelyn. After the young woman moved away from their table to take someone else's order, Evelyn excused herself to go to the salad bar. Horace stood and pulled back her chair.

Once downstairs, Evelyn made a run to the ladies' room to gather herself before filling a plate with greens and other salad items. She looked closely in the mirror. Time had changed her skin, but inside she felt like the same girl she'd been all those years ago when she and George had roamed all over Santa Cruz.

Time had also altered the coastal town. More buildings and traffic had made the area less desirable in her eyes, but it still could evoke feelings of carefree days and the end of her dream of marrying George MacAllister. Evelyn washed her hands and dried them on a paper towel. She'd better grab her salad before Patty came looking for her.

A few minutes later, Evelyn joined her party with a plate of brightly colored fruits and vegetables. Once again, Horace stood and helped her to her seat. This time it grated on her. Did he think she needed to be babied? She was an independent grown woman who could take care of herself. She plastered on a smile. "Thanks, Horace."

"You're welcome." Horace sat and picked up his half-eaten fish taco and looked at Ronald. "You were telling me about your friend. The one who was a missionary." He took a large bite.

Evelyn sucked in a breath. Were they talking about George? She thought Patty and Ronald had lost track of him. They hadn't mentioned her young love in years knowing the way her relationship with him ended.

Patty gave Evelyn an "I'm sorry" look.

"What? Did I say something wrong?" Horace shrugged his shoulders, a pained expression on his face.

"We heard from a classmate that George came back to the states with a high fever and gangrene in his leg. It didn't look good. Wish we knew more."

Evelyn felt like someone had punched her in the gut. Her mouth went dry and she grabbed her water, downing half a glass. She'd hoped to find out what happened to George during her vacation and wanted that now more than ever.

During the meal, Horace attempted to include Evelyn in the conversation, but more than once she responded with one-word answers and polite smiles, her mind on her long-ago love. Yes, Horace was an attractive man and a gentleman to boot, but after tonight she'd never see him again. And that was fine with her.

As they walked out of the restaurant into the cool night air, Patty hugged her and invited her out for coffee, just the two of them, the following morning. Evelyn readily accepted and thanked Ronald for the meal.

"May I walk you to your car?" Horace held up his elbow for her to take hold. As long as he didn't try to end the evening with a goodnight kiss! My, she was being presumptuous.

"That would be lovely, thank you." Evelyn cupped his elbow with her hand and waved to Patty and Ronald. Her facial expression must have shown her trepidation because Patty called out to her as she and Horace walked away.

"See you in the morning!"

Evelyn and Horace kept on walking through the parking lot. She spotted her sedan and gestured. A few more feet and she'd be free.

"How long will you be in town?" asked Horace.

"Not long." Hopefully, he'd get the hint. "I could leave at any time if my daughter calls begging me to come home." Horace didn't need to know she'd planned on staying another two weeks. She purposefully avoided asking him the same question.

Once they reached her car, she fumbled for her keys. She was ready to go back to her cozy beach house, change into her pajamas, and read until she felt sleepy. *Where are those keys? Ah, there they are.*

"Thank you for joining us." Horace held out his hand. "It was a pleasure to meet such a beautiful woman."

Evelyn's heart sped up at his compliment. She placed her hand in his expecting him to give it a shake. Instead, he brought it to his lips and kissed the back of her hand. *Smooth move.*

Horace let go of her hand and dipped his head. *Was he from the movies?* "I leave in a couple of days. Ronald knows where I live in case you'd like to stay in contact. Good night, Evelyn."

She hit the remote unlocking the door and slid inside. Putting the key in the ignition, she was grateful for the sound of her car's engine. She couldn't get away fast enough. Horace stood behind the neighboring parked car and watched her leave. As much as she enjoyed the man's attention, he wasn't the one she longed to be with. But from what she heard this evening, George was more than likely in heaven with Edward. Tears clogged her throat.

She gunned the gas pedal and her tires screeched against the pavement. In her side mirror she caught sight of Horace scratching his head, watching her drive away. She passed Patty and Ronald on the side of the road as they walked to their car.

Evelyn was positive Patty would question her in the morning.

17

How many clubs do you need?" the ticket clerk asked.

Jessica glanced around the Boardwalk's Neptune Kingdom. The indoor miniature golf course had a pirate theme and was an eighteen-hole two-story creative maze. Jacob would've loved it.

"Two adults, please." Nick whipped out his wallet from his jeans pocket.

Jessica fished for hers in her purse. "Oh, here—"

"No, I've got it." He pulled out a ten and set it on the counter. "You can spot for a coffee afterward if you like." He grinned.

The clerk replaced the money with two balls and clubs. "Have a good time."

Nick grabbed them both, along with a pencil and a scorecard.

"Are we really keeping score?" Jessica cringed.

"You bet we are. It's the only way to play miniature golf. Don't worry, I'll keep tally. What color do you want? Blue or yellow?" He opened his palm for her to decide.

Jessica tentatively took the blue one. "It's my lucky color." She'd need it. She hadn't played miniature golf in years. They stood behind an older couple still trying to get the ball in the first hole.

When Holly had suggested she go out with Nick, Jessica had no idea what to expect, where they'd go, or what they'd talk about. Nick was a nice guy—attractive, too. If their circumstances were different, she could imagine dating him. The thought shocked her and sent a ripple down her spine.

"Ladies first." Nick gestured once the couple moved on to the second hole, then wrote their names on the scorecard.

Jessica set her ball down on the middle hole on the mat. The dings on the wood where most people aimed the ball caught her eye and she decided that would be her target, too. Only her club didn't cooperate. She completely missed the ball. Laughter bellowed behind her. She glanced over her shoulder. A group of rude teenagers had gathered behind Nick. She looked at him for reassurance and was encouraged to find he wasn't laughing.

Nick stepped in front of the kids to block their view and nodded in her direction. She swung again. This time the ball flew down the lane and bounced out. Jessica could feel heat flooding her neck and face. Nick ran to retrieve the ball.

"We're going to be here all day," one of the kids called from behind. "Maybe we should go bowling?"

Jessica wished they would.

"Third time's a charm." Nick handed her the ball and leaned in. "Ignore them, okay?"

Jessica met his gaze and was momentarily encouraged. She placed the ball on the mat, held the club between nervous fingers, and gave a practice swing before stepping forward and taking another shot.

She let out the breath she was holding when she heard the dinking sound of the ball falling into the hole. She hit a hole in one—on the third swing.

"Nice one. I'll give you a point for that. The rest we'll say was practice." Nick winked and wrote down her score, then tucked the pencil and card in his back pocket. He proceeded to make the hole in two shots.

Out of the corner of her eye, she saw a man resembling Andrew with his five o'clock shadow and tousled dark hair peeking out from under his red baseball cap. He wouldn't have come to Santa Cruz, would he? Butterflies danced in Jessica's stomach. The man moved out of her line of vision.

Throughout the course, Jessica felt on edge. If Andrew saw the address of Pacific Coast Manor on the envelope on her kitchen counter, he'd no doubt come looking for Jacob. Every time she'd talked to him, she heard desperation in his voice, like nothing would stop him from seeing his son. Maybe she was being overprotective. Would it hurt to allow Andrew the opportunity to see Jacob just this once? She felt her resolve slipping.

Jessica followed Nick into a dark section of the course. The balls glowed, as did the holes and pirate-themed décor. She putted the ball.

"You doing all right? You're quiet." Nick took his turn.

"Thinking about Jacob. I hope he's doing okay. I feel guilty for leaving him tonight." She banked her blue ball off the side and came within inches of the hole.

"Is your cell phone on? I'm sure Holly would call if Jacob needed you." Nick took a shot and the ball fell in.

Jessica pulled her phone out of her pocket and checked. The battery was low, but should have enough power until she could charge it at the hotel. "I'm good."

"What about the volume? A couple of times today I noticed you didn't answer your phone." Curiosity edged his tone.

"The sound is turned as high as it will go." Jessica put her phone back in her purse, then took a shot missing once again.

"What can I say? I screen calls." A low chuckle escaped. It didn't sound genuine, even to her ears. She chewed her lip and tapped the ball into the hole, avoiding his gaze and grateful for the darkness.

"Is that right? Good to know." He wrote down their scores.

After two more holes, they came into the light once again. Jessica scanned the crowd of miniature golfers. The man with the red cap was nowhere to be found. She was probably just being paranoid.

People had been known to come to the Santa Cruz Beach Boardwalk from all parts of the world. If Andrew were in town, it wouldn't surprise her. He loved roller coasters, and the Giant Dipper was one of the best. If she were going to enjoy the evening, she'd need to put all thoughts of Andrew out of her mind. Jessica bumped Nick's arm playfully as they waited for the elderly couple to finish a hole. "How far behind am I? I know you've got it all calculated in your head." She teased.

He grinned, resting an arm on her shoulder. "I'm ahead by twelve strokes."

"Don't be smug. Let me see that." Jessica snatched the scorecard from his hand. "Twelve? I think you've been cheating." She knew that he'd been beating her at every hole, but she enjoyed the banter and having him close enough to smell his cologne.

"The scorecard doesn't lie." Nick arched a brow.

She concentrated as she added the numbers, but his nearness made it difficult. He was ahead by thirteen points. "Your math is wrong." She left it at that and stuck the card in his shirt pocket. There were only a few holes left. She couldn't catch him now.

"Okay, it's thirteen but I was trying not to make you feel bad—since you're playing with your lucky color and all." He grinned. "Maybe next time you should take the yellow."

She'd show him. Letting out a breath, she set her ball on the mat and wiggled her hips before putting.

"No distractions, please." Nick shook his head and crossed his arms.

She was never one to use her feminine charm to get a man's attention, but knowing she distracted him if only for a brief moment brought a satisfying smile to her face. She hit the ball again and it dropped in.

Nick followed her with a hole in one.

Figures. By the end, he beat her by fourteen points, almost as many as the entire course. She wasn't being very competitive today, an unusual occurrence. Why did she want to win all the time? Is that what was going on between her and Andrew?

Truth was, she wanted the upper hand where Jacob was concerned. She'd been his only parent for six years—taking care of him, making daily decisions, and supporting him financially. She didn't need Andrew's help, nor did she expect him to step in and be a caring father. In fact, she'd rather forget he called and go back to the way things were before he dialed her number.

Her mind took a turn. Even if Andrew tried to pursue custody, he'd never win. A judge would side with her. She had Andrew's signature on the termination of parental rights paperwork and his apparent drug and alcohol use would restrict him from spending time with Jacob alone—unless he'd changed his ways and had gotten help in the form of rehabilitation. But wouldn't he have told her that on the phone? No. Andrew was still the same guy. Controlling. Demanding. Selfish.

And as far as she was concerned, Andrew had seen Jacob the day he intruded on her home and saw a picture hanging on the wall.

A shiver ran through her. *Andrew knows what Jacob looks like.* Time to get out of here.

Jessica set her club next to Nick's on the rack. "Thank you. I enjoyed it even though you creamed me. And we left those teenagers in the dust."

"Glad you had fun." Nick grabbed her hand and directed her out of the building. "But I can tell you have a lot on your mind."

Jessica liked the feel of Nick's strong hand in hers. She could easily fall hard for a guy like him, but at this point in her life with Andrew pursuing Jacob, a relationship was out of the question. "I'm sorry, you're right. I'm preoccupied. Mind if we grab a coffee to go? I want to get back to Jacob."

"I have a better idea. Let's skip coffee altogether and go straight home. I'd like to know how Jacob's doing myself."

His words were like a salve on an open wound.

"Thank you." Jessica leaned in to him. The man had muscles. A smile curved her lips remembering Ryan's announcement from the day before.

Yes, she could easily fall for him—but she wouldn't allow herself. She let go of his hand and tugged at the collar of her jean jacket.

"Chilly?" asked Nick.

"I'll be all right. The sooner we get back to your place the better."

When Jessica and Nick returned to the house, the children were playing a game at the table and Holly and Aaron were watching a show on television, sitting close under a blanket. Jessica felt a mixture of relief and envy.

Aaron hit the off button on the remote. "You're back early. Miss us?"

"Wanted to see if Jacob was doing okay." Nick hung up his coat and offered to take Jessica's.

"I'll leave mine on," said Jessica. "We should get going—"

"He's doing fine." interrupted Holly. "He's only complained of pain once, but that was right after you left."

"The pain medication must've kicked in." Jessica moved across the room to the dining area where Jacob, Ryan, and Sarah played and stood next to her son. She laid a hand on his shoulder, pulling his attention from the game. "How's your arm?"

"It hurts when I think about it, but I'm having fun." Jacob made a move with his playing piece.

"We need to go back to the hotel. It's been a long day."

"Can we wait a little while? We're almost done."

"I'll give you a few more minutes, okay? Mommy's tired." Jessica covered a yawn. "Tomorrow's a big day. We're moving Uncle George."

The blanket hugged Holly's shoulders as she approached. "You found a place. That's great news."

"Thank you for giving me the list of apartments. I checked them all out, but none were right for my uncle. Then—"

Jessica heard the men talking in the background. Aaron was asking Nick what time he needed him in the morning to help demolish the cabin.

Jessica directed Holly to the men's conversation. "Nick will tell you."

"Changed my mind—at least for now," said Nick. "Jessica's uncle needs a place to live until he can get settled somewhere else. Thought I'd help him out for the time being."

"That's kind of you," said Holly. "I know it will be the perfect spot for George to get back on his feet."

Jessica grinned. "I hope so."

"Let me know if anything in the cabin needs fixing," said Aaron. "I'm a good handyman and have some extra time."

"Not for long," Holly encouraged. "He has two interviews lined up."

"That's great, man." Nick punched Aaron on the shoulder.

After saying their goodbyes, Jessica returned to the hotel with a sleepy Jacob in her arms. She was worn out. It had been an overwhelming day. She dug in her purse for her room key. Her cell phone dinged, signaling she had a text message.

Jessica slipped the card inside the metal box and the green light flashed. She opened the door, then laid Jacob down on one of the queen-sized beds.

She pulled her cell phone from her purse and read Melissa's message.

He came again. Made me nervous. Staying with my sister until you come home. Call me ASAP!

18

Melissa's text message was embedded in Jessica's mind. Andrew had made her roommate nervous? She wasn't afraid of anything—or anyone. Andrew must have threatened her in some way for her to feel she had to go to her sister's house. Jessica's hand shook as she called Melissa.

Three rings. Four. When her roommate's spunky voicemail kicked in, Jessica hung up. She looked at the text message again. It was written hours ago. Why had she only now received it?

She peered over at Jacob lying on the bed next to hers. He looked sweet and young, his long eyelashes and soft cheeks beckoning her for a goodnight kiss. She acted on her instincts and covered him with a blanket.

He let out an audible sigh. "Mommy."

"What is it, sweetie?"

Jacob's eyelids fluttered open. "My arm hurts."

"Need more medicine?" She rubbed his shoulder.

"Uh-huh." His brows knit together.

"Why don't you sit up and I'll get you some." She propped pillows against the headboard and helped Jacob scoot back.

Tears filled his eyes. "I'm really sorry, Mom."

"About what?" She grabbed his stuffed bear and handed it to him.

"For not listening and jumping off the swing."

Her heart swelled. It took a lot of courage for him to admit his mistake. She could learn from his example. Jessica sat on the edge of the bed and snuggled her son close. "You're forgiven. I wish you never broke your wrist, but I think you've learned your lesson."

"I did."

"That's my boy." She kissed the top of his head. "Now let's get that medicine inside you. It'll make your arm feel better."

Jessica went into the bathroom and dug through her toiletry bag for the pain medication. Never in her wildest dreams did she imagine Jacob would break a bone. Her jaws clenched. If only she could reverse time.

As she poured the proper dose into the small measuring cup, her mind darted to her roommate. She'd try to call her again as soon as her son fell asleep. Maybe Melissa would answer this time.

<hr />

Not long after Jessica and Jacob left, Aaron and his family decided to go, leaving Nick alone on the couch with his thoughts. He wavered with whether or not he'd made the right decision allowing Jessica's uncle to stay at the cabin. Ever since he'd met the cute brunette and her son, his plans for tearing down the small house had all but disappeared.

In a sense, it was the charitable thing to do. He grabbed his Bible and flipped to Deuteronomy 15:10, the verse his pastor read in church the other week. "Give generously to them and do so without a grudging heart; then because of this the Lord your God will bless you in all your work and in everything you put your hand to."

With a sudden jolt of energy, he set the book down, darted off the couch and gathered cleaning supplies from the cabinet under the kitchen sink. It wouldn't do to have Jessica's uncle come to a dirty cabin. Nick had more pride than that.

For the next couple of hours, he mopped the kitchen floor, vacuumed the shabby carpet, and washed and dried the bed linens. He also gave the walls a good wipe down and dusted the furniture. He cleaned the hard water stains from the toilet, bathtub, and sink, and made sure they were in working order. The plumbing knocked and groaned reminding him of the many years he'd lived there, but at least the place was clean.

A gnawing feeling grabbed him. He was glad he was living in his new home and not this beat-up place. Honestly, he was surprised Jessica saw the cabin's potential. Everything was old and worn. Then again, her uncle was a missionary and maybe was used to living in less than desirable conditions.

He moved to the kitchen, pulled out the few dishes stacked in the cabinet, and filled the sink with soap and hot water, his mind taking a new direction. One of the first times he'd fixed a meal in the small kitchen, his friend A.J. had come to town and chopped the vegetables for homemade salsa. He insisted on making it himself, saying he'd learned from the locals in Mexico.

That evening turned out to be one of the best Nick ever had with his friend, despite their differences in lifestyles. A.J. had always been the life of the party and a magnet for women, while Nick was loyal, seeing friends through thick and thin. He was more cautious with those he'd dated, making sure they believed in the same things he did—like God, family, and serving his community. A.J. had always teased him, telling him to lighten up. And Nick would get after A.J. to be responsible for his actions.

That dinner was the last Nick had heard of or seen A.J. It was as though he'd fallen off the map—until a few days ago when Nick saw his picture on TV. Had A.J. sold the woman drugs? Impossible. Anger started to bubble inside and Nick threw the sponge in the water, refusing to believe his friend had anything to do with her death.

He grabbed a towel and swiped at the droplets that had sprayed onto the window. Dust and grime clung to the cloth. Nick had never known A.J. to get in trouble with the law. Everyone makes bad choices now and then, but sooner or later people grow up. Hadn't A.J. learned from his mistakes? Apparently not.

The sound of tires crunching on his gravel driveway drew his attention. Who would come to his house at this hour?

The minute Jessica pulled into Nick's driveway, she wondered if it was a hasty decision. What reason would she give for why she came back? She wanted to tell Nick the truth—that after talking with Melissa, she'd learned Andrew could already be in Santa Cruz and she didn't want to be alone with Jacob. But how much did Nick need to know? She'd rather not involve him in her mess.

Her phone conversation with Melissa replayed in her mind.

"His eyes were bloodshot, like he'd been drinking." Melissa's voice had lowered to a near whisper. "He pushed me aside and came into our apartment."

"Did he hurt you?"

"No, but he forced me to tell him where you were."

Jessica closed her eyes and pressed her lips together. "What did you say?"

"That you and Jacob were taking a much-needed vacation."

She wished it were true. So far, it had felt like anything but. "That could be good, right?"

"I'd like to think so."

Jessica could hear the hesitation in Melissa's voice. "What are you not telling me?"

"Andrew stormed into the kitchen and rummaged through the drawers. I'd hidden the letter from Pacific Coast Manor inside the phone book, but he found it and tore off the address."

Jessica dug her fingernails into her palm. "Is he on his way?"

"I don't know," Melissa had said. "He left without saying another word, but I'd be on the lookout if I were you."

Jessica had battled whether to stay put, transfer to a different hotel, or go to Holly's, but in the end her heart won out and she drove to Nick's. Now she questioned whether to stay—or leave while she had the chance.

A light was on in the cabin and she could see Nick through the small kitchen window. She turned off the engine, stole a breath, and walked to the cabin door, knocking lightly.

The door opened and the smell of cleaning supplies wafted from the cabin. Nick's forehead crinkled. "Jessica? What's wrong?"

"You're going to think I'm crazy, but I'd like to spend the night . . . to be sure the cabin's the best place for my uncle." She clutched her arms around her waist and willed her voice to remain calm. Did he buy her story? In a way, she spoke the truth.

"Having second thoughts, huh?" He eyed her suspiciously. "Come on in. Where's Jacob?"

"In the car sleeping. I was only going to wake him up if you agreed for us to stay. I was planning on cleaning the cabin tonight, but by the fresh smell you beat me to it. Thank you for being so considerate."

Nick stepped forward and placed a hand on the doorframe, his nearness bringing her comfort. "Are you sure nothing's troubling you?"

How did she answer that question and remain discreet? "I'm having a difficult time with everything that's been happening lately. Between finding a place for my uncle, Jacob's broken wrist . . ." She let the rest go unsaid. As much as she considered Nick someone she could trust, she didn't know him well enough to divulge the whole story, nor did she want to go into detail about Andrew.

"Yeah, it's been quite a day. Is your luggage in the car? I'll get it for you."

"Thank you. I'll bring Jacob inside." An overwhelming urge to hug Nick came over her, but she didn't want to create an awkward moment or make him feel like her intentions weren't pure.

As the moon and stars shone above, she had peace for the first time that day. God was watching over her. He brought Nick into her life when she needed a friend and housing for Uncle George.

Andrew would never find Jacob here.

Evelyn padded across the room in her robe, flannel pajamas, and slippers and stuck the DVD of *Pride and Prejudice* into the player, her choice among the dozen or so from the cabinet. As the music started, she sat on the sofa, propped a pillow behind her back, and dug in the pocket of her robe for the small bag of trail mix she'd brought from home.

Time flew as she got wrapped up in Elizabeth and Darcy's push-pull romance.

"May I have the next dance, Miss Elizabeth?" The dark-haired hero asked Miss Lizzie at the Netherfield Ball.

Evelyn's heart stirred at Darcy's request and a memory of George asking her to dance at the Cocoanut Grove flashed through her mind. Like Miss Elizabeth Bennett, she'd said yes. The Grand Ballroom, with its wooden dance floor, balcony seating, and tiered stage, reflected the glamour and romance of the 1940s, perfect for Patricia and Ronald's wedding reception.

George had pulled Evelyn close as the melody of "Just Once in My Life" by the Righteous Brothers played in the background. "I haven't seen you in a while. Where've you been?"

"That's a funny question coming from someone who's been gone the last few months. I could ask you the same thing." Evelyn tilted her head to look into George's eyes and pouted her lower lip.

"I told you I wasn't going to be gone forever. Only for the summer." George turned her around the dance floor, one hand clasped in hers, the other on her lower back as their bodies swayed to the rhythm of the music.

She smiled, and laid her head on his shoulder. "But you're home now."

"Not for long. I'm hoping to go back in six months. Come with me." His voice was husky in her ear.

Evelyn felt in sync with George, except when he talked about his desire to be a missionary. She'd always thought she'd be able to enjoy all the luxuries her parents could afford with her father being a prominent lawyer in the Bay Area. She loved God and didn't mind sharing her faith, but that didn't mean she could be a missionary full-time in order to be with George. My, she was getting carried away. He hadn't asked for her hand, only to go on a mission trip. "Let's enjoy the song, and talk about it later."

Disappointment had shone in his eyes, but it quickly disappeared as he whirled her around the dance floor.

Darcy and Elizabeth's dance ended, bringing Evelyn back to the present.

Her life was definitely not like the movies. She'd chosen to marry someone like her father instead of stepping out in faith and marrying for love.

And now, if what Patricia and Ronald suggested was true, she might never see George again.

19

Nick balanced a tray in one hand and knocked on the cabin door with the other. He hoped Jessica and Jacob were up and dressed for the day. Last night, she told him she needed to be at Pacific Coast Manor at nine o'clock to pick up George. Exactly one hour from now.

The door opened a crack. "Nick?" Jessica's groggy tone indicated she hadn't talked this morning.

"Room service, madam?"

"Can you give me a minute?"

From what he could see, she wore turquoise pajamas. *Cute.* "Sure, I can wait."

"I'll hurry." The door closed.

A couple minutes later, Jessica reappeared wearing jeans and a sweatshirt, her hair pulled up in a ponytail. "What did you bring?" She inhaled deeply and stepped aside so he could pass. The smell of eggs and bacon floated in the air. "You're going to spoil us."

Nick set the tray on the small table. "Is Jacob awake?"

"Not yet. I'll go get him." Jessica moved toward the back bedroom, then stopped and turned around. "You're staying for breakfast, right?"

The question brought a satisfied smile to his face. "Don't mind if I do. Thanks for asking."

While Jessica checked on Jacob, he gathered the plates, silverware and cups from the cabinet and brought them to the table. He dished up the food and poured coffee into the cups.

Jessica returned without her son. "I didn't have the heart to wake him. He had a rough night last night, and so did I." She yawned.

"Maybe I should've let you sleep, too—"

"Oh, no. I needed to get up. Besides the breakfast looks delicious." Jessica sat by the table. "I'll get Jacob up in a little while."

He liked the boy, but it would be nice to get to know Jessica a bit better. Nick handed her a cup of coffee and took his place beside her. "I like this—just the two of us."

"Not a family guy, huh?" Jessica brought the steaming mug to her lips.

"That's not it at all. I like kids a lot and I'd like to have some one day—"

"You just don't like spending too much time with them." She picked up a piece of bacon with her fingers and took a bite.

"I didn't say that." Why did he suddenly feel as though he needed to defend himself? All he wanted was to eat a good breakfast with a beautiful woman, but it appeared Jessica didn't understand where he was coming from.

"Last night when Holly and Aaron came over and suggested we go out, it seemed you couldn't get out of the house fast enough." She took a bite of her eggs.

He couldn't allow her to think he hated kids. She had him all wrong. "Did it ever occur to you that I want to spend more time with you—alone?"

By the surprised look on Jessica's face, the thought apparently hadn't crossed her mind.

He considered last night a date, scrubbed the cabin clean, and made the breakfast mainly for her. Why *was* he doing all these things for someone who would be gone in a few days? "What can I say? I'd like to get to know you. Is that so terrible?"

Jessica's face flushed. "I guess not."

"Good." Nick took a swig of his coffee. "Can I ask you a question?"

"You already did." She teased.

"Very funny." Nick smiled, then sobered his expression. "Why do you wear that diamond ring? Are you engaged?"

Jessica dropped her eyes and twisted the ring around her finger. "So men leave me alone. My Uncle George gave it to me when I found out I was pregnant."

"You mean to tell me you haven't dated anyone since?"

Jessica shook her head.

"And Jacob's father? Does he ever see the boy? Send him birthday gifts?"

"Never. He's not in the picture, nor will he ever be." Her eyes darted to the left. From what he'd learned as a fireman, her gaze indicated she was hiding something.

Jacob padded into the room wearing his dinosaur pajamas and rubbing the sleep from his eyes.

"Jacob, look what Nick made for us." Jessica reached out her arms and he came toward her. "Sit down. We have a plate for you."

Nick wanted to know more about the brunette sitting across from him and what she was hiding. He had a feeling there was more to the story than what she was willing to tell him. But with Jacob now in the room, it would have to wait for another time.

Jessica arrived at Pacific Coast Manor, her senses on high alert at the risk of running into Andrew. When Nick offered to keep an eye on Jacob while she helped her uncle pack and get settled in his new environment, she'd jumped at his offer. Before walking into her uncle's room, Holly pulled her aside.

"You're going to have to be patient with George. Seems he's afraid you're going to push him to wear his prosthesis. He said he was going to demand you take him back here if that happens. Truthfully, he doesn't need us anymore. We've taught him well."

"Is it painful for him to use his prosthetic leg?"

"Yes." Holly nodded. "Scar mobilization can keep the skin flexible and pliable, and make his prosthesis easier to wear, but the skin on the retaining limb still needs to develop a tolerance to the socket. Phantom pain or sensation is normal and should gradually disappear."

Suddenly Jessica felt overwhelmed and ill equipped for the road ahead. How could she return to her apartment in Fresno by the end of the week? "Will George be able to handle life on his own?"

"Don't worry. George is a strong man. He's had training and knows exactly what to do. When he decides to wear his prosthetic leg for longer periods of time, a whole new world will open up to him."

Jessica let out a breath. "I stayed at Nick's cabin last night. It won't be easy for him to move around in his wheelchair."

Holly raised a brow and a grin spread across her face. "You stayed at Nick's place? I thought you left to go to the hotel."

"I did." Jessica's neck heated. How could she get out of explaining Melissa's text message? "But I returned to the cabin to clean it before my uncle arrived, but Nick already took care of it." It *had* crossed her mind. The more she talked the more vulnerable she felt. The less she said the better.

"You're right. It won't be easy for George to move around the cabin. That's why it will be perfect. He'll need to use his crutches, but hopefully he'll want to make life easier for himself by using his prosthesis. It'll be his decision."

"Are we talking about *my* uncle?" Jessica laid a hand on her chest. "I'm sure you've noticed he's been withdrawn and grouchy lately. He doesn't seem interested in using his prosthesis. If the size of the cabin doesn't encourage him, I don't know what will."

"It will all work out," Holly encouraged. "Somehow, it usually does."

Jessica didn't know if she agreed with that statement. Take her life. She didn't understand how allowing Andrew to see Jacob would have a positive outcome. The man had a drinking problem, and from what Melissa told her, Andrew sounded out-of-control and dangerous.

Maybe Holly was referring to her own situation being pregnant with a husband who was out of a job.

After George signed the release papers, Jessica pushed him out of the room and into the hallway. "Here we go, Uncle George. Aren't you glad to be out of this place?" She maneuvered his wheelchair down the corridor and out the back door.

"Slow down. You trying to kill me?" He grumbled, his knuckles white as he gripped the armrests.

She didn't have time to waste. Andrew might show up any minute. But she slowed her steps to please her uncle. "I can't wait to get you out of here. I think you're going to really love Nick's cabin—"

"I was fine where I was." His words shot out like bullets.

As rehab facilities go, this one was top-notch, but who would want to live there permanently? It appeared her uncle did.

She'd have to figure out a way to change his mind.

"So, what did you think of Horace?"

Evelyn would swear people could see Patricia's bright orange jogging suit from a mile away. The woman wasn't shy when it came to dressing in lively colors. Evelyn kept up the pace beside her friend as they walked down the path on West Cliff Drive. "He was . . . nice."

Patty whipped her head around. "Nice? That's it?"

"Okay, he was also good looking—in a Hollywood sort of way."

"And?" Patty moved her hand in small circles, signaling Evelyn to keep going.

"And, he was a gentleman."

Patty rolled her eyes. "Horace was quite smitten with you. Said you were as cute as a button. But he was surprised you brushed him off at the end of the evening and wondered why you drove off the way you did. Ronald and I are curious as well. What gives?"

"I told you I didn't want to be set up with anyone and you assured me it wasn't a date." Evelyn picked up the pace. The wind threatened to blow her sunhat off her head. She pushed it down and zipped up her jacket.

Patty caught up to her. "It felt good to be noticed by a man, right?"

A hint of a smile curved Evelyn's mouth.

"You can't fool me." Patty lifted a finger in Evelyn's direction. "I see that grin. You enjoyed Horace's company."

Evelyn adjusted her sunglasses and pushed her hat lower over her eyes. "I don't know if I'd go that far. He was a little over the top."

Patty laughed and linked arms with Evelyn. "Okay, I agree with you there. He's quite suave, but he knows how to handle a woman with care. You deserve to be treated like a queen."

"I'm doing fine on my own." Evelyn didn't sound as convincing as she hoped.

"I'm sure you are, but wouldn't you like to start dating again? You're still young and vibrant."

They slowed as they neared the lighthouse. Did she dare admit to her friend how much she'd been thinking of George? It didn't matter now that he might be dead. Evelyn sat on a bench and Patricia joined her.

"I have been thinking of someone." Evelyn fingered the simple gold chain at her neck.

"Do tell." Eagerness laced Patty's voice. She inched closer.

Evelyn removed her hat, tucked a strand of hair behind her ear, and allowed her young love's name to roll off her tongue. "George MacAllister." The crash of the waves against the rocky shore threatened to drown out the timbre of her voice.

"George? But . . ." Patricia's expression fell.

"When I married Edward, I closed off my feelings and that chapter of my life, but in the last few days I haven't been able to think of anyone but him. Last night when I heard Ronald say George had been sick, I immediately thought the worst. And now it might be too late."

Patricia patted Evelyn's hand. "When George returned from the Philippines after learning you were married, he separated himself from Ronald and me and, I suppose, most everyone we knew. Soon afterward, he returned to the mission field. We heard he bought a mobile home and would come back to

Santa Cruz every once in a while, but he never once contacted us."

"How could I have broken up with him in a letter?" Evelyn covered her mouth with a hand to halt herself from saying more.

"You did what you thought was best at the time."

The sound of the ocean's tide filled the lull in the conversation.

"Do you wish you'd never married Edward?" asked Patty.

"Of course not. I have Amy and Bella." Evelyn shifted in her seat, uncomfortable with where this conversation was going.

"But there was something special between you and George. Anyone with eyes could see that."

Evelyn stood and moved to the railing overlooking the surf. If her love for George was obvious, why didn't anyone stop her from marrying Edward? Seagulls flew overhead, and her eyes followed their path.

Patty came up beside her. "You want to know what happened to George, don't you?"

Evelyn hesitated from answering. Could she handle knowing what became of George even if she discovered he was married, or worse . . . dead?

Yes, she had to know. "Will you help me find him?"

"I'll do everything I can." Patty wrapped an arm around Evelyn's shoulder. "Now let's get that coffee we talked about last night."

20

Jessica pulled into Nick's driveway as close to the cabin as possible. "There it is. Your new home."

"It's not much to look at, is it?" George griped, folding his arms across his chest. "How old is the place? Looks rundown."

"It's definitely rustic but everything inside is in working order." Jessica tried to sound as cheerful as possible. She expected this kind of reaction, but it frustrated her just the same. "Do you think you could use your crutches for now and I'll set up your wheelchair inside?"

"If it'd be easier for you." His tone indicated she was asking a lot, but pushing him over the gravel driveway would be too difficult.

"Thank you." She got out of her car and pulled the crutches from the trunk.

Jacob hadn't greeted them. Nick's dog, Rosco, was usually roaming about, but even he was nowhere to be found. She opened the passenger's side door and handed her uncle the crutches. "Do you need help standing?"

George shook his head. He turned his body toward her, and hoisted himself up using the armrest. Quickly, before he lost his balance, he stuck the crutches under his arms.

Jessica scooted to the front door and turned the knob. Good, Nick had left the door unlocked. She pushed it wide. The small kitchen was clean and a thin vase of wildflowers sat on the table. She let out the breath and turned to see Uncle George coming toward her. A new wave of sadness washed over her as she watched her uncle hobble toward her without a lower left limb, his pants tucked up and pinned.

"You don't need to look at me that way." George barked.

"Like what?" Jessica challenged.

"With pity." He spat the words as he walked by and into the house.

"I don't pity you." Jessica shook her head. "You do enough of that yourself." She turned her back and strode to her car, her blood pressure rising a few notches.

Truth was, she did pity him a little. But it had more to do with his sour attitude than his missing limb. She reached in and attempted to pull out his wheelchair, but it wouldn't budge. She leaned over to see what was the matter.

"Need some help?" called Nick.

She stood and bonked her head on the lid of the trunk. Rubbing the sore spot, she peered around to see Nick standing on the front porch wearing a baseball hat and holding two glasses of water.

"Where's Jacob?"

"Around back. I'm teaching him how to throw a spiral with his new football."

And to think she accused him this morning of not liking kids. She'd need to apologize. Her fear of the chemistry between them caused her to say things she regretted.

"And Rosco?"

"Asleep on my bed in the house. Didn't think your uncle would appreciate the kind of reception he gave Jacob."

Nick had thought of everything.

"Would you mind helping me get George's wheelchair out of the trunk?"

"No problem. I'll swing around back and let Jacob know you're here." Nick drank from one of the glasses he was holding.

"Okay," said Jessica. "I'll wait for you."

Once he rounded the corner of the house, an unsettling feeling gripped her. The picture she painted of her uncle was not the man inside the cabin. But if she understood anything about Nick, he was caring and thoughtful. She'd rely on that. Maybe she'd warn him before he met George face-to-face.

She opened the side door of her car and grabbed one of the suitcases sitting on the back seat and set it on the ground, then retrieved the second one.

Jacob returned with Nick. "Is grouchy Uncle George here?"

"Jacob! Shh." Jessica reprimanded. "Don't let Uncle George hear you."

Nick pressed his lips together, suppressing a grin. He tugged at the wheelchair and hoisted it out of the trunk. "One of the wheels was stuck on a box."

The tattered cardboard box her uncle insisted he take with him carried important papers and mementos or so he said.

Jessica stood close and lowered her voice. "About my uncle—"

"Jacob's already told me all about him."

She cringed. "He's been going through a rough patch, but all those things I told you were true. Before his illness."

"Don't worry about it. I've dealt with plenty of difficult people in the past." Nick lowered his tone. "A little tough love will crack his facade in no time."

"I hope you're right."

"Mommy," asked Jacob. "Can I stay outside and play?"

"A quick hello to Uncle George would be nice. Besides, you should take it easy with your wrist."

"Do I have to talk with him?" Jacob worked his lip.

Jessica opened the wheelchair and unlocked the brake. "Show him your cast. I'm sure he'll ask about it."

"I don't think he'll notice." Jacob's shoulders slumped and he ambled to the cabin.

Had her uncle become so disconnected with life that her son would think he wouldn't notice something as obvious as a broken arm? She crinkled her brow. Uncle George had changed. It frightened her as much as it caused the ache in her chest for the man who lovingly helped her through her pregnancy. Now it was her turn to show him the same compassion.

Jessica lifted one of the suitcases and placed it on the seat of the wheelchair. "Mind getting the other bag?" She directed her words at Nick.

"Not at all. I'll grab the box, too."

The box. On the drive, George had wanted to carry it in his lap, but she'd insisted there was enough room beside his wheelchair. "Thanks."

Once inside, Jessica found Jacob sitting next to George on the couch showing him his cast. "I didn't listen to my mom. I shouldn't have jumped off the swing."

"Ach." George cocked his head and waved a hand in the air. "Kids jump off swings all the time. Landed wrong, is all."

A worried expression covered Jacob's face. "But Mommy says—"

"It happens," George interrupted. "Now this here is senseless." He pointed to his amputated limb, his face contorting into a grimace. "After a few weeks, your wrist will be fine. My leg won't. If God knew what he was doing, he wouldn't have let this happen." George's voice turned angry.

Jacob bolted off the couch and ran out the cabin door.

"Uncle George did you have to talk to Jacob like that? You've scared him. He's only a six-year-old boy!"

Jessica took off after Jacob, leaving Nick to make his own introductions.

∽∾∽

"If Jessica babies that boy, he'll never amount to much." George lifted himself to a standing position. "You must be the owner."

"Yes." Nick set the box down, stepped forward and shook George's hand. "I'm Nick Fuller. Nice to meet you."

"George MacAllister. How'd Jessi find this cabin? Seems a bit remote." He plunked back down on the couch.

"The Branson family and I have been friends for years." Nick took a seat in the overstuffed chair across from George. "Holly Branson mentioned the cabin would be a great place for your rehabilitation, and I obliged. Simple as that." George didn't need to know how he'd changed his plans. "Have you had a chance to walk through the entire cabin? It wouldn't take but a minute."

"I haven't made it past the couch."

"You might notice the hallway's a tad narrow and the bedroom quite small, but it ought to do until you find a more permanent situation." Nick placed his hands on his knees and stood. "Do you want me to bring the suitcases to the back room?"

"Please." The man had manners. Maybe George wasn't as cantankerous as Jacob made him out to be. "Can you hand me that box over there?" He pointed to the kitchen table where Nick had put it minutes ago.

"No problem." Nick did as George asked, then brought the luggage to the back bedroom. A twin bed hugged the corner

151

of one wall, and a dresser sat opposite the other. A small end table and lamp completed the furniture. Not much to speak of, but adequate.

When he returned to the front room, George was digging into the box as though he were looking for something important.

"Is there anything else I can do for you?" asked Nick.

"No." George answered, without looking up.

"Then I'll leave you to get settled." Nick moved to the door.

"There is one more thing." George called after him. "How much do I owe you?"

"Jessica and I worked it out—"

George shook his head. "I won't allow my niece to pay my way. I don't have much money, but I do have a watch I can give you. If you cash it in, you'll find it's quite valuable."

Nick stopped him with a hand. "George, I'm not taking your watch."

"But I don't accept handouts." He untied the clasp, slipped it off his wrist and held it up.

"Believe me, I should be paying you for staying here." Nick laughed. "I'll go find Jessica. The two of you can decide who handles payment. For now, it's taken care of. Have a good day." He slipped out of the cabin before George tried to give him something else.

After a quick search of his property, Nick found Jacob and Jessica on the far side of the house sitting on a wood bench near the small flower garden he'd planted a few years ago in honor of the little boy who lost his life in the Santa Cruz apartment fire. The child hadn't been more than two years old. Nick's partner had pulled Nick from the burning building before he'd also be listed as one of casualties. The toddler's remains were discovered in a closet the next day, the one place Nick didn't look. His fire captain told him countless times not to take responsibility for the boy's death, but beside the man who started the fire, who else could Nick blame? He was a fireman and it was his job to save lives. He shook off the painful memory and approached Jessica and her son. "I set your uncle's things on the bed in the back room."

"Thank you." Jessica took a deep breath. "Jacob, you ready to go back?"

"No."

She patted his knee. "Remember what we talked about."

Nick would love to know what Jessica said to Jacob, but thought better than to probe.

"Can I hang out with you, Nick?" The corners of Jacob's mouth turned down and his eyes held a pleading look.

Nick didn't mind, but he'd rather not contradict Jessica. "You need to listen to your mom."

Jessica mouthed a word of thanks and got to her feet. "Come on, buddy. Help me unpack Uncle George's things, then afterward we'll play a board game." She held out her hand. "I'm sure Nick has other things to do."

"All right." Jacob stood, slipped his small hand in hers, and the two of them walked off toward the cabin.

Nick stared at the patch of flowers that grew despite the lack of attention he gave them. Much like Uncle George, Nick wasn't willing to face what God allowed to happen that terrible night when the boy lost his life. He balled his fists, then released his grip.

His phone vibrated in his pocket. He pulled it out and answered.

Nick slumped on the bench when he recognized the voice on the other end of the line, his heart plummeting to the pit of his stomach.

21

"Are you sure Joyce won't mind us popping in like this?" Evelyn tossed her empty coffee cup into the trash receptacle outside the church office, her nerves a-flutter.

"If we're going to get to the bottom of what happened to George, Joyce will know. She's our best resource," said Patty.

"But to come unannounced—"

"Honey, church secretaries expect people to show up asking questions. That's what they're there for." Patty linked her hand inside the crook of Evelyn's arm and pulled her along. "Remember, she's the one who told Ron and me about his condition a few months back when we bumped into her at the mall. I didn't spend the last thirty minutes calling around to find out where she worked for nothing."

True, it had taken Patty a good half hour to find out where Joyce spent her days. Besides Patty had told her their random meeting at one of the largest stores in Santa Cruz was a divine appointment since she and Joyce didn't associate within the same circles nor attend the same church.

"Slow down. Let me catch my breath." Evelyn halted in her tracks, closed her eyes, and inhaled deeply. She wasn't ready for her fear to be confirmed or to let go of the idea of seeing George again.

When she blinked her eyes open, Patty was staring at her. "What?"

"I never imagined that after all these years you'd be pining for George. Makes me feel like a teenager again."

"You and me both." Evelyn grinned and relaxed her shoulders.

Patty squeezed her hand. "I'm here for you, whatever the outcome."

Evelyn toyed with her earring. "Now I feel like the shy girl I was years ago."

"You used to do that when you were nervous." Patty teased.

"What are you talking about?"

"Your earring?"

Evelyn's cheeks heated. She pulled Patty toward the church door. "Come on!"

The minute they walked in, the sound of praise music from the local Christian radio station played from the speakers. The phone was attached to Joyce's ear and she was rattling off the times for the church service. She glanced at Evelyn and Patty, then did a double take, her smile widening and her red curls bouncing as she turned her head. She ended the call and hung up the receiver. "Patty, good to see you."

"Thank you. You, too." Patty motioned to Evelyn. "This is Evelyn Sweeney, my dear friend from way back."

"Nice to meet you." Joyce placed her elbows on the desk and folded her hands in front of her. "Is there something I can do for you ladies?"

"I hope so," said Patty. "Several months ago you'd mentioned George MacAllister was back in California and was quite ill."

"Oh, yes." Joyce nodded. "I remember."

Evelyn jumped in. "Do you know if he recovered?"

"No, I haven't heard." Joyce wrinkled her brow. "Do you need to get in touch with him?"

"Evelyn knew George a long time ago and would like to find him. If you hear of anything or know of someone who might have information, can you give them my phone number?" Patty took out a business card from her purse and handed it to Joyce.

"I'd be glad to." Joyce pinned the card to the bulletin board by her desk. She tapped her chin. "I'm sure this sounds silly, but have you checked the phone book?"

Why hadn't they thought to do that instead of hunting Joyce down? Evelyn nudged Patty. "Now that would be a smart idea."

Patty looked in Joyce's direction. "We were too busy trying to find you."

"Here, let me help." Joyce dug into her desk drawer and produced the white pages. She flipped through and scrolled down the list of names with her finger. "Here we are. George MacAllister. Would you like to call or shall I?"

Evelyn's heart quickened. What would she say?

Patty touched her arm. "Why don't you write down the number and we'll call him."

"All right." Joyce jotted the number on a piece of paper. "His address is also listed here. Do you want me to write that down as well?"

"Please."

After Joyce penned George's address, she gave Evelyn the slip of paper. She felt as though she'd won the lottery. Not only did she have George's phone number, but his location as well.

"I knew you were the right person to help us." Patty winked at Joyce. "Have a good day."

"You, too. Let me know how George is doing." The desk phone rang and Joyce waved as the women walked out the door.

Evelyn and Patty stepped out of the office and stood under the eaves as rain began to fall. The smell of plants and wet pavement filled the air. At the moment, nothing would dampen Evelyn's mood. "Want to make a run for it?"

Patty zipped up her orange sweatshirt. "You bet."

Evelyn tucked the piece of paper in her pocket, then put her purse over her head and took off. The two women shrieked and giggled as they sprinted across the parking lot to Evelyn's sedan.

Once Patty settled in the passenger's seat, she removed her hood and ran her fingers through her highlighted hair. "Call him now. The suspense is killing me."

"You and me both." Evelyn dug into her pocket for the slip of paper, and reached for her cell phone and punched in the number. She pressed the phone to her ear and willed her heart to slow down.

"We're sorry. The number you have dialed is disconnected and no longer in service . . ."

Evelyn turned her head toward the side window and grimaced.

"What's wrong?" Her friend's concern pulled her back.

"The number is disconnected." Her voice wavered.

"That doesn't mean . . ."

Evelyn tossed her phone in her purse. "I'm in the mood for a drive. How about you?" She handed Patty George's address.

"Sounds like a plan. I'll navigate."

Evelyn wasn't going to give up yet!

The car inched forward as Evelyn drove through Surf and Sand Mobile Home Park. "What was the space number?"

"Fifty-seven," said Patty.

The modular homes were an eclectic mix of old and new, but most were on the smaller side of the beachside community that bordered Jade Street Park and the ocean.

Evelyn noted the bikes and toys lying about. "Must be an all-ages park."

"I think you're right." Patty agreed. "I wonder how long George has been living here."

Evelyn could picture George sitting on the porch of one of the mobile homes with an ocean view, sipping iced tea and planning his next trip to the Philippines. She couldn't imagine him staying in California for long whenever he came home.

They wove around to the right.

"There it is." Patty pointed to an older singlewide trailer. The curtains were drawn in the windows and the surrounding plants were overgrown. "There isn't a car out front. I wonder if he's home."

Evelyn parked in the space available. "I don't have a good feeling about this." Her mouth went dry. She dug into her purse for a piece of gum and offered one to Patty.

"It will be all right, don't you worry." Patty cupped Evelyn's hand between her own and squeezed, then unwrapped her stick of gum and popped it into her mouth. "We'll knock on a neighbor's door if George isn't home."

Evelyn exhaled a breath. "I'm glad you're here with me."

"I wouldn't miss this reunion for the world." Patty tossed her a playful grin.

The women exited the car and climbed the few porch steps to the door. Evelyn knocked. After a few minutes, she rang the bell. When there was no response, they moved to the sliding glass door and took turns peering through the slit in the curtain. From what Evelyn could see, the trailer was dark and unkempt like it was being used as a storage locker.

"I don't think anyone lives here." Patty voiced Evelyn's assumption.

"May I help you?"

Evelyn turned when she heard the raspy voice. Even though the hour was fast approaching noon, the older woman wore a terrycloth robe, her flowered flannel pajamas showing down the open center. Her white hair was askew as if she'd rolled out of bed and she carried a newspaper in her hand.

"Yes, I'm looking for your neighbor. George MacAllister." Evelyn stepped down from the porch. Patty followed.

"I'm sad to say he doesn't live here anymore." The woman shook her head, and her mouth twisted into a hard line. "The new owner is rarely here and when he is . . . I shudder at what's going on."

"What do you suspect?" asked Patty.

"I have no idea, but I don't think it's on the up and up. Most of the time I see him bringing boxes of items into the house, but rarely does he take things out. I haven't called the police, but I'm seriously thinking about it."

"Back to George." Evelyn hoped she wasn't being insensitive to the woman, but she had to know what happened to him. "Did he pass away or sell the mobile home?"

"Was George sick? I never knew." The older woman grabbed the neckline of her robe and drew the top of it closed. "He rarely lived here, but when he did he was a lovely man. Kind and generous. Do you know he always brought me a gift from his travels to the Philippines? One time he gave me a bracelet. Said he didn't have a special woman in his life and wanted me to have it. Wasn't that sweet?"

The woman described the George she remembered. The thought that George had remained single sent a ripple of pleasure down Evelyn's spine. But she quickly sobered at the realization that George could be dead. A lump formed in her throat. Evelyn swallowed hard and pushed down her fear. "Did you ever see a For Sale sign? Maybe the mobile home went to a relative."

"There was no sign, but I wouldn't put it past George to sell it without a realtor. One day someone new arrived and that was that."

"What about George's stuff?" asked Patty.

"The mobile home was furnished when George bought it. He lived simply. If someone did come by to collect his things, I never saw them."

Evelyn tucked a strand of hair behind her ear and touched her earring. "Thank you for your time."

"I didn't catch your names."

"I'm Patty. And this is Evelyn."

"Nice to meet you both. I'm Doris. If you find out what happened to George, will you please come back and let me know? In the meantime if my neighbor returns, I'll be sure to ask him if he knew George."

"Thank you." Patty smiled. "Have a nice day."

Doris turned toward her house and Evelyn and Patty moved the few steps to Evelyn's sedan.

"Wait a minute." Doris called after them. "Did you say your name was Evelyn?"

"Yes." She nodded.

"By any chance did George call you Eva?"

A smile crinkled the corners of Evelyn's eyes and warmth filled her chest at the reminder. "Yes, he did."

"Well, glory be! You're the only woman who ever captured George's heart. I've heard countless stories. Come by again sometime and I'll tell you some of the special memories George shared with me."

"I'm sure you know I'm the one who broke it off and married someone else."

Doris nodded.

"Is tomorrow too soon?" Evelyn hoped she didn't sound too eager.

"I'm leaving for a week to visit family, but I'll be back."

"Some other time, then. Have a safe trip." Evelyn wished she could follow Doris into her home right now and find out some of the things George had told her over the years. There were details about his life she wanted to know about him, too.

The bigger question was whether George had ever forgiven her for breaking his heart. Even if he had, she'd never forgive herself for not finding him sooner and apologizing to him face-to-face. And now, it might be too late.

She waved to Doris as she and Patty climbed into her car.

"Where to now?" asked Patty.

"Your guess is as good as mine." Evelyn heard the melancholy in her voice as she backed up and drove out of the mobile home park.

Patty glanced at her watch. "Oh dear. It's almost noon. I have a lunch date with Ronald."

"I'll bring you to your car." Evelyn was relieved. She needed time alone to sort through her feelings.

By any chance did George call you Eva? You're the only woman who ever captured George's heart.

As much as she had loved Edward, Evelyn wished she could reclaim her romance with George. If only she could see him again.

If only . . .

22

Perspiration dotted the back of Nick's neck. He leaned forward on the bench in his backyard with his elbows on his thighs, his head resting in one hand as he talked to A.J. on the phone.

"Ready to make some salsa?" A.J. sounded unusually chipper for someone evading the police. Was it only an act or was he innocent of the crime?

"Tonight?" Nick's voice cracked as if he were the guilty one. He'd gone over what he'd say to A.J. if he ever called or showed up at his door, but now that he was faced with responding to him the words vanished.

"Why not? You got plans?"

How would he answer without letting on he knew A.J. was a wanted man? Nick would rather A.J. divulge the truth. "I've got guests. New tenants, actually." Maybe he would get a clue and not expect to stay the night in the cabin.

"Did you finally do it? Build the house you were talking about the last time we saw each other?"

"Yes. Finished and moved in not long ago."

"That's great. How many bedrooms you got?"

Nick gritted his teeth. "Three."

"Plenty of space for a wife and kids. Is that the plan?"

"Eventually." The image of Jessica and Jacob walking hand in hand moments ago popped into his mind.

"So you've got a room to spare." A.J. hinted.

"It's amazing how the place fills up." Nick inwardly groaned at the half-truth. Each of his spare rooms had a few items, an old sofa in one and boxes of childhood memorabilia in the other, but there was definitely enough space for someone to crash for the night. Truth be known, he didn't want A.J. coming to his house especially now that the police were looking for him. Nick should come right out and ask him if what he saw on the news was true, but he couldn't form the words.

"Do you have a live-in girlfriend or something?" A.J. probed, his voice a mixture of teasing and disbelief.

"You know me better than that—"

"Then what gives?" Impatience laced A.J.'s words.

"What do you mean?" Nick didn't feel good about avoiding the obvious, but his emotions were swinging back and forth between wanting to help and frustration with being contacted.

A.J. exhaled into the phone. "I need to talk to you—"

"I'm listening." Nick's brows puckered and he leaned back on the bench.

"In person."

Nick hesitated. What would it hurt to hear A.J. out? Maybe Nick would be able to encourage him to give himself up. "Can we meet somewhere in Santa Cruz? A coffeehouse? Restaurant?" He paused. "Or a park?"

"I don't want to meet in a public place."

The problem lay with his new tenants. How could he with good conscience allow A.J. near his home? "Look, you can't come here—"

"You're breaking up." The sound of whooshing air filled the line as if A.J. were in a wind tunnel. "I'm . . . my way . . . your place. I'll . . . there . . . few minutes."

"No!" The word burst from Nick's lips. He took a breath and softened his tone. "Pull over and I'll meet you. Give me your location—"

"Almost there." The line went dead.

At this point, Nick couldn't stop him. All he could do was wait for A.J. to arrive. He stood, tucked his phone in his pocket, and kicked the dirt, aggravation twisting his insides at the turn of events.

He'd need to ask Jessica and her family to leave. But with George's physical limitations, it might be easiest to keep them hidden from view.

Was it time to notify the police? His stomach clenched. Maybe he'd give A.J. a chance to explain himself before he'd make the call. One thing was for sure. The less he got involved with A.J. the better.

Nick walked to the cabin and rapped on the door. A couple minutes passed before Jessica answered it, a smile lighting her face when her eyes met his.

"Hey. We're finishing putting George's things away. Then Jacob and I are going to play a game. Want to come in?" She gestured.

From his view over Jessica's shoulder, he could see George still sitting on the couch going through the contents of his tattered box. Nick dug his hands into his jeans pockets. "I'd love to, but I can't." He let his hands drop to his sides. He needed to stop fidgeting or else Jessica would see right through him. "I'm expecting a visitor and won't be available this afternoon, but I'll swing by once my company leaves to make sure nothing needs fixing."

"All right." Jessica eyed him carefully. "I'll make sure Jacob doesn't bother you. I'm sure George won't go anywhere."

"That would be good. Thanks." Nick had the sudden urge to glide his finger down Jessica's cheek. Besides being beautiful, she was a courageous woman who loved her family—a trait he admired. The attraction he had for her was growing rapidly and he'd protect her from A.J. if the need arose.

Jessica tilted her chin toward him. "Everything okay?"

Nick nodded. "Yeah. Yeah, fine." He would've liked to tell Jessica the truth, but he was afraid he wouldn't have time before A.J. arrived.

"Enjoy your company and we'll see you in a little while." Jessica touched his forearm, then reached out and grabbed the door.

Nick stepped forward. "Oh, before I forget. You might want to close the front curtains. The sun streams in during the day and makes the place as hot as an oven." There was truth to what he'd said, but he was more concerned with A.J. seeing them through the windows.

"Good idea." Jessica leaned toward him and whispered. "I don't want George complaining about the heat on top of everything else." She gave him a knowing smile.

Nick grinned, distracted by her nearness. "I'll be by as soon as I can." He gave in to his impulse and caressed her chin with his thumb and index finger, then turned and strode toward his house, his heart thumping a strange rhythm.

The sound of the cabin door closing brought a sense of relief. He hoped Jessica would keep an eye on Jacob to make sure the boy stayed within the confines of the four walls. If what the newscaster said was true, Nick didn't know what A.J. was capable of and he didn't want to find out.

Once inside his house, he glanced through the kitchen window and saw Jessica closing the cabin's front curtains. *Good.*

He moved to the refrigerator, pulled out a soda, popped the lid and took a long hard swig.

At the sound of tires hitting the gravel driveway, Nick set the can on the counter and peered out the window. A small truck he didn't recognize came to a stop in front of his house. His childhood friend stepped out, his frame tall and lanky, and his usual clean-shaven face now sporting a beard. Was he trying to disguise his appearance?

Nick collected his thoughts and went to the door. He pulled it open before A.J. had a chance to knock and gestured him inside, wanting to get the encounter over with as soon as possible.

Jessica moved her playing piece. "Your turn."

Jacob rolled the dice. He counted out the spaces and landed on the same square hers occupied, sending her home. "Sorry." Her son covered his mouth and giggled.

"Okay, mister. That's the third time you've done that. Knock it off," she teased.

"I'm thirsty," Uncle George called from the sofa. "Any iced tea around here?"

"I haven't had time to stock the refrigerator, but let me see if there's anything to drink." Jessica scurried to the kitchen and looked. Nothing but leftovers from the morning's breakfast. "After I finish the game with Jacob, I'll run to the store. Water will have to do for now." She pulled a glass from the shelf and filled it from the tap.

"With ice, please."

Jessica appreciated her uncle's well-mannered request. "Will do. Jacob, would you like a cup?"

"Nick told me he bought soda. Can I go ask him if I can have one?"

"He's expecting company. We can't drop by Nick's house anytime we want."

"But he told me this morning that I could—"

"That may be true, but right now he has a guest and it wouldn't be polite. Plus, I don't want you drinking that stuff." Jessica filled two more cups. "Let's finish our game. Then we'll go to the store. I'll treat you to something special. Okay?" She set two glasses on the table and handed the third to George.

"Don't forget the iced tea," George reminded and took a drink.

"Don't worry, Uncle George, I won't." Jessica pointed to the item on the end table and sat beside him. "Where did you get the paper fan?"

"I brought it back from the Philippines many years ago. Was saving it to give to someone special. You want it?"

"Sure. Thanks." Jessica opened it up and stared at the embroidered sequins and painted flower motifs, then fanned herself with quick movements. "It's beautiful."

"The people there call it an *abaniko*. Did you know there's a fan language in the Philippines?"

"A fan what?"

"A fan language. For instance, when you move it rapidly, you're telling me you're uneasy."

How right he was. She hadn't felt comfortable around her uncle since his illness. Maybe if she kept him talking about the things he was interested in, she'd see the man he used to be. Jessica stopped fanning. "Tell me more."

"If you cover your chin, it's a sign of modesty."

"Like this?" Jessica placed the fan on her chin.

George nodded. "Now if you were with your beau, you could glide the fan over your cheek to signal you love him, or touch your lip to tell him you want a kiss."

"Eww." Jacob called from his place at the table. "That's gross."

"And if you fan by your left ear you'd be telling people to stop bothering you." George let out a breath and diverted his attention back to the contents of his box.

Jessica could take a hint. She nudged her uncle's knee with her own. "Mind me asking what happened to the woman you wanted to give this to?"

"Married someone else." George's voice was low and soft.

Jessica looked at her left hand. "Is this the same woman you bought the ring for?"

"The one and only—"

"Mom, can we finish our game now?" Jacob interrupted.

George cocked his head toward her son. "Go on. He's waiting."

"Thanks again for the fan. It might come in handy one day." Jessica made a move toward the table. "Here I come, Jacob." The few minutes she shared with Uncle George were a good reminder of their former relationship. She hoped he was turning a corner for the better.

Yes, the fan might be useful. She could communicate her frustration with her uncle without saying a word. And the next time she was with Nick, she might touch her lip. The thought brought a grin to her face. She rolled the dice.

"Why are you smiling? You can't move." Jacob pointed to the board.

Jessica shrugged a shoulder. "Thinking about my new fan."

The game ended ten minutes later when Jacob rolled the right amount bringing the last of his playing pieces home. "I win! Can we go to the store now?"

"All right, buddy. Let's go." Jessica ruffled his hair. "Will you be fine by yourself, Uncle George?"

"I'm not a baby." George's tone turned sour.

"That's not what I meant." Jessica grabbed her purse from the kitchen counter. "Don't go anywhere. We'll be back soon."

"Now where would I go?" George mumbled.

"Maybe you need a nap. Mom always says I need one when I'm grumpy." Jacob walked over to the door and pulled it open.

Jessica pressed her lips together to suppress a smile. "See you in a little while."

A dingy blue pick-up sat in Nick's driveway. Nick sure acted strange when he came to her door, almost secretive like he was concealing something—or someone.

Who was she to talk? She was hiding a secret of her own. And she hoped Andrew was as far away from her and Jacob as humanly possible.

"Mom, can I *please* ask Nick for a soda?"

"Get into the car and I'll buy you something special to drink at the store." Jessica pressed the remote and unlocked the doors. "Maybe by the time we get back, his guest will be gone."

A silhouette inside Nick's house caught her attention. Who was visiting? And why did she sense the need to leave as quickly as possible?

23

Once back at the beach house, Evelyn tossed a salad of spring greens and raw vegetables with balsamic vinegar, and sat in the wicker chair on the front porch. After thanking God for her simple meal, she watched the assortment of people walking by. Young and old enjoyed the path bordering the cliffs from Natural Bridges Beach to the Lighthouse. A motorcycle roared past bringing another memory of George to the forefront of her mind.

"I'm not going to ride that thing!" Evelyn had shaken her head and folded her arms tight across her chest the minute she saw the motorcycle in the church's parking lot.

"Come on, Eva. Hop on," George encouraged. "You can wrap your arms around my waist. I promise you won't fall off."

Evelyn bit her lip. More than anything she wanted to spend more time with George before he left for another mission trip. The thought of sitting close to him sent a rush of excitement through her. But how would she explain the motorcycle ride to her father? He'd told her more than once not to trust men who rode these "two-wheel death traps." Said they were wild and risky. "My parents expect us for dinner at five."

"We have plenty of time to drive up the coast and back." George prodded. "I hear the elephant seals have returned to Año Nuevo."

One thing was certain, George couldn't have been more conservative. He was not the wild man her father would assume by the vehicle he rode. Why, the man lived and breathed his love for God and took every opportunity to spread the gospel. But if they drove up on a motorcycle to her parents' front door with her seated behind him clutching his waist, her father would get the wrong idea.

"Are you sure we can't borrow Ronald's car?" She'd wanted George to make a good first impression. Edward Sweeney already had. He'd come over for dinner the other night at her parents' bidding. He was a lawyer like her father and handsome, too, soon to be employed with a prestigious law firm in San Francisco. But she wasn't interested in the attention he lavished on her. No, she fancied George MacAllister.

George grinned. "Your folks aren't too fond of motorcycles, huh?"

"Not particularly."

"If it makes you feel better, we'll stop by Ronald's house after we get back and see if we can borrow it then."

"Okay. But let's hurry." Evelyn put on a helmet and straddled the motorcycle behind George. She wrapped her arms around his middle, and took in his musky scent.

Her legs hugged George as he drove the motorcycle up and down the stretch of highway along the coast, the wind whipping her hair at the base of her helmet. Each minute seated behind George had been worth it—even if her parents, especially her father, would be upset. She was a grown woman who could make her own choices.

Two hours later they'd stopped by Ronald's house, but he wasn't there.

"Must be out with Patty." George shrugged nonchalantly, as if it didn't matter to him one iota what her parents thought.

Evelyn's heart tripped as she stood on Ronald's covered porch beside George. An idea sparked. "I know. We can park the motorcycle down the street and walk to my house."

George thrust his hands on his hips. "Now you're being silly. Why would it matter to your parents what I ride?"

George's leather jacket and tattered jeans wouldn't make a positive impact on her mother and father either, but she wasn't about to debate her parents' thoughts on proper grooming. It didn't matter to her. Why should it be important to her parents? Then why did she have the sudden urge to defend them? "George, you're not being fair. All I'm saying is—"

"You'd rather hide the fact I ride a motorcycle."

"Is that so bad?"

George hesitated.

"Would you do it for me?" Evelyn cocked her head and batted her eyelashes. "At least until my parents have a chance to get to know you. Once they do, I promise we'll tell them all about your motorcycle. You never know, my father may ask you to take him for a spin."

George laughed out loud. "Doubtful."

"Okay, we don't need to go that far." Evelyn grabbed his hand.

He placed a kiss on her cheek, then found her lips. "And what would your father say about that?"

"George!" She giggled and gave him a playful shove.

"Come on." He tugged her toward his motorcycle. "If we have to park down the street, we'd better leave now. I don't want to be late. I get the feeling being on time is also important to your parents."

Evelyn shook off the memory and scraped the bottom of her bowl. She'd eaten the salad without tasting it. She felt numb, like the day she allowed her parents to convince her that Edward was the proper person for her to marry, leaving George to find out in a letter.

She pushed up from her seat on the porch and ambled into the house, wondering what life would have been like as George's wife.

No, she wouldn't allow herself to have any regrets. She'd grown to love Edward and had a beautiful daughter, and now a precious grandbaby. He'd given her security and stability, and a wonderful forty years together. She'd not tarnish what they had because of her past mistakes.

But her husband was gone now and she had the chance to discover what became of George. She rinsed her bowl and placed it into the dishwasher, then moved down the hall to the bedroom for a short rest—her eyelids were growing heavy, along with her heart.

"Amy, Daniel? What a surprise!" Evelyn welcomed her daughter and son-in-law into the vacation rental an hour later and held her arms out to hold Isabella.

Amy handed her the baby. "Wow, Mom. Nice beach house."

Evelyn kissed Bella's cheek and held her close. "Not too shabby, huh?"

"Did you find this place online?" Daniel stepped toward the front windows facing the surf. "I could watch the waves crashing against the rocks all day."

"Yes, it's quite addictive, isn't it? Besides the water, I like to people watch." Evelyn swayed back and forth. "What brings you by? Checking up on me?"

"Oh, no, nothing like that." Amy shook her head. "Daniel took the day off and wanted to get me out of the house. My choices were to either take a drive down the coast or go to the doctor's office for some anti-depressants."

Evelyn raised her brows. "And you chose to come visit me—"

"Only for a short time," said Daniel. "We don't want to barge in on your vacation."

"Who says you're barging in? I don't mind. In fact, I'm glad you came." Evelyn pushed the pacifier back in Bella's mouth with an index finger. The baby sucked vigorously. "Amy, how are you feeling?"

"Let me take Bella and the two of you can talk. The stroller is all set up. I'll walk her down to the lighthouse." Daniel scooped the baby into his arms, grabbed the diaper bag, and went outside.

Evelyn sat on the denim loveseat and patted the seat beside her. "Now tell me what's on your mind."

Amy dropped beside her. "I'm tired, but I've talked with several of my friends and they all say motherhood takes a while to get used to."

"Yes, but if you need to see a doctor please don't hesitate. I'm worried about you."

"Spoken like a mom." Amy rested her head on Evelyn's shoulder. "I've missed you."

"It's only been a few days." Evelyn refused to give in to the guilt and cut her vacation short. She'd been a new mother once and knew her daughter could take care of Isabella with her husband's help.

"I miss Dad, too." Amy was a grown woman and yet now was acting like a young girl.

Evelyn could understand. She'd been feeling like a teenager these past few days hunting for George. She stroked her daughter's hair. "I miss your father as well."

"He's not alive to see his granddaughter and Bella will never have a chance to meet him. I'm always going to be sad about that."

"Life has no guarantees, does it?"

Amy expelled a breath. "Daddy worked a lot, but you had a good marriage, didn't you?"

"It wasn't always easy and we had our disagreements, but for the most part we were very compatible."

Amy sat up straight. "Is that why you wanted to get away? So that you could think about Dad and all the memories you shared?"

Evelyn's neck heated. "I *have* been reminiscing about the past." How could she tell her daughter that it wasn't Edward that had filled her thoughts these last few days, but George— someone Amy had never heard of before?

"I thought so. You seemed distracted on Easter."

"Really? I didn't think you noticed. What, with your eyes half closed most of the time." She nudged her daughter with an elbow, her tone playful. She'd put off sharing about George until she knew whether or not he was still alive. Why hurt her daughter with talk of another man?

"I'm still living in a daze." Amy covered a yawn. "But back to your memories about Dad. Which ones have you been thinking about?"

Evelyn avoided the question and jumped to her feet. "What time does Daniel need to be at work tomorrow?"

"Thursdays are his late days. He starts at ten." Amy shrugged a shoulder. "Why do you ask?"

"You're all more than welcome to stay the night. The house has three bedrooms."

"We'd only planned on being gone during the day. We don't have pajamas or toothbrushes, and I don't know if I have enough diapers for Bella." Amy dug through the diaper bag. "Three. I'll need some more."

"While Daniel is walking Bella, why don't you lie down and take a nap? The store is down the road. After I make a quick call to the owners to confirm, I'll pick up more diapers and a couple of toothbrushes along with a tray of sushi and some fixings for stir-fry."

"Really?" Amy brightened. "You'd do that for me?"

"Yes, sweetie. Now go on and check out the bedrooms. You'll see which one I've occupied by my suitcases."

"Thank you, Mom. This is exactly what I need." Amy squeezed her hand and then disappeared down the hall.

Evelyn had noted the grocery store after dropping off Patty. She gathered her purse and keys. It'd be nice to clear her head in case Amy peppered her with more questions.

"Mom?" Amy's voice rose. "Who's George MacAllister?"

Evelyn dug into her pocket. Empty. She must have dropped the slip of paper containing George's phone number and address.

So much for time away to gather her thoughts.

Evelyn's cheeks heated. "George is a friend from long ago." She set her purse and keys on the counter and played with her earring, wishing the subject didn't make her feel as though she'd downed a cup of caffeinated coffee. "I wanted to see if he still lived in the area. You know, since we knew each other way back when."

"Oh, that's nice. Have you been able to see him?" Amy handed her the slip of paper and covered a yawn.

Evelyn's heart rate returned to normal with Amy's response. Maybe her daughter wouldn't be offended that she was searching for an old love. Still, she needed to tread lightly. "No, I haven't seen him. His phone number is disconnected and he doesn't live at this address anymore."

"Do you know of anyone else who might know where he is?" Amy's question encouraged her further.

Evelyn shook her head. "George didn't live here full time. He was a missionary but recently returned to California when he became ill."

Amy leaned against the wall in the hallway. Dark circles lined her eyes. Her daughter definitely needed some sleep. "Is he all right?"

Evelyn shrugged. "Remember my friend Patty? She and I have been trying to locate him. But so far . . ." She shook her head.

"Was George a friend of Dad's, too?" The questions kept coming.

Guilt pricked at Evelyn at the sudden mention of Edward, the man she'd loved and Amy adored for many years. "No. They never met."

"Well, if George was a friend of yours, I'm sure he would've gotten along with Dad." Suddenly Amy's eyes widened and nervous laughter bubbled from her lips. "He wasn't Dad's competition was he?"

"Competition?" Evelyn worked her lower lip.

"You know, the guy you had a thing for when Dad swept you off to San Francisco."

"What are you talking about?"

"You didn't know Grandma told me that story? Yeah, the summer after college when I broke up with Daniel and stayed with Grandma and Grandpa. She said you'd loved someone else besides Dad. She never told me his name, but that you were heartbroken and cried the night before you and Dad married. Grandma wanted to talk with you, but Grandpa insisted she keep quiet. He said you'd made your choice. She never understood why you didn't follow your heart. But it turned out okay, didn't it?"

Evelyn's stomach clenched. She'd placed the blame of her breakup on her parents all these years instead of owning her decision. She took the easy way out. What kind of a woman would hurt George the way she did? "Your dad and I had a good, stable marriage. He was kind to me and was a faithful friend." Her throat clogged.

Amy sat on the edge of the bed, her tone light. "Personally, I'm glad you married Dad. Otherwise, I wouldn't be here. Bella either."

"You know what? I'm glad, too." Evelyn twisted the blinds closed. "Now get some sleep while I run to the store."

"But you'll still hunt for George, won't you?" Amy slid under the comforter, her voice more curious than defensive.

Why would Amy want her to continue the search? "We'll see. Now go to sleep." Her motherly instincts kicked in.

"I think you should. If I were you, I'd want to know." Amy's eyes closed.

Evelyn padded from the room and shut the door. She snatched her purse and keys from the kitchen counter and headed out the door. Apparently her daughter knew her better than she thought.

Yes, she'd follow her heart. If George were alive, she'd find him—if for no other reason than to ask for forgiveness.

24

"Can I get you something to drink? soda? coffee?" Nick offered A.J. once he entered his living room and sat on the sofa.

"I don't think you have what I'm craving."

"Try me."

"Got a beer?" A.J. kicked his feet up on the coffee table and brought his arms up, locking hands behind his neck.

"You're right, I don't have alcohol." Nick didn't want A.J. to get too comfortable.

"Soda's fine."

Nick went to the kitchen and snatched a Coke from the refrigerator.

"On ice, if you don't mind." A.J. called from the other room.

Nick pulled a glass from the cabinet, and added ice. Out of the corner of his eye he saw Jessica and Jacob coming out of the cabin. He stepped away for a moment to grab a bag of chips from the pantry, sending a silent plea that they wouldn't come to his door.

"I really like your house."

Nick's shoulders stiffened when he heard A.J.'s voice directly behind him. *Hurry Jessica, leave.* He handed A.J. the soda and chips. "Thank you. Have a seat at the table and I'll be there in a minute. Need to grab the dip."

A.J. laughed. "Like old times." He took the food.

When A.J. walked away, Nick stole another glance out the window. Jessica was backing her Honda from its spot near the cabin and pulling away. He breathed a sigh of relief, then snatched a jar of French onion dip and joined A.J.

Nick remembered the countless times he and A.J. had raided his parents' pantry. They'd known each other since they were kids and liked the same girl in junior high. They played football together, went to summer camp, and hung out at each other's homes. Their parents were the best of friends until A.J.'s family moved away.

How could Nick question whether or not he had any part in his girlfriend's death? *People change.* He and A.J. had only kept in contact through a smattering of phone calls. The few times they'd met over the years Nick felt the distance widening between them.

He didn't want to beat around the bush any longer. "What've you been up to and what brings you by?"

"You get straight to the point." A.J. tore open the bag and popped a chip in his mouth.

Could he pull the truth out of him? "Usually I know you're coming to town. Today you showed up suddenly. San Diego is a good nine-hour drive from here."

"Been traveling a while. I've had time off work and thought I'd drive up the coast." A.J. poured Coke into his cup. His hand trembled and he spilled some on the table. Looked like his nerves were getting the best of him. Was it a sign of guilt?

Nick handed him a napkin from the holder. "How long you plan on being in town?"

"Don't know. I'm hoping to see someone. We haven't been in touch in a long time and I know she has family in the area."

"A woman, huh?" Nick eyed him. A.J. always had a way with the ladies. Had he been two-timing? Runaway thoughts threatened to overtake him. But this was A.J. The funny, goofy kid that made friends wherever he went.

"She doesn't know I'm in town. I'd like to surprise her."

"Like you did me?"

"Something like that." A.J. took a long drink. "Mind if I grab a shower? I've been camping and it's been a few days."

Maybe that was the reason for the beard. "If it'd make you feel better. But before you do, was there something you wanted to tell me?"

"It can wait." A.J. smelled the collar of flannel shirt and scrunched his nose. "Seriously."

"I'll show you where the clean towels are." Nick cocked his head for A.J. to follow him down the hall.

"Hold on. My duffle bag is in the truck." A.J. raced out the door.

Nick rubbed the back of his neck to ease the mounting tension. Why couldn't A.J. come out and tell him what happened? He should demand the truth before he came back inside.

But Nick didn't want to make a scene outside with George in the cabin less than fifty feet away.

An army green duffle bag hung from A.J.'s shoulder as he entered the house. "Now where is that shower of yours?"

"Follow me." Nick led the way down the hall to the first door on the left. He snagged a towel from the linen closet and placed it on the bathroom counter. "By the way, you do look scruffy."

A.J. set the bag on the tile floor and rubbed his chin. "You don't like my new look? I'm thinking about keeping the beard."

"Your lady friend might not recognize you." *Or the police.* "I hear women prefer men without much facial hair." Nick raised a brow, then closed the door behind him.

The water turned on and Nick moved to the kitchen and looked out the window. No sign of Jessica yet.

Maybe the police had it all wrong and he was worried for nothing.

No, there were too many things he questioned—the unexpected visit, the request for alcohol, the tremor in his hand, and the beard. The one thing that he couldn't put out of his mind was A.J.'s face plastered on the television and the number to call if anyone knew of his whereabouts. Nick never wrote down the number and now wished he had. He didn't plan on losing all that he'd worked hard for, even for a childhood friend.

Jessica's comment a couple of days ago stuck in his mind. *You like to be a hero.* She didn't know how right she was. But it wasn't for attention. Nick needed to make amends for the child he wasn't able to save. He realized he couldn't rewrite the past, but he could protect the people on his property.

Nick dropped onto his couch, turned on the television and flipped through the channels, his emotions doing a number to his head. A familiar comedy show was on and he sank deeper into the sofa cushions, grateful for the momentary diversion. Ever since he heard A.J. on the other end of the line, he'd been uptight. But now he'd made a decision. Until he heard A.J.'s side of the story, he'd give him the benefit of the doubt.

The ugly blue truck was still in Nick's driveway. Jessica cut the engine and dropped the keys in her purse. Four bags of groceries sat in her trunk and Jacob sipped from a can of juice in the back seat. They stepped out of the car.

"Can I invite him?" asked Jacob. He belched and a giggle erupted. "Excuse me."

"Nick's company is still here."

"But what if *he* asks *his* company for dinner? Then he won't come over."

Her son had a point. "We'll wait a little while longer. And I'll do the asking."

"All right." Jacob downed the last of his drink.

While at the grocery store, Jessica imagined the person visiting Nick. Maybe it was a woman. He'd inquired if Jessica was seeing someone, but she'd never asked him the same question. She mentally kicked herself. But Nick had been nothing but sweet and caring since the day they'd met and from what she'd learned about him from Holly, he was an outstanding guy. By the tender way he'd looked at her when he came to her door earlier, she would've guessed he'd wanted to kiss her. Maybe this whole time she'd been reading him wrong. She opened the trunk. "Jacob, help me carry the groceries into the house."

Jacob set the empty can on the ground and stomped it flat. "Okay."

"Hmm. Let's see. What can you carry with one arm?" She handed him the bag of boxed items, including the box of cereal he'd begged for at the store. "Go on in. The door's not locked."

Jacob scurried toward the house.

Three bags remained as well as two gallons of milk. She'd need to make two trips. Curiosity at Nick's guest niggled once again. Would it be rude to knock on his door to invite him to dinner? She wouldn't need to meet the person who'd come over. No, she only wanted to make sure Nick was available before she spent the time making her special lasagna. Otherwise, she'd save it for another night and open a couple cans of soup. Seemed logical.

Jacob was inside the house, no doubt already opening the box of cereal. She hurried to Nick's door and knocked. She twisted the ring around her finger and shifted from side to side waiting for him to answer. She glanced at her watch. What were Nick and his guest doing? She reigned in her thoughts and climbed down the stairs, the invitation for dinner shoved aside.

The door creaked open.

"Jessica." Nick whispered, barely loud enough for her to hear.

She turned around.

He motioned for her to come toward him through the slightly opened doorway "I can't talk now. Please, go to the cabin and stay there."

"Nick, what's going on? You're acting strange."

Nick glanced over his shoulder. "Please, do as I say."

"If you're dating someone just tell me. It's no big deal. You can see whomever you want." She crossed her arms, her words far from the truth. If Nick did have a girlfriend she'd be crushed like Jacob's juice can.

The pained look on Nick's face startled her. "You've got it all wrong, but I don't have time to explain."

His words and expression caused her to take a new approach. "Then come for dinner. Six o'clock."

"Believe me, I want to be there." Nick's smile didn't reach his eyes.

Something was bothering him, but who was she to expect he'd share his thoughts or life with her? She was someone he'd known for only a few days. After all, she hadn't yet opened up to him about Jacob's birthfather.

"Great. I make a mean lasagna. I'll start cooking, but don't worry if you can't make it. I didn't mean to pry."

"Nick, where'd you go?" A deep voice called in the background. *Andrew?*

Jessica rocked back on her heels. "I'll let you get back to your company."

"Remember what I said. Don't come out of the cabin."

"Come at six." She hurried down the front steps toward her car.

The door clicked shut.

She hoped if Nick came over for dinner, he'd open up and tell her exactly whose voice she heard. Once at the car, she hoisted the milk out of the trunk, her thoughts drifting to Nick's guest. A shiver ran through her. Could it be Andrew . . . or was it her imagination?

Nick leaned back against the door and took a breath. That was close. He joined A.J. in the family room.

He wore clean clothes, his hair was slicked back, and he still had a couple weeks' growth on his face. "Mind if I turn the television off?"

"Don't mind at all." Nick sat on the couch. "You ready to talk? 'Cause I'm ready to listen."

A.J. clicked the off button on the remote and sat across from him. "Now is as good a time as any."

"I'm all ears," said Nick. "I'd like to know the truth."

"Good, because I've got an unbelievable story to tell you."

"Try me." Nick said, for the second time since A.J. arrived.

25

Nick sat speechless and listened as A.J. paced the room, the story of his girlfriend's demise tumbling from his lips. "We'd been dating a few months and I found out Crystal was only going out with me because of my connections."

"What kind of connections?" Nick had an idea, but he wanted A.J. to voice exactly what he meant.

"I know you'll be disappointed." A.J. stopped wearing a hole in the carpet and wagged his head. "I'd been using drugs, marijuana mainly."

The admission stung like a hornet. Nick's jaw clenched.

"Over the past month, Crystal was becoming less interested in me and more interested in using my apartment for her own benefit." He sniffed, then bent his head back and made a motion with his hand like he was tipping a bottle.

"Then what happened?"

"Last week she stopped by with a couple of her girlfriends and a sack of groceries, mostly bottles of booze. I informed her she was going to have to take her party elsewhere, but she didn't listen to me. Said I was a killjoy and to lighten up, that she and her friends wanted to have a good time."

"Why didn't you force her to leave?" Nick was one to talk. He should've done the same thing when A.J. showed up at his door.

"What can I say? She promised to make it up to me."

Nick really didn't want to hear all the sordid details, but he had to know one way or another if A.J. was guilty. "Go on . . ."

"I told Crystal I'd be at the gym working out and that I wanted everyone gone by the time I got back."

"And were they?" Nick probed, a sickening feeling squeezing his gut.

"No." A.J.'s words came out between clenched teeth. "In fact, when I returned there were more people at my apartment than when I'd left."

"What did you do?"

"I let them know I was going to call the police before one of my neighbors did and to get out. It worked for the most part, except for the few stragglers that were too drunk or stoned to move—including Crystal."

Nick sat forward on the couch, his elbows resting on his knees. He was having a hard time separating the facts from his emotions. Since when had A.J. gone off the deep end? "Then what happened?"

A.J. dropped onto the couch opposite Nick and continued. "I covered them with blankets, took a shower, and went to bed. The following morning I was awakened by one of the women screaming. I ran into the family room and found her kneeling over Crystal, shrieking and crying, and saying she had no pulse. I asked her to call 911 while I performed CPR. The paramedics arrived and took her to the hospital where they pronounced her dead." A.J.'s voice hitched. "And now I'm being accused of providing the drugs and liquor that killed her."

Nick moved to A.J.'s side and rested a hand on his shoulder. Guilty or not, he'd been through a terrible ordeal. "But you were trying to save her. What evidence do they have against you?"

A.J. bolted from the couch and began pacing the floor again. He threw his hands up in the air, then pointed his thumb against his chest. "Since the party was at my apartment, they hold me responsible."

"You had a host of people at your house that could've provided Crystal with the drugs and alcohol," said Nick.

"After they took her in the ambulance, I made the mistake of cleaning up. I was upset and wasn't thinking clearly. My fingerprints are all over the place." A.J.'s mouth was set in a grim line. "Most of the people who were at the party know me, which doesn't help my case. And worst of all, I found out Crystal was underage, a fact she kept hidden from me."

Although entangled with the wrong crowd, if A.J.'s story was true he was innocent of the crime. Running only made him appear guilty. And it wouldn't be long before he was caught. Nick toyed with the corner of a magazine on the coffee table, flipping through the pages. "What do you plan to do now?"

A.J.'s facial features softened. "Find my child before I go to jail."

"Your what?" Nick's voice rose. What other surprises did A.J. have up his sleeve? A.J.'s life was becoming more complicated by the minute.

"My son. I relinquished my rights years ago and have yet to meet him."

Nick attempted to put two and two together as he recollected their earlier conversation. "Is this the woman you hoped to see?"

A.J. nodded. "Yes."

Nick stood and squeezed the back of his neck. "Does she know you're here?"

"No. I've left messages, but she won't return my calls.

"I'm not surprised. Your photo was plastered on the news."

Realization dawned on A.J.'s face. "You knew I was wanted by the police and you still let me in?"

Nick let out an audible breath. "Crazy, huh?"

"But I'm innocent. You believe me, right?"

Did he? A.J. might be mixed up in a horrible situation, but he was no killer. "Yes, I believe you. But it doesn't change the fact you need to turn yourself in. I don't want to be the one making the call."

"And I will. But first I want to see my son—to lay eyes on my boy. You can understand that, can't you?"

Nick hesitated. He couldn't imagine being in A.J.'s shoes. "As long as you promise me you'll call the police after you see him."

"Promise." A.J. stuck out his hand.

Nick locked eyes with his long-time friend then pulled him close in a manly embrace. "Oh, one more thing. My tenants can't know about you. I've been invited over for dinner tonight. You'll need to park your truck somewhere else."

"All right." A.J. scratched the stubble on his chin. "What's the story? You sweet on someone?"

"She's something special. But that's all I'm going to say." Nick held up a hand.

"I get it." A.J. cocked his head. "You don't want me near her. You did say tenants, didn't you? Who else lives in the cabin?"

"Extended family."

"Parents? Siblings?" asked A.J.

"Uncle and her son." Nick pressed his lips together. He wasn't about to give A.J. any more details. He'd already said too much.

A knowing look flashed across A.J.'s face. "I get it. You don't trust me. I'll go move my truck and come in the back way. They'll never know I'm here."

"Thanks." An overwhelming urge to call the police surfaced as Nick watched A.J. hoist his duffle bag over his shoulder and leave his house, doubt boring a hole into his heart.

God, I want to do the right thing.

———— ❀ ————

Jessica pulled the lasagna out of the oven and set it on the top of the stove. The cheese bubbled and the Italian spices mingled in the air creating an enticing aroma. She placed the French bread in the oven and gathered salad fixings from the refrigerator.

Jacob ran his small truck over the edge of the counter. "What time is Nick coming over?"

It took her only a few minutes after talking with Nick to decide that it wasn't Andrew's voice she'd heard. She was being paranoid. The chances of him knowing Nick were slim to none. Jessica washed the vegetables. "Six o'clock."

"What time is it now?" asked Jacob.

She couldn't wait for the day when her son could tell time. "The small hand is on the six, and the big hand is on the one. That means it's five minutes after six."

Jacob's brows puckered. "Should I go knock on his door? Maybe he forgot."

Jessica peeked out the kitchen window. The blue truck was gone. She didn't see any harm in Jacob giving Nick a friendly reminder. After all, she'd spent a long time in the kitchen preparing the meal. Then again, if Nick could come he would. "Let's wait a few more minutes. I still need to fix the salad.

Why don't you finish setting the table?" Jessica pointed. "The silverware is in that drawer."

With his good hand, Jacob counted forks, spoons, and knives, and carefully put them next to each place setting. "What else do you need, Mom?"

"Glasses. Let me get them for you." Jessica reached into the cabinet and set four down on the counter. "When you're done you can go play in the back room till I call you for dinner."

Jacob set each glass in place, then grabbed his truck and disappeared around the corner.

"Hungry, Uncle George?" Jessica called to her uncle, who was reading on the couch.

"Famished," George replied without looking up. "Smells good. That your mother's recipe?"

She hadn't seen her mom in a long time, not since Jacob was two. "No, it's mine. I've tweaked it over the years. My roommate says it's the best she's ever tasted."

"Trying to impress the landlord, I see." George grinned.

Jessica chopped the tomatoes. "I'll have you know I purchased the ingredients before I invited Nick over. I wanted to make *you* happy."

"Thank you, that's nice." His smile faded. "But I don't know what will satisfy me these days. Even reading my Bible doesn't do it for me like it used to." He shut the book in his lap and placed it on the end table.

"I'm sorry for how your life has changed, I really am. At the end of the week, Jacob and I need to go back to Fresno. He has school and I've got a business to run." Whether or not she'd go back to her apartment was still up in the air. She couldn't risk running into Andrew until she understood exactly what his agenda was for wanting to see Jacob. Before she drove home, she'd suck it up and give him another call.

"How many clients do you have?" asked George. "Is business good?"

That was the first time her uncle had asked about her life since she'd arrived in Santa Cruz. It did her heart good to know he cared. "Plenty to keep me busy. I work with clients of all ages, but mostly children."

George pushed himself to standing and hobbled across the room on his crutches. "You doing okay financially?"

"Yes, fine. I make enough to get by." Jessica cut carrot wedges into the salad, her insides dancing at the fatherly concern in her uncle's eyes.

"I plan on paying you back every penny you gave Nick—"

"Uncle George, I don't want to hear another word," Jessica interrupted before the conversation took a turn for the worse. "You're forgetting all the times you sent me money over the years. Think of it as family helping one other."

The grin was back on her uncle's face, and the corners near his eyes crinkled. "You're feisty, you know that? Guess you've had to be in order to take care of the boy on your own. I'm glad this Nick fellow is coming for dinner. He seems like a good, honest sort—"

"Though a little late."

"Aw, give the man five more minutes."

"Only a few. Otherwise, I don't think he's coming. Plus, I'm hungry." Jessica chomped on a carrot.

George set his crutches against the wall and plunked down in a kitchen chair by the table. "There was a time when my life ran by the clock. Evelyn's parents couldn't stand it if I was a minute late to pick up their daughter. Mind you, I didn't want to be early either. Her father would give me the once over and by the looks he shot my way, I knew he didn't approve."

"What became of Evelyn? Did you keep in touch?"

"She married a lawyer—someone her parents could be proud of. But that was forty years ago. Once she married, I tried to put her out of my mind."

"And did you?" Jessica set the salad bowl on the table and sat beside her uncle.

"I had to give her up. She was another man's wife. But I've thought about her numerous times over the years, and more so lately. I don't know why."

Jessica touched her uncle's hand. "You've had a big change in your life. Have you thought about contacting her? For old times' sake?"

George slipped his hand away and crossed his arms over his chest. "I don't want her see me like this."

"I'm sure it wouldn't matter to her. You could always practice using your prosthetic leg." She purposely added a lilt to her voice.

"Doubt I'll ever be ready." George's tone reflected his deflated attitude.

Before Jessica had a chance to respond, a knock sounded on the door.

Nick had come for dinner.

26

While A.J. had moved his truck, Nick called the fire station and found someone to cover for him the next couple of days. Truth was, he wanted to make sure A.J. followed through with his promise of notifying the police and to make sure Jessica's uncle was satisfied with his living conditions.

When A.J. returned, he propped his feet on the coffee table and thumbed through a magazine.

"I won't be long," said Nick. "A couple hours at the most."

A.J. tossed him a look, and then lowered his eyes to the reading material in front of him. "Take your time. I wasn't planning on going anywhere."

Now standing at the threshold of the cabin, Nick's mind took a turn. The police might work with him if they knew A.J.'s whereabouts.

The door opened.

"Nick, glad you came." A smile lit Jessica's face. She moved to the side so he could enter.

The aroma wafting from the cabin reminded him of stepping inside an Italian restaurant. He inhaled deeply. "Thanks for inviting me. Smells wonderful."

"For a minute there, I didn't know if you'd make it." Jessica's eyes darted to the clock on the wall above the kitchen sink.

"Sorry I'm late." He'd wait till after dinner to explain the situation to Jessica, a decision he'd made on his short walk from his house to the cabin. She had a right to know he had a wanted man in his house. Whether Jessica and her family would stay or leave was up to them, but he'd not say a word until after they ate. By the delicious smell, Jessica worked hard to prepare the meal and he wouldn't spoil it.

Jacob ran up to Nick and wrapped his arms around his waist. The boy's cast bumped against him. "You're finally here."

He ruffled the top of Jacob's head. "It was nice of your mom to invite me. I bet she's a great cook."

"The best." Jacob grabbed his hand and pulled him toward the table. "Sit by me, okay?"

"You've got it, squirt." Nick glanced at Jessica. Her eyes shone with warmth, and a grin tugged at the corners of her mouth. Apparently, she liked the idea, too.

Jessica donned a pair of oven mitts and carried the lasagna to the table, then went back into the kitchen and retrieved the bread. "Dinner is ready."

During the meal they made small talk around the table. It surprised Nick how comfortable he felt eating with Jessica's family—especially her uncle after the awkward moment about payment. George's facial features were relaxed and he appeared more at ease. The prayer he uttered before dinner was not only eloquent, but heartfelt as well.

Every once in a while during the meal, Nick caught Jessica staring at him. He wished he could read her thoughts. Now more than ever, he wanted to call the police and let them handle the situation. Who was he to think he could orchestrate helping A.J. see his son and keeping Jessica and her family safe? He had an overwhelming urge to grab the phone and make the call.

He set his fork down on the plate, and leaned toward Jessica. "Can we talk after dinner?" He hadn't intended to sound so serious.

Her eyes grew round and she nodded. "There's something I'd like to speak to you about as well." Her tone matched his.

George cleared his throat. "Jacob, why don't you and I go in the back room and read a story. I think your mom and Nick would like to be alone."

"What about dessert?" Jacob eyed George cautiously. "Mom bought vanilla ice cream, chocolate syrup and machine cherries for the top."

Nick suppressed a grin at Jacob's word for maraschino. The boy was a character—forthright and full of energy. If he had a son, he'd want him to be exactly like Jacob.

"It's okay, Uncle George," said Jessica. "We can have dessert first. Otherwise, I'll never hear the end of it."

Jacob pumped his fist. "All right!"

"But then you'll need to go to the back of the cabin with Uncle George so I can talk with Nick." Jessica stacked the plates and took them to the sink. "Jacob, help me clear the table while I dish up."

The boy bounded from his seat and grabbed the empty salad bowl with one hand.

"Let me help." Nick stood and carried the remaining lasagna to the kitchen.

"I'll wait right here." George leaned back, stretched, and patted his stomach.

The simple dessert turned into a sundae-making contest.

"The trick is to drizzle the chocolate if you want it to look nice." Jessica made a show of carefully adding syrup stripes on her ice cream.

"I say pour it on and add a cherry. It tastes the same going down." Nick demonstrated by squirting a mound of chocolate, scooping a spoonful and bringing it to his lips.

"I have to agree with Nick," said George, laughing.

"It does look good, Mom," Jacob defended. "But you need more ice cream. You only have one scoop."

Ten minutes later spoons clattered against empty glass bowls.

"I wish we could go to Nick's house to watch TV." Jacob muttered as he and George went to the back of the small cabin. Nick was thankful Jessica didn't flinch at the idea. The last thing he wanted was for Jacob to go to his house and see A.J. sitting there.

Once they were alone, he offered to wash the dishes but Jessica declined.

"I'll do them later," she said. "Want a cup of coffee?"

"I'd like that." He'd never refused a cup in his life and wasn't about to start now. After all, what he had to tell her could put a wedge between them and he might as well have a cup of joe while he told her the truth about his guest.

But first, he'd listen to what she had to say. He stood beside her as she put fresh grounds in the coffee maker, her flowery scent doing a number to his senses. She'd worn her hair up when he first came, but had since released its hold. Her hair now cascaded around her shoulders and he fought the urge to push a lock away from her face. "What do you need to talk to me about?"

She took a deep breath and turned toward him. "It's about Jacob's father."

Nick leaned against the counter. "What about him?"

"He keeps calling me wanting to see Jacob."

The irony of her and A.J.'s situation wasn't lost on Nick. "How long has it been since you've heard from him?"

"Six years. He's never been involved in Jacob's life. Don't you find it odd that after all these years he's suddenly interested in him? First, he'll want to see him, and next he'll want visitations, and before long, he'll be fighting me for custody, though I doubt he'd win." She pressed her lips together and blinked back moisture that had formed in her eyes.

"Whoa. Aren't you getting carried away?" He reached up and gently pushed back the lock of hair that called to him earlier. "I'm not a father, but I can imagine the curiosity. What would it hurt to have him see the boy?"

"Whose side are you on?" She shook her head and looked heavenward. "I've been Jacob's only parent for six years and now suddenly I'm supposed to accept his dad with open arms?"

"Have you asked him what his intentions are? Seems that would be a fair question."

"But how can I believe what he says?" Jessica shrugged a shoulder. "Since I've been in Santa Cruz, he's come to my apartment twice, and according to my roommate he wasn't sober the second time around. He seemed desperate, like he was crazed."

Alarm bells went off in Nick's mind. What were the chances A.J. was Jacob's father? Impossible.

Jessica continued. "I'm afraid to go home, but I can't live here in the cabin with George forever. Like I told my uncle, Jacob needs to go back to school, and I have a business to run." Her brows lowered. "I'm sorry if I've said too much." She poured hot coffee into a mug and handed it to him. "Was there something you wanted to discuss with me?"

Nick's throat tightened. How would he be able to explain A.J.'s sudden appearance and still maintain sympathy for her situation? Seemed cruel to expect her to understand. "No need to apologize. You have a lot on your mind. Are you sure you don't want to talk about it further?"

"If you're asking me to be open-minded, you might as well forget it. Jacob's dad has a drinking problem, and I wouldn't be surprised if he's used drugs." Jessica poured herself a cup of coffee and added vanilla creamer. "Mind you I wasn't innocent during my college years, but I've since rededicated my life to God and want to raise Jacob in a Christian home."

"I respect that. In fact, I want the same thing for my family one day."

"Then you can understand why Andrew's influence would be detrimental for Jacob."

Andrew. No, God, please? Not A.J.

His fear was confirmed. His childhood friend was the father of Jessica's child. It wasn't a coincidence A.J. showed up in Santa Cruz. His hands grew moist and his mouth went dry, despite the coffee he was drinking. What would Jessica think if she found out Andrew was not only on his property but less than fifty yards away? His plan for discussing A.J.'s visit all but disappeared.

"Nick, say something. You're making me nervous."

If he were able to figure out a way to have A.J. see his son so that he could phone the police, he'd do it in a heartbeat. Nick set his mug down on the counter and took her hand, his voice low and gentle. "Jessica, maybe Andrew only wants to see the boy and nothing else. Would you reconsider then?"

Her hand felt good in his. Dainty and light. But she was strong if she needed to defend her child. He'd witnessed her protectiveness more than once.

"But how can I be sure? You can't promise me that's all he wants." Jessica didn't pull her hand away.

"No, I can't guarantee anything." He rubbed his thumb against her soft skin. "I do know that if Andrew got to know Jacob, like I have, he wouldn't want him out of his life."

"That's what I'm afraid of."

In that instant, Nick feared that and more. He found himself caught in the middle between his childhood friend and the woman he now couldn't imagine his life without. Either way, he'd lose.

With their faces inches apart, Nick leaned forward and gently caressed her lips with his own. The kiss was over in an instant, but it would forever stay in Jessica's mind. Soft. Gentle. Leaving her wanting more. She didn't know why he chose that moment to kiss her, but maybe he wanted to let her know he'd be there for her. "I'm glad I can trust you."

Nick's gaze lowered to the floor. "I care about you—Jacob. And your uncle." His tone sounded melancholy, not like a man's should when he's sharing his heart with the woman he'd just kissed.

Something was wrong.

"Ever since you came to my door and told me you were going to have company, you've been acting strange. Are you in some kind of trouble?"

"Me? No . . . um, I don't want to be."

"What do you mean?"

"Jessica, have you been watching the news? TV?"

"No, I haven't. Jacob watched cartoons a couple of days ago, why? What does it have to do with you or your company?"

Squeezing his eyes shut, Nick took a deep breath. He placed his hands on Jessica's shoulders and looked squarely into her eyes. "I've known A.J. since I was a kid, but never knew he fathered a child—your child." He pressed his lips together, then continued. "The other day A.J.'s . . . Andrew's . . . face appeared on the news. The police are looking for him . . ."

Heart in her throat, Jessica shifted her stance. "I need to sit down."

With his hand on the small of her back, Nick guided her to the couch. Once seated, he wrapped an arm around her shoulder and spoke with measured words. "Jessica, his underage girlfriend died a week ago, and now he's wanted for providing drugs and alcohol to her. But I believe he's innocent—or want to believe." He lowered his voice.

"That's why he's so desperate to see Jacob." Jessica covered her mouth with a hand, her mind spinning. "I'm relieved I didn't give in. There's no way I'd allow Andrew to see him now."

"Please remember I didn't know A.J. was Jacob's father. I would never have allowed him to set foot on my property if I had known."

"What are you saying?" Jessica's voice shook.

"Andrew, or A.J. as I've called him since I was twelve, is sitting in my house right now. He called me this afternoon and told me he was on his way. The line was breaking up and I felt I had no choice but to wait for him to arrive."

Jessica clutched her middle, her stomach winding into a knot. "Why didn't you call the police?"

"I've wanted to many times, but I felt as though I needed to hear him out." Nick pulled Jessica close. "Listen, A.J. only wants to see Jacob—"

"And if he's innocent like you say? Then what? I don't want Jacob dragged into a custody battle."

"Innocent or guilty, I doubt anyone would award him custody rights with his history of substance abuse."

"This is all too much to take·in." Jessica bolted off the couch and moved to the far side of the room, the recliner between them. "Can you give me tonight to think it through?"

Nick stood and closed the gap. "I understand. But the sooner you decide, the quicker this whole ordeal will be over with. I'll keep Andrew away from the cabin and I'll stop by first thing in the morning."

Jessica walked Nick to the door. He planted a kiss on her cheek and thanked her for the meal.

"You're stronger than you think." He ran his hand down her arm, his parting words like a warm embrace, and quietly slipped into the night air.

Strong or not, she wouldn't be there in the morning. She couldn't allow Andrew, a possible murderer, into her son's life. But if she left, she might never see Nick again. Her shoulders sagged and her heart felt heavy.

It was a chance she'd have to take.

27

Jessica checked the time on her cell phone. 2:00 a.m. All the bags were packed and loaded in the car. No sense in telling her uncle or Jacob of her plan. She hoped they'd go without making it more difficult than it had to be. Dropping her phone inside her purse, she walked quietly to her uncle's room and laid a hand on his shoulder, shaking gently. "Uncle George. Wake up."

He startled. "What's the matter?"

"Come with me."

"Where are we going?" Uncle George's voice was a mixture of shock and annoyance.

"I know it's the middle of the night, but I'm not comfortable staying here."

"If you'd rather sleep on the twin bed, I'll move to the couch."

It was sweet of her uncle to offer, but he had no idea the news Nick shared with her. She wouldn't be able to sleep knowing Andrew was in such close proximity to Jacob.

"No, Uncle George, I don't want to be here in Nick's cabin."

George sat up. "Did you two have a disagreement last night?"

Jessica shook her head. "Nothing like that. Can we please leave and I'll tell you on the way?"

"You're being fickle. Why do we have to sneak away? Can't you and Nick work this out?"

"I talked with Holly Branson and she's expecting us."

"You're bringing me back to the rehabilitation facility?"

"No. Her house. It has nothing to do with your progress and everything to do with Jacob."

George scooted to the edge of the bed. "I don't know what you're up to—"

"The car is packed and ready to go. The only problem is that I can't fit your wheelchair, but we'll bring your prosthesis and your crutches."

"Is this a ploy to make me use that blasted thing? Because if it is, I might as well go back to bed."

"I promise that's not what I'm doing." Jessica patted her uncle's shoulder and motioned him to follow her. "I'll get Jacob in the car."

"I need to get dressed—"

"Like I said, all your things are packed. You'll have to go as you are. Let's hurry."

Jessica's heart beat a staccato rhythm and she willed her hands to stop shaking. If they could leave without Nick and Andrew seeing them, she could catch her breath. She'd thought about calling the police herself, but she hadn't seen Andrew in person or his face on the television screen and she didn't want to explain the whole situation without implicating Nick. No, she'd leave and let him decide whether or not to make the call.

Stepping into the other bedroom, Jessica reached down and ran her fingers through her son's hair. When she looked at him, she didn't see Andrew in him at all. Jacob was her boy, all hers. She'd raised him from birth and she wouldn't share him with an addict. "Come on, buddy. We're going for a drive."

Jacob rolled over and settled under the covers. Jessica hated to wake him. She sat on the bed and maneuvered him on her lap, then hoisted herself to standing, shifting her stance to even out the weight of his body.

She met her uncle in the hallway.

"You're sure we can't wait till morning? After you and Nick have a chance to talk?"

"No, Uncle George, definitely not. Please, no questions." With Jacob in her arms, Jessica led the way and grabbed her keys from the kitchen table. "Stay quiet," she called over her shoulder before opening the door.

The moon was full and the stars twinkled overhead, the sky clear and brisk. She inhaled the smell of the redwoods, knowing she'd miss this place.

"Mom, where are we going?" Jacob's small voice cut into the silence.

"Shh, baby," Jessica whispered. "I'll tell you in a minute." She opened the car door and helped her son into the car. Her uncle climbed into the passenger seat while Jessica made her way to the driver's side.

No lights were on inside Nick's house and the blue truck was nowhere to be found. She sent a quick plea heavenward that Nick and Andrew wouldn't hear her engine as they rolled out of the driveway.

"Having second thoughts?" asked George.

Jessica shook her head. "Saying a prayer." She turned the key and backed up, then glanced at the house before pulling away, the memory of Nick's kiss on her mind.

After Nick had left the cabin and Jacob and her uncle had gone to bed, she'd called Holly and explained the situation as best she could without giving away too many details. Since Holly had the following day off work, she'd been more than willing to house them for the remainder of the night and help them find George a new apartment once the sun came up.

"Sorry it didn't work out at the cabin," Holly had said. "I thought for sure the Santa Cruz mountain air would lift George's spirits."

She'd been right. Jessica had seen a change in George's mood and she hoped he wouldn't digress the farther they drove away.

"The boy's asleep. You going to tell me what's *really* going on?"

Jessica relaxed her tight grip at Uncle George's caring tone. She glanced in her rearview mirror and saw Jacob's head bob to the side. He was asleep all right. "Jacob's birthfather has been trying to find him. When Nick was over tonight he told me he and Andrew have been friends since childhood and that he was the one who came to Nick's house today."

"Jessi, sooner or later you're going to have to give a little where Andrew is concerned. Now I know he gave up the boy years ago, but why not let Jacob meet his father? It's bound to happen sooner or later."

Jessica glanced in her rearview mirror again. Jacob was still asleep, but she spoke in a hushed tone. "Because the cops are looking for him."

"The police? What for?" George's tone lifted.

"Shh. Apparently he supplied drugs and liquor to his young girlfriend and she overdosed. Oh, Uncle George." Her voice hitched. "If I'd stayed with him, I could've been sucked into that life. I'm glad I walked away when I did."

"I'm surprised Nick would associate with that type of fellow. I'd assumed he was a Christian man—"

"He is. I don't think he and Andrew are close. In fact, it came as quite a shock to Nick when he saw Andrew's face on the news."

"News? Then you made the right decision."

She was pleased at her uncle's words, but a slight niggling stirred inside. Was she making the best choice? Nick would be disappointed in the morning when he came to the cabin door and discovered they weren't there. She hated to let Nick down and put him in the awkward position of calling the police on his own.

But she'd do anything to protect her son. Even drive to the Bransons' home in the middle of the night.

Nick woke with a start. Darkness enveloped him, as it should at three o'clock in the morning. He'd tossed and turned attempting to get some sleep and had finally succumbed, but a nightmare jolted him awake. He sat up trying to recall the threatening images. All he could remember was trying to get away from something—or someone. Then it came to him. A.J. was in the other room, probably asleep on his living room sofa. And if the police knew Nick was helping him in any way, he'd wind up in trouble as well.

One more day. He'd give A.J. twenty-four hours before he'd force his childhood friend to make the call, or call the police himself. Jessica was the one who held the key. If she allowed A.J. to see his little boy, then it would be over and the police could be notified. But the fear he saw in Jessica's beautiful green eyes when he told her about Andrew made him question himself for even asking.

She had to know how much he cared for her by the kiss they'd shared. He'd never intentionally put her or Jacob in harm's way. In years past, he'd never known A.J. to be dangerous.

Nick hung his legs over the side of the bed and stretched. An eerie silence enveloped him. He pushed himself up and looked out the bedroom window.

Jessica's car was gone.

His bad dream was slowly turning into reality. Quickly, he slipped on jeans, a sweatshirt and a pair of shoes, and went outside to the cabin. If Jessica and her family left, he might never see them again. The thought sucked the air out of his lungs.

He pushed the door open, walked inside, and fumbled his way to the back of the cabin, looking through both rooms and finding empty beds. He was about to leave when he saw a lone figure sitting on the couch. Before he had a chance to react, A.J.'s voice cut in.

"He was here, wasn't he?"

Nick flipped on a light.

A.J. clutched Jacob's stuffed teddy bear.

"What are you doing here?" Nick's words were laced with disgust. "And what right do you have to come into my cabin when I told you I had tenants?"

"I heard them leave. When you mentioned the woman was here with her uncle and son, I wondered if it was Jessica. I'm right, aren't I?"

Nick thrust his hands in the air, then clutched them behind his head, his mind whirling.

"I was so close," A.J. muttered.

Nick could smell alcohol on the A.J.'s breath. "Listen, she doesn't want anything to do with you. I tried to convince her to let you see Jacob, but she wasn't having it. Time to let it go and turn yourself in. If you're innocent, you have nothing to worry about. You'll be out of jail before you know it. Clean yourself up and give her time."

"You don't get it, man." A.J.'s eyes looked hard, evil. "I don't have time."

"Care to explain?"

208

A.J.'s face contorted, pain evident on his features. "Crystal loved me. Said she wanted to marry me. Start a life together."

Nick's gut twisted. "Go on."

"She'd hoped we'd get straight and stop using." A.J. swiped at his eyes. "But I ruined everything."

"What do you mean?" Nick attempted to swallow the lump that had formed in his throat.

"I organized the party. Planned the whole thing. I asked her to marry me that night and she'd said yes. I wanted to celebrate and so did she. I went out and bought the stuff, and we had a good time." A.J. let out a wry laugh, then sobered. "Before we went to sleep, she told me she was going to have my child. But in the morning, she was dead." He squeezed the stuffed animal to his chest with white knuckles.

Nick's lungs constricted and he couldn't breathe. He gasped for air as his doubts were confirmed. A.J. was guilty of providing the drugs that killed his underage girlfriend. Nick moved to the kitchen and splashed water on his face, then cupped his hands for a drink. And here he'd asked Jessica, nearly begged her to consider letting A.J. meet her son. Nick's shoulders slumped. He'd failed to protect them and was glad Jessica had the foresight to escape. A.J. couldn't be trusted.

"It's time to make the call." Nick turned on his heel, but A.J. was gone.

He'd run off and taken Jacob's stuffed toy with him.

Nick raced to the door and looked out. The cover of darkness concealed A.J.'s whereabouts. He wished he'd thought to write down the blue truck's license plate number. Once again, he failed. With sweaty palms, Nick picked up the phone and dialed 9-1-1.

28

With suitcases in hand, Jessica led her son and uncle into the Bransons' home. "Thank you for letting us stay."

Holly, clad in a fluffy blue robe, stepped aside to let them enter. "No problem, I wish it had worked out at Nick's place." Her hushed tone matched the quiet of the night.

Jacob tugged on Jessica's arm. "Mom, we didn't even say goodbye to Nick. Won't he be sad?"

Jessica's throat constricted and she pushed down the emotions. She'd never planned on getting involved with someone while helping her uncle, but that was exactly what she'd done. If only her son had never met Nick, it would make their parting less painful. She squeezed Jacob's shoulder. "He'll be okay and so will we."

"Follow me and I'll get you settled," said Holly. "George, I hope you don't mind sleeping on the pullout couch. It has a queen mattress, though not as comfortable as I would like."

"Right now I could sleep on a meat hook." George hobbled behind on his crutches. "Show me the way."

Holly cinched the belt on her robe and grinned. "I like your attitude, George." She winked at Jessica and moved in the direction of the family room. The bed was already made, complete with a pillow, sheets, and a comforter.

George dropped on the bed, set his crutches on the floor, and waved the women on. "See you in a few hours."

"Can I sleep in Ryan's room?" asked Jacob.

Holly guided them down the hall. "Maybe another night, okay? You'll see Ryan in the morning. I have you and your mom set up in here." She turned into a bedroom and flipped on a light.

Jessica and Jacob followed. The room was beautiful. A queen-sized bed hugged the far wall flanked by matching lamps and nightstands. A cozy stuffed chair sat in a corner and wispy curtains draped the windows.

"Let me know if you need anything else—especially a listening ear. I'll be in the kitchen for a half hour or so. I'll heat enough water for two if you'd like a cup of tea."

Holly's gentle smile warmed Jessica. Yes, she'd like something hot to drink, but more than that she needed a friend. Over the years her roommate Melissa had been her trusted confidant, but she was miles away. "Thank you, I'd like that. Give me a few minutes to tuck Jacob in."

"Take your time. No rush." Holly closed the door, leaving Jessica to tend to her son.

She moved the mound of decorative pillows and turned down the covers. "This big bed looks comfortable. Let's give it a try."

Jacob slipped off his shoes and leapt on the bed. "Mom, I'm not sleepy anymore. Can you read me a story?"

"If you promise me you'll try and go back to sleep." Jessica reached into the side pocket of her suitcase and produced *Goodnight, Moon*, one of Jacob's favorite picture books since he was a toddler.

"I will." Jacob snuggled under the covers.

As Jessica read the simple words, she couldn't help but long for the uncomplicated routine before Andrew interrupted their life and she'd left for Santa Cruz. And yet, for a short time she'd dreamt of the exciting possibilities of a future with Nick. She forced all thoughts of the handsome firefighter out of her mind and turned her attention to the bunny in the story as he said goodnight to the various objects in his bedroom.

"Hey, Mom." Jacob turned the page. "The number of books changes on the bookshelf. And so do the stripes on the bunny's shirt."

"You're right." Along with several other bedtime favorites, they'd read *Goodnight Moon* for years and she'd never noticed. There were other things that had caught her eye, like how the pictures of the room's lighting progressively darkened, or how the moon rises in the left-hand window.

Once the last page was turned, she kissed Jacob on the cheek and said a prayer before switching off the light. A night-light glowed in the corner. "Holly is making me a cup of tea. I won't be long."

"Okay, but hurry." Jacob's small voice beckoned her from across the room.

Jessica left the door ajar and ambled down the hall toward the kitchen. She was tired and the weight of the day sat on her shoulders, but it would be nice to spend a little time with her gracious host.

From the aroma floating in the air, Holly was making lemon tea. "Have a seat and I'll pour you a cup. You're welcome to some cookies." She patted her belly. "The nausea is worse this time around and the ginger snaps have helped." Holly now appeared to be taking her pregnancy in stride, compared to how upset she'd been the other day.

Jessica sat on a stool by the counter, thankful to think about someone other than herself for the time being. "You doing all right?"

"Took me a little while to accept this pregnancy. It came as quite a surprise. Selfishly, I'd recently gotten back in shape and with Aaron being laid off, it was more than I could take." Holly poured steaming water in a cup and passed it to Jessica, along with an assortment of flavored tea bags.

Like Holly, Jessica chose the lemon.

"To be honest, I'm quite embarrassed about how I acted on Easter. Aaron and I shouldn't have run off the way we did leaving you and Nick to tend to the kids."

An image of Nick patting soggy pieces of pizza with a napkin came to mind. Jessica smiled at the recollection. "Really, it was fine. No need to apologize. I'm happy you're feeling better about the pregnancy."

"It's been faith building. My husband and I are learning to trust God in a whole new way. The other morning Aaron received a phone call from a company in Texas wanting to interview him for a position. It would mean a huge promotion and Aaron would love it if I could stay home with the kids."

"Holly, that's great." Jessica swirled her teabag around in her cup, attempting to stifle the envy that would grow like an ivy plant if left unattended.

"He should be home by the weekend." Holly reached for a ginger snap. "What am I doing? I'm going on and on when I wanted to be the one to listen."

"It's been nice to hear what's been going on with you and Aaron. I know he's Nick's good friend and I was hoping our sudden visit wouldn't put you in an awkward position."

"Jessica, what really happened between you and Nick? I sensed a spark between you from the first day you met."

"That's what makes this difficult. Nick and I are drawn to each other, but there's something standing in our way." Jessica wrestled with how much to share. On the one hand, Holly was a mother and would relate to her need to protect her child, but on the other she had a solid relationship with her husband and wouldn't understand the pressures of being a single parent.

"Whatever it is, I'm sure the two of you can work it out. Besides Aaron, Nick's one of the most caring men I know, almost to a fault. He'd do almost anything for someone in need."

Like allow her uncle to move into his cabin. Or help a friend wanted by the police.

"Was it unlivable? I know the cabin is small—and old." Holly interrupted her wayward thoughts. "I was hoping it could be a good in-between house until he's ready for something more permanent."

Jessica sipped her tea. "The cabin is fine."

"Only not suitable for your uncle?"

Suddenly, Jessica didn't want to answer all the questions Holly was tossing her way. The less she knew the better, if Nick wanted to confide in Aaron, that was his choice. "Until Nick and I work out our differences, George can't stay there."

"It won't be long before he'll be up and about with his prosthesis. I've seen it happen many times before."

"He did seem to come out of his shell while at the cabin." Jessica stared at the small pool of liquid where her tea bag sat on the saucer. Had she put her negative feelings about Andrew ahead of her uncle's progress? What if A.J. had only wanted to see her boy like Nick had suggested? Her head spun from lack of sleep. She wouldn't make any more decisions tonight.

"I can see you're tired. Why don't you bring your tea to your room and we'll talk in the morning." Holly set her empty cup in the sink and closed the box of ginger snaps.

"Good idea." Jessica stood. "Thanks again for the tea. And for letting us come in the middle of the night."

"We mothers need to stick together." Holly's off-hand comment jolted Jessica. Had Holly known all along what this visit was *really* about?

"You're right. We do."

Jacob padded into the kitchen, tears streaming down his face.

Jessica rushed toward him and knelt down, her hands clutching his shoulders. "What's the matter, sweetie?"

"I left my bear at Nick's cabin. I can't sleep without him!" Jacob rubbed his eyes with clenched fists.

There would be no sleep tonight.

The policeman stood in Nick's entryway, a small pad of paper in his hands and a pen poised to take notes. "So you say Andrew Lawson came to your home yesterday afternoon?"

"Yes." Nick rubbed the back of his neck, then stuffed his hands in his jeans pockets.

"Why do you think he came here?" The officer pursed his lips and looked at Nick, eyebrows raised.

"We were childhood friends. He must've figured he could stay in the cabin—but I had tenants."

"Had? When did they move out? Did Mr. Lawson confront them?"

Nick released the breath he was holding. The last thing he wanted to do was drag Jessica and her family into the story, but he didn't see any way around it. "No, they never saw him. At first, they didn't know he was here."

"How many tenants were there?"

"A woman, along with her uncle and son."

"Did Andrew threaten them?"

Now that was a loaded question, one that Nick would need to be careful when answering. "Like I said, they never saw him. But you can say they felt threatened. They left in the middle of the night. I woke up at three o'clock and Jessica's car was gone."

"When did you notice Andrew's disappearance?"

"I spoke with him shortly after I noticed Jessica was no longer here. I went inside the cabin and Andrew was sitting on the couch."

A flicker of disbelief crossed the police officer's face. "Why do you think Andrew went inside the cabin?"

Time for Nick to get straight to the point. "Because he's been looking for his six-year-old son, but the boy and his mother had left before Andrew had a chance to see him."

"Are you telling me the child that was living in your cabin is Andrew's son?"

"Yes."

The officer looked at his notepad. "You said the mother's name is Jessica?" His tone lifted.

Nick nodded. "MacAllister. Jessica MacAllister."

"Are Andrew and Jessica married? Separated? Divorced?"

"From what I've heard, they never married. A.J. relinquished his rights to the child years ago, but he wanted to see his son before he notified you of his whereabouts."

"I take it the child's mother doesn't agree to this."

"I was trying to arrange a meeting in the morning, but Jessica took off. And now so has Andrew. I suggested he wait till he cleans up his act, but . . ." Nick let his words dangle.

"Is there anything else you'd like to tell me?"

"Jessica's son left his stuffed animal, a teddy bear, here and A.J. found it and took it with him. Jacob won't be able to sleep without it."

"Is that all?"

"Jessica's uncle needs his wheelchair. She left it behind. Probably not enough space in her car when she took off."

"We'd like to speak with Jessica. If she comes back to the cabin to collect the wheelchair or notifies you in any way, please let us know."

"I will. Thank you, officer."

"And if Andrew returns or calls, please contact us. You wouldn't want to be charged with harboring a fugitive." The officer handed him a Santa Cruz Police Department business card with his name and phone number on it. Officer Timothy O'Leary. "We'd like to get him off the streets as soon as possible."

Nick tucked the card in his shirt pocket, then shook the man's hand.

The officer left and Nick closed the door behind him.

Nick had done the right thing by contacting authorities, something he should've done hours ago. If he had, A.J. would be in police custody and Jessica and her family would still be in the cabin.

He'd only wanted to help. Or had he tried to play God?

29

Jessica questioned whether or not she should be driving when her eyes felt like sandpaper. But unless she picked up Jacob's teddy bear and her uncle's wheelchair before the sun came up, Nick and Andrew might spot her at the cabin and come knocking on the door.

The car tires crunched on Nick's gravel driveway. She cut the engine, and hurried to the cabin. The door was locked. Either her uncle locked it on the way out, or Nick had done it after they'd left. Or maybe Andrew now slept inside.

At that frightening thought, she stepped back a few paces and her breath came out in short bursts. She turned, and stifled a scream when she smacked right into Nick.

"Come with me." He stuck the key in the door and pulled her into the cabin, locking it behind them. He wrapped his arms around her shoulders. "I thought I might never see you again."

Jessica drew back, her words frantic. "I'm here for the things we left behind and then I'm leaving—"

"Andrew's not here." Nick caught her gaze.

Jessica sagged against him, his familiar masculine scent bringing comfort to her tired bones, and allowed Nick to hold her for a few moments. She stood upright, and stepped away from Nick's embrace. "Jacob's upset. I need to get his bear."

She moved to the back bedroom, checked between the covers, then knelt on the floor and looked under the twin bed. Nothing.

"Andrew came in after you left." Nick's strained voice interrupted her search. He pressed his lips together, brows drawn. "Jessica, it's not here." He helped her up. "A.J. took the bear."

Jessica dropped onto the bed. "What am I going to tell Jacob? That his father, the person who abandoned him, also stole his bear?" Her words sounded as angry as she felt.

"I understand why you're furious." Nick sat beside her and took her hand. He let out an exaggerated breath. "I'm sorry that I tried to push you. I'd never intentionally—"

"But you did." Jessica stared at their entwined fingers. His hands were thick and strong, and made her feel cherished. And yet they didn't see eye-to-eye where Jacob and his birthfather was concerned. She loosened her grip. "After I get the wheelchair in the car, I'll be on my way."

"You should rest a while. Do you have to rush off? You look exhausted."

"I need to get back to Jacob."

"But you shouldn't drive."

"I'll be fine."

"At least let me know where you're staying—"

"Why? So you can tell Andrew?" The question was a low blow, but she didn't care. If he was interested in her well-being he wouldn't have tried to arrange a meeting between her and Andrew in the first place.

"No, Jessica." Nick pushed himself off the bed. "So I can give Jacob his bear if I find A.J."

"You're going to look for him?"

"I would if it meant you'd forgive me."

"Nick, you don't have to do that. Don't you think you've gotten involved way over your head?"

"I called the police. They might want to talk with you."

"You told them about me? And Jacob?" Jessica stepped back a few paces, the betrayal like a knife to her heart.

Nick hung his head. "I didn't see any other way. He's guilty. Told me as much before he took off. Andrew has an agenda and that's to find Jacob."

"I've got to go." Jessica marched to the front room and grasped the handles of the wheelchair and pushed it across the room.

"Wait. Here, let me help." Nick opened the door.

"I think you've done enough already." Tears clogged her throat. She forced the wheelchair through the doorway and pushed it to her car, trying not to let her mind get caught up with the fact that she cared for Nick—too much, perhaps. She fumbled in her purse for the keys, and opened the trunk, feeling his presence behind her.

Without saying another word, he folded the wheelchair and placed it in her car.

"Thank you." Now was not the time for her to break down or linger. He would see right through her. Reluctantly, she moved to the driver's side door and got in, regret for how she was acting already taking root.

What would it hurt to give Nick her cell phone number . . . in case he found Jacob's bear?

She reached into her purse and tore the corner off a scrap of paper, scribbled her information on it, and handed it to him through her opened window. "Call me if you find Jacob's teddy bear."

Nick held tight to her hand. When she didn't look in his direction, he took the piece of paper from her and let go. She kept her gaze forward not wanting to encourage him. Her life was too messy and she didn't want to drag Nick into it any further. She knew he cared, and yet he was the one who could've called the police when Andrew first arrived on his property. True, Nick didn't know A.J. was Jacob's birthfather, but he saw the newscast and A.J.'s face plastered on TV. Andrew would be behind bars already and out of her life.

And now she had to go back to Jacob and tell him the bear was gone.

Jessica started the engine and stepped on the accelerator—needing to put distance between them. As she drove back to the Branson home, a twinge of remorse for keeping the bear in the first place crept inside. Of course, Andrew would recognize the brown stuffed animal with the blue bow. He was the one who'd purchased the toy and had given it to her for their soon-to-be-born son along with the signed relinquishment papers. At the time, it felt like a contradiction, giving her hope that one day he'd return and act like a father. But as the years wore on, her hope turned to anger, anger to indifference, and indifference to relief to have Andrew out of her life.

But a question remained in her mind. What kind of a father would willingly give up his child?

Deep down she knew Nick never would.

Once Jessica rounded the corner, Nick stared at Jessica's cell phone number on the piece of paper in his hand. He clenched his fists determined to hunt A.J. down. The reality that his friend was the father of Jessica's son did a number to his head. How could A.J. walk away from them six years ago? If it weren't for his recent girlfriend's pregnancy and death, he might not be looking for Jacob now.

What right did Nick have to expect Jessica to forgive A.J. so easily? A wave of remorse washed over him. He shouldn't have pushed Jessica and expected so much from her. They'd only begun to care for each other in a deeper way, and he blew it.

At this point, he couldn't go back to bed. Maybe the time had come to let the authorities do their job. He'd learned his lesson trying to fix things on his own, but he had to do *something*. But first, he'd read his Bible and pray. He'd need a ton of wisdom if he were going to win Jessica's confidence back and help A.J. remember his childhood faith.

Each time Bella cried during the night, Evelyn had difficulty going back to sleep. She stretched and glanced at the clock. 8:00 a.m. Apparently, she did get a little, but not enough to keep her going through the day. No wonder Amy was tired.

Evelyn covered a yawn and rose from the bed. While at the store yesterday, she'd picked up a dozen eggs, a pound of turkey sausages, and some pastries. Besides cooking the sausage, she'd fix scrambled eggs, her daughter's favorite, and heat up the cinnamon buns. But if she didn't make coffee straight away, she'd turn around and drop back in bed.

"Good morning, Mom." Amy sat on the loveseat in the family room nursing Isabella.

"Oh, you scared me."

Amy laughed. "Sorry. Didn't mean to. You're usually an early riser. Did Bella keep you up last night?"

Evelyn didn't have the heart to be completely honest. She flipped the switch on the coffeemaker. "You forget I'm on vacation."

"When I was a kid, you were always up with the birds— even on vacation." Amy eyed her suspiciously.

"Okay, fine." Evelyn kept her tone light. "I did hear Bella a time or two."

"Sorry about that. By the way, we'll be leaving as soon as Daniel loads the car."

"Not until I've fed you breakfast." Evelyn shook her head and crossed her arms, challenging her daughter to contradict her.

Amy brought Bella to her shoulder and patted her back. "Wish we could stay, but Daniel is eager to get back to work. Remember, he has to be there by ten."

"You did mention that didn't you?" Evelyn had forgotten that they needed to return mid-morning. It would be pointless to argue. She wasn't used to sleeping late and thought she'd have plenty of time to send them on their way with full stomachs. "But what about breakfast?"

"We'll grab something on the way." Amy laid her daughter on her lap and buttoned her blouse.

Evelyn's heart warmed at her daughter's positive attitude this morning. Maybe she'd turned a corner. Evelyn grabbed a mug from the cabinet and poured a steaming cup of coffee. The aroma aroused her senses. "Want some?"

"Sure. I think I have a minute or two." Amy situated Isabella in her car seat, and joined Evelyn in the kitchen. "Bella's asleep. I'm hoping she stays that way the whole way home."

"You doing okay?" Evelyn handed her a mug and poured another cup.

"For now. Daniel and I had a good talk last night. I've agreed to go see the doctor. He reminded me there's nothing to be ashamed of if I need medication to help me cope. Lots of women suffer from postpartum depression."

"He's right, you know." Evelyn smiled.

"So I'm not a failure as a mother?" Amy's voice lowered and a pained expression crossed her face.

"Of course not, sweetie. I'm glad you're seeking help. And from what I've witnessed, you're a fantastic mother. I'm proud of you." Evelyn cupped Amy's cheek with the palm of her hand.

"Thanks, Mom. If Daniel hadn't taken me away from home and you hadn't invited us to stay the night, I don't know if I'd have been receptive to the idea. Now I see my depression in a whole new light."

Daniel strode into the house. "The car is packed. Ready to go?"

"Yes." Amy nodded.

Evelyn hugged her daughter tight. "I'll call you first thing when I return home."

"Thanks, Mom. For everything."

Daniel picked up the baby's car seat. "Thanks for the dinner last night and the comfy bed."

"Don't let him fool you. He didn't sleep much," Amy whispered. "We took turns getting up with Bella."

Evelyn walked her daughter to the door. "He's a wonderful husband."

"The best." Amy waved, then followed Daniel to the car.

As they drove away, Evelyn realized Amy hadn't even taken a sip of her coffee. And what was she going to do with all those eggs and cinnamon buns?

30

Jessica bolted upright, her mind fuzzy from the few hours of sleep. She glanced at the clock on the bedside table and rolled out of bed, the morning half gone.

She slipped into a pair of sweats and a T-shirt and pulled her hair up in a ponytail. By the time she'd returned to the Branson home from Nick's cabin, all was quiet. Jessica had found a note from Holly saying she was able to calm Jacob down once he had a cup of warm milk, a stuffed animal from Ryan's toy chest, and given the option to sleep in Ryan's room. Holly was amazing.

Jessica rolled her eyes and shook her head. Why hadn't she thought of that? Instead, she traipsed across town and ran the risk of running into Andrew. As happy as she was that he was no longer at Nick's house, she'd wished she were able to get Jacob's teddy bear back. Now Andrew was in control and the only way Jacob would have his precious stuffed animal again would be to allow a meeting between him and his birth-father. She shuddered as she donned a pair of socks and athletic shoes. For the past five days she'd held her ground, but if seeing Andrew face-to-face meant he would give himself up, it would be worth it knowing he'd go to jail for a long time.

But could she do it? She popped a breath mint into her mouth and moved toward the sound of giggles and small voices coming from the kitchen.

"Mommy, you're up! I thought you were going to sleep all day!" Jacob teased. He sat on a stool by the counter next to Sarah and Ryan and shoved a forkful of waffles into his mouth. At least he hadn't asked for his teddy bear straight away.

She smiled at her son and directed her words to Holly, who poured small mounds of batter onto the griddle. The dough hissed as it started to cook. "Sorry I slept so late." Jessica inhaled through her nose. Her mouth watered at the smell of maple syrup.

"No problem." Holly flicked her wrist. "Thought you might sleep in a little longer. We didn't wake you, did we?"

Jessica shook her head. "No, not at all."

"By the way, I've arranged for you and George to look at a wheelchair accessible apartment later this afternoon."

When Jessica had entered the kitchen, she'd noticed the pullout couch was back to its original state with the comforter and sheets neatly folded and piled on the corner cushion. "Speaking of my uncle, where is he?"

"Out back." Holly gestured to the yard with the spatula. "Thought he might like some peace and quiet while I feed the kids. Hey, you want to bring him a plate?"

"Good idea." Jessica forked a waffle onto a dish, then placed a dab of butter and syrup on top.

"Why don't you join him? I've got it covered in here."

"Are you sure you don't mind?"

"Positive." Holly nodded. "I'm certain you two have plenty to talk about."

"You're right about that. Thanks." Jessica repeated the waffle preparations, grabbed two forks and napkins, and headed out the back door.

She found Uncle George by the patio table, his crutches leaning against the seat beside him, and his Bible in front of him. He'd shaved. Wow, what a difference.

"I love the new look. Mind if I join you? Holly thought you might enjoy breakfast outside."

"Pull up a seat." George moved his Bible off to the side without closing it, like he'd done many times before his illness. "My stomach was rumbling, but I didn't want to go inside. Mind you, it's not that I don't enjoy children. I'm not used to their constant chatter."

The corners of Jessica's mouth turned up. She understood completely. Her uncle never married nor had a family and was used to peace and quiet. She set the plates and forks on the table and handed him a napkin. After a moment of silent prayer, they dug into their food. "Do you ever wish you had kids?"

"Didn't have much experience with babies," said George. "Come to think of it, I haven't spent much time with school-aged kids either. If I had some of my own, they'd be long grown by now. But it would've been nice."

"I've always been able to come to you for guidance, so in a way you're like a father to me." Jessica meant every word.

Moisture formed in George's eyes and he blinked rapidly, then sliced a forkful and brought it to his mouth.

She must have touched a chord. As of late, George's demeanor had softened and she might as well keep the conversation going while he was open with his feelings. "Holly said she'd made an appointment for us to see an apartment."

"Is that so?" George took another bite.

"We have a couple of hours to kill, how about a walk along West Cliff Drive? The path is paved and would be a great place to practice with your prosthetic." She kept her eyes averted, but stole a glance when he didn't respond.

George's forehead crinkled and his mouth puckered. "Don't know if I'm ready for that. I'd rather ride in my wheelchair if it doesn't inconvenience you too much."

"It's all right. I don't mind." Jessica made squiggly lines with her fork in the extra syrup on her plate.

"That reminds me, I'll need my wheelchair. We'll have to go by Nick's place and pick it up." He raised his eyes and met her gaze. What was that look? Was he trying to play matchmaker or challenging her to meet *her* obstacles head on?

"Already picked up your wheelchair." Jessica shrugged a shoulder. "Jacob left his teddy bear at the cabin and I went back for it in the middle of the night."

"I heard Jacob crying. Thought he might be having a nightmare."

"Yes, that was Jacob. I could've waited. Should have, really. Holly got him settled in Ryan's room with one of his stuffed toys."

"That's it? You don't have any other reason to communicate with Nick?" George dropped his fork and raised a hand. Her uncle was far from subtle. Obviously he'd like her and Nick to have a relationship.

"That's right." She tried to sound nonchalant, but she could hear the sadness in her tone.

"I see." George wiped his mouth on his napkin, his voice resolute. "Well, did you at least find the boy's bear?"

Jessica shook her head. "Andrew took it."

Her uncle's face clouded. "What? You mean to tell me Andrew went inside the cabin? Of all the nerve."

As touched as she was that Uncle George sounded ready to pummel Jacob's birthfather, she'd rather not pursue this line of conversation any further. If Jacob overheard, she'd have some explaining to do and at this point he hadn't asked her about his bear. She pushed her plate away. "Are you up for that walk, because I need to clear my head."

George grabbed his crutches. "Lead the way."

Evelyn had opted for a quick breakfast—half a grapefruit and a slice of toast, before making her plans for the day, now that her daughter, son-in-law, and grandbaby were on their way back to Daly City.

Now as water slid down her back in the shower, she decided to go shopping before continuing her search for George.

Her condo in San Francisco was filled with antique furniture. She enjoyed the hunt for the perfect piece to complement any given space and scoured many antique stores for the right find. But every nook and cranny of her home was complete and she didn't have the room in her car to bring back any furnishings. She turned off the shower and wrapped herself in a towel, her mind taking a turn. A new piece of jewelry to remember her vacation in Santa Cruz, the first as a widow ready to move on with her life, would be the perfect keepsake.

Excitement bubbled inside as she pictured antique earrings or possibly a necklace dangling around her neck. She didn't need to break the bank with this purchase, only find something to help her take the next step as an independent woman making her own choices. She hurried to her bedroom and looked through her clothes hanging in the closet. Khaki cargo pants and a brightly colored V-necked top jumped out at her. George had always complimented her when she wore something blue. He said it matched her eyes.

After dressing, she applied dark raspberry lipstick on her lips and ran a brush through her bobbed hair. Once she stepped into a pair of sandals, she moved to the front room and thumbed through a phone book to find nearby antique shops. The description of *Santa Cruz Jewelers* on Pacific Avenue caught her eye: "Specializing in Antique & Estate Jewelry, Unique Picture Frames & Home and Garden Decor. Expert jewelry and watch repair. Open daily 10-6."

Perfect.

Fifteen minutes later, Evelyn stood at the jewelry counter eyeing the rings and earrings, lockets, brooches, and stunning diamonds as they glistened under the lights hanging overhead.

"May I help you?" A middle-aged woman approached. "See something you'd like to try on?"

Evelyn wasn't prepared. "You have many beautiful pieces."

"Thank you. Is there something in particular you're looking for?"

"No. I'm here on vacation and would like a keepsake to remember my trip. I used to live here long ago and haven't been back in quite some time. Santa Cruz holds special memories for me—some painful, too. In fact, that diamond ring reminds me of the one George bought me." She leaned down and pointed to the heart-shaped diamond ring, realizing how foolish she sounded. A slight pang gripped her chest. Would George have sold her ring? The resemblance was uncanny. Of course if he did sell it, he'd probably done so years ago.

"Would you like to try it on?" asked the clerk.

Evelyn worked her lower lip. Should she? Why not? It wasn't like she was going to purchase it, as tempting as that might be. "All right."

The woman unlocked the cabinet, reached inside the glass case, and pulled out the box holding the ring. She looked at the description and handed it to Evelyn. "This is a ½ carat heart-shaped diamond solitaire ring in 14k white gold."

Evelyn slipped it on her left ring finger, her pulse quickening at the perfect fit. George had known her size all those years ago. Could this be her ring? Impossible! The band looked and felt right on her hand, but before she had a chance to fall in love with it all over again she pulled it off and set it on the counter. She'd never buy a diamond ring for herself. It wouldn't be right. An engagement ring should be given to a woman out of love. Besides, the price tag was more than what she was willing to spend. "It's beautiful, simply elegant. But not quite what I've come in for today."

"All right." The clerk repositioned the ring back inside the case. "We do have other heart-shaped pieces. May I interest you in a pair of earrings . . . or a necklace, perhaps?"

Evelyn's budget wouldn't accommodate diamond earrings. She stepped to the right a couple of paces and studied the necklaces. Her breath caught in her throat when she saw a heart-shaped filigree pendant necklace in sterling silver. It was feminine and romantic. And would remind her of George and the time they'd spent together all those years ago.

Would she disregard Edward's memory by purchasing the piece? Her insides were having a tug of war as she battled the question in her mind. A favorite Bible verse popped into her head. "For I know the plans I have for you," declares the Lord, "plans to prosper you and not to harm you, plans to give you hope and a future."

Evelyn tapped the glass with her index finger. "May I please see the heart-shaped necklace?"

"A wonderful choice." The clerk looked at the small white tag attached to the chain. "It has a .01 carat single cut diamond amidst a radiant glade of filigree scrollwork. I'm sure it will make you feel special every time you wear it." She laid the necklace in Evelyn's hand. "There's a mirror at the end of the counter. I'd be happy to help you put it on."

Evelyn looked closely at the beautiful design and nodded. "I'd like that, thank you."

The woman came around the counter and fastened the chain around Evelyn's neck while she looked in the mirror. The heart pendant rested on the perfect spot against her skin, and the chain was the ideal length.

Evelyn let out a breath. "It's lovely."

The clerk smiled over Evelyn's shoulder. "And there's a 10% discount today on all jewelry."

Evelyn's throat tightened and she hesitated. Why wasn't she able to confirm the purchase? Her confidence waned. Was she ready to move on with her life no matter what the outcome— even if she never found George? She let out an audible sigh. She was being silly. All she was doing was purchasing a necklace. It wasn't the biggest decision of her life.

And yet, that's exactly what it felt like. By purchasing a necklace that reminded her of George and everything they held dear, she was truly moving on.

I need to do this, Edward. You were a good husband, and provider . . . and I miss you, but I must follow my heart. She laid a hand on her chest and touched the pendant between thumb and index finger, the delicate scrollwork matching the tentative nature of her heart. One last thought bolstered her resolve. *Amy gave me her blessing to search for George.*

"I'll take it." Evelyn smiled at the clerk.

"Would you like me to box it, or would you rather wear it out?"

"I don't know when I'll ever take it off." Warmth rushed up her neck and settled on her cheeks.

The clerk laughed. "I only need the price tag and payment, then you'll be good to go."

As the woman removed the tag, Evelyn took her wallet out of her purse. She couldn't wait to show her friend Patty her new purchase.

But first, she'd take a walk along the path on West Cliff Drive. Now that she'd taken a bold step to move on with her life, she needed to commit the next phase to God. She had a feeling He was preparing her for something big.

31

Driving down Highway 17, Nick wracked his brain trying to think of all the places he'd been in Santa Cruz with A.J. Who's to say his childhood friend wouldn't go somewhere they'd never been, but Nick had a hunch he'd stick to familiar territory. A.J. wouldn't run the risk of being caught before he had a chance to see his son.

Nick glanced at his watch and noted the time. Almost noon. Would A.J. stop at a restaurant for a bite to eat or at a convenience store for a six-pack of beer? He'd always been an avid hiker and loved to camp. Nick wouldn't put it past him to hide out at a state park until he'd made arrangements with Jessica. Henry Cowell Redwoods State Park was the closest one to his house. He veered right, taking the Mount Hermon exit toward Graham Hill Road.

He stepped on the brake when the light turned red. An older man stumbled across the road pushing a grocery cart filled with what looked like all his worldly possessions. Nick's gut twisted. Sadly, he could picture A.J.'s life turning out the same way unless he got help, serious help. And Nick wanted to be the person to get him on the right path, but he needed God and a host of people to help A.J. see the error of his ways.

The light changed to green and Nick maneuvered his Jeep Cherokee toward CA-9, heading south. He drove slightly over a half a mile before turning left on N. Big Trees Park Road. Once he spotted the sign for Henry Cowell Redwoods State Park, he pulled his car into the parking lot and turned off the engine.

Before he'd left his house, he'd thought to bring a photo. A.J. looked a lot different now with his full beard and sallow color skin from the hard life he'd been living, but hopefully someone might recognize his deep-set eyes or the curve of his jaw. Nick glanced at himself in the picture and had to laugh. He looked different, too. His hair had grown since the days he wore a buzz cut, and his shoulders had filled out from the heavy physical work as a fireman. People on the trail might not recognize him either, but he tucked the photo in his pocket anyway and grabbed a baseball cap to keep the sun out of his eyes.

The first people he came across on the fifteen miles of hiking and riding trails were two women, both fit and in their late twenties or early thirties. They smiled at him as he approached and were more than willing to share all they knew.

"I'd remember this guy if he walked past." The petite blonde's eyes widened and she nudged the brunette beside her. "Wouldn't you?"

"You bet." The woman grinned. "What did you say his name was?"

"I didn't," Nick answered, keeping his tone light.

"Everyone has a cell phone. Why not call him?" said the shorter of the two. "In fact, if you give me his number I'll call him myself."

Oh boy! Nick hadn't taken into account he'd run into the flirty kind. "Tried that already. He's not answering his phone. I've left several messages."

"Why are you looking for him?" The brunette folded her arms across her chest. "He's not in trouble, or missing, is he? It would be a shame, what with his boyish good looks." Her eyes met his. "Say, you're not bad yourself. Got a girlfriend?"

"Not in the market for one."

Jessica's image flashed in his mind. He couldn't quite say what she was to him, but he had a good idea what he'd like her to be. Nonetheless, these two women were definitely not his type.

"Thanks, anyway." Nick slipped the picture back in his pocket, maneuvered around the pair and kept walking. His plan wasn't to draw attention to himself or have someone recognize A.J.'s face from the recent newscast, only to bring the man to justice before he did more damage to himself and others.

As he continued down the trail between rows of redwoods, mixed evergreens, riparian, and ponderosa pine, he was convicted of the true reason for his search. *Jessica.* He wouldn't be able to forgive himself for running her, Jacob, and George off his property. From what Jessica told Nick, George's heart grew bitter when he'd become ill and lost his leg, but at dinner last night the man appeared relaxed and grateful for the roof over his head. Nick kicked at a small rock. Who was he fooling? His hunt for A.J. had more to do with getting the stuffed toy back so he could call Jessica and be the hero in her eyes once again.

A man with a Yellow Labrador came down the trail. His eyes were downcast as he walked and he appeared deep in thought.

"Excuse me," said Nick. The man was clearly in another zone. Nick noticed the white chords hanging from the hiker's ears and tucked into the collar of his jacket. Nick waved an arm and the guy stopped and removed one of his earbuds. The Yellow Labrador sat beside its owner, panting.

"What's up?" The man swung his backpack to the ground and poured water into a small bowl. The dog lapped it up.

"Looking for my friend—about 6'2, my age, brown hair, a beard. Have you seen him?"

The man shook his head. "No, but I haven't been paying attention." He rubbed the dog's head, then put the empty bowl back into his pack.

Nick chose not to pepper him with more questions. "Say, I like your dog. Should've brought mine. Rosco would've enjoyed these trails."

The man stroked the dog's fur. "I don't go anywhere without Bailey. She's been my best friend for ten years."

"Mind if I pet her?"

"Go right ahead. She loves everyone."

Nick leaned down and scratched behind the dog's ears. Bailey's pink tongue darted out of her mouth and she licked Nick's face. He chuckled and wiped his chin on the sleeve of his sweatshirt. "I'll let you get back to your music."

The man nodded. "Good luck finding your friend." He put the earbud back into his ear and strode down the trail, his dog by his side.

Where else would A.J. go? Nick hadn't thought to look in the parking lot for his blue truck, but he doubted A.J. would leave it out in the open. Then why would he let people see him in the park? Nick had a feeling he was wasting his time.

He thought back to when he got his job at the firehouse and A.J. was in town to help him celebrate. They were having dinner at a pub-style restaurant on Walnut Avenue in the heart of downtown Santa Cruz when a friend of A.J.'s stopped by, encouraging them to try several different beers. Seemed to know what he was talking about. After he'd left, A.J. mentioned he'd known the guy since junior high and that he was surprised he was still alive the way he'd used drugs over the years.

Come to think of it, the last time A.J. was in town he'd mentioned wanting to visit an old school friend from junior high days. They must've kept in touch. Nick picked up a twig from the ground and snapped it in half. He was positive A.J. would search him out. What was the shady man's name? It was unusual . . . something to do with nature, if Nick remembered correctly.

A couple he guessed to be in their early sixties rounded the corner of the trail. They wore hiking gear, complete with hydrating packs and walking sticks. "I'm positive you can fish in the San Lorenzo River," the woman said, her southern drawl thick.

"The Department of Fish and Game won't allow people to fish during the spring. And believe me, the rules are enforced," the man said, his accent as prominent.

"Then we'll have to come back." The woman smiled.

Nick enjoyed listening to the two bantering back and forth, but he couldn't let more time pass before he searched for A.J. somewhere else. If this couple hadn't seen A.J., then Nick doubted he'd find him here. "Hi, there."

The woman set her walking sticks against a tree. "Thirsty? I always pack extra water. Would you like some?"

"No, thank you." Nick held up a hand. "Looking for a friend. He's slightly taller than I am, has a beard and brown hair."

The man shook his head and pressed his lips together. "Seen plenty of people on the trail, but no one with a beard."

"How far down the trail have you hiked?" asked Nick.

"Four miles, give or take."

The sandy-haired woman glanced at a device hooked to her belt. "Good guess, dear. According to my pedometer, we've gone exactly four point two miles."

Time to turn around or Nick would be burning daylight. "Thanks. You two have a nice day." He waved and turned the way he came.

"You sure you don't want a drink?" the woman's southern voice called after him.

"Thanks. I'm good," Nick called, leaving the couple on the trail. *Forest, Rain, Stone.* Words from nature rattled through his head, trying to conjure up the name of A.J.'s friend.

He had to admit he was a little thirsty, but he'd rather get back to his jeep as soon as he could—

River. That was it!

Nick quickened his pace. He would head straight to Pacific Avenue, the main thoroughfare in downtown Santa Cruz, near the restaurant where they'd seen him last. Maybe someone would know River's last name. And where he lived.

The fog lifted and the sun shone across the water overlooking Steamer Lane. Jessica pushed George closer to the guardrail so he could watch the surfers below. Before they'd left, Holly had offered to keep an eye on Jacob, which suited Jessica just fine. He would've been bored looking at the apartment. She didn't tell him they were stopping by the beach first or he might have protested.

George let out an exaggerated breath. "I've always loved this spot."

The other day her uncle barely said two words when they were here. Jessica liked the improvement. "Any particular reason?"

"It's where I asked Evelyn to marry me." George grinned, then shrugged a shoulder.

Jessica nudged his arm in a playful gesture. "Uncle George! You never told me that story."

"She told me she'd think about it. If I'd known she'd go and marry someone else while I was in the Philippines, I never would have left."

"If you ask me, Evelyn didn't deserve you."

"Thanks, Jessi, that's kind of you to say, but I don't know. Eva grew up with money and I was a poor missionary."

"That's no excuse." Jessica crossed her arms. "If she loved you, she would've given it all up to be with you. Besides, what kind of woman would put money first? Sounds like she was two-timing and playing with your heart."

"I have a hard time believing that, but anything is possible. She did send me a letter to let me know she was getting married. Her father must have been happy. The guy was a rich lawyer."

"I still say Evelyn had ulterior motives."

George looked down at his folded hands. "I'll never understand what happened, but I have to believe God worked it all out for the good."

"I think that's true about Evelyn, but can you say that about your leg?" Jessica challenged.

"I'm working on it. I don't feel whole, but I know my worth isn't based on having two feet."

Jessica appreciated George's honest answer. He'd made huge strides in accepting his amputated limb since she'd been in Santa Cruz. She enjoyed witnessing his change of heart.

The surf pounded against the rocks, and the spray flew up creating a waterfall effect. What a view! She inhaled the misty air, her mind taking a turn. "Do you regret giving me the ring?"

"Goodness, no. I held onto it far too long, but didn't have the heart to put it up for sale. I'd rather see you wearing the ring and keeping it in the family."

"Maybe Jacob will want to give it to a special woman someday." Jessica grinned.

George nodded in agreement. "Say, don't you think it's about time to switch it to your other hand? You don't want to keep the right man away."

Now that the subject had shifted to *her* love life, it was a good time for a walk. She stepped back from the guardrail and grabbed the handles of George's wheelchair. "Feel like a stroll? It's such a beautiful day."

"You can't fool me, Jessi," George called over his shoulder. "I see the way you and Nick look at each other."

At least her uncle hadn't witnessed the kiss.

"Reminds me of Evelyn and myself years ago."

"Well in that case, I'm going to forget Nick ever existed." Jessica tossed her words into the wind. She hoped her response didn't hurt George in any way, but if he was reluctant to find Evelyn again—even to discuss what really happened between them, than what was the use of pining for old memories? *Even those made less than twenty-four hours ago.*

"If you're able to forget about Nick, let me know your secret," said George.

Jessica didn't know if it was possible, but she didn't want to be stuck in the past years later like her uncle. She stopped pushing and maneuvered around George's wheelchair. "Let's make a pact." She made a fist and stuck out her pinky finger. "I'll never mention Nick's name again, and you'll not talk about Evelyn. They've hurt us and we don't need them in our lives." The gesture was something she would've done in high school, but Jessica didn't care. She had to move on with her life and George needed to do the same.

"That's foolishness." Her uncle pushed her hand away. "I have no intention of ever seeing—"

"George?" The timbre of the woman's voice behind them sounded kind, but the paleness of her uncle's face told her otherwise. It was as if he'd seen a ghost.

32

Evelyn couldn't believe her eyes. Time had grayed George's hair and etched lines around his eyes, but he was the same handsome man she fell in love with all those years ago— except now he sat in a wheelchair, a blanket covering his lap. It saddened her to find out the rumors he'd been ill were true.

"Jessica, take me back to the car." George grabbed the wheels of his chair and turned himself in the opposite direction, putting his back to her.

Evelyn had expected such a reaction. She'd have done the same thing if the roles were reversed. Why had she dreamed of a different response?

"I'm sorry, and you are?" asked the young woman with George.

"A friend. At least I'd like us to be friends again. It's been a long time."

"I'm George's niece Jessica MacAllister—"

George cleared his throat. "Jessi."

His niece leaned over. "What is it, Uncle George?"

He spoke in a low voice. "Please, get me out of here."

Jessica stood to her full height and shrugged a shoulder as if to apologize for her uncle's behavior. She gripped the handles and pushed the wheelchair down the path.

"Please." Evelyn caught up to them and touched Jessica's arm, stopping her movement. "If you could give George and me a few minutes alone?"

Jessica leaned over once again. "Uncle George, this woman wants to talk with you."

George raised his fist and stuck out his small finger. Evelyn didn't understand the gesture, but the soft features around Jessica's mouth suddenly hardened into a grim line.

"It's her, isn't it Uncle George?" Jessica's words sounded clipped. Her head turned in Evelyn's direction and her eyes narrowed. "How did you know where to find him?"

"I didn't." Evelyn took a step back, surprised at the protective reaction from George's niece. "I'm renting a beach house a couple of blocks from here." She pointed down the path, then laid a hand against her chest feeling the new pendant beneath her fingertips. How could she explain how much she'd longed to see George again and apologize for hurting him the way she had?

"How convenient." Jessica shifted her stance. "Well, my uncle isn't ready to speak with you."

"I understand." Evelyn's voice wobbled. "I'm grateful to know he's alive."

Jessica's shoulders sagged. "You knew he was sick?" Her voice softened.

"Only for the few days I've been looking for him."

"You two are talking like I'm not here," George called over his shoulder, his tone gruff.

"I'm sorry, Uncle George." Jessica laid a hand on his shoulder. "But maybe you should talk with Evelyn—"

"I asked you to get me out of here!" George lowered his head in his hands.

"Okay, we'll go." Jessica mouthed an apology behind George's back and pushed his wheelchair down the path.

"Wait," called Evelyn, snatching Jessica's attention once again. "If he changes his mind, please come see me." She rattled off the address of the beach rental. "I'll be there for another week." She infused as much hope as she could muster into her voice and raised her hand in farewell.

As the distance grew between them, Evelyn's heart sank. By George's reaction, she doubted she'd ever see him again. Lovely as the beach house was, she'd end up spending the rest of her vacation pacing inside the four walls anticipating George's arrival—a long shot at best.

Maybe it was time for her to go home.

Nick's feet hurt from all the walking he'd done up and down Pacific Avenue. He'd stopped and inquired at a number of shops and restaurants but no one had heard of a man named River. Nick leaned up against the building housing the Del Mar Theatre. A line had formed. At this point, he'd rather join the throng of people escaping their regular lives to be entertained for the next two hours, but he didn't have that luxury. Time was of the essence. He needed to find Andrew before the authorities.

He watched people of all shapes and sizes pay for their ticket and walk into the theatre. Maybe he was asking the wrong crowd. Plenty of musicians dotted the sidewalks to earn a dollar or two, as well as others walking around who appeared to be stuck in the hippie era. They might offer information if

Nick played his cards right, but he'd need to give them something in return.

He reached inside his pocket and produced his wallet. A twenty-dollar bill sat wedged between a pair of receipts. He pulled the bill out and stuck it in his pocket. Not much, but he'd pay almost anything to find A.J.

An odd-looking character wearing an army-green trench coat and tattered jeans, walked past. On any given day, Nick wouldn't have chosen to approach this type of fellow, but under the circumstances he might be the exact person with the information Nick needed.

He pushed himself away from the wall of the theatre and hurried to keep up. One thing was certain, the man was in good physical shape and appeared to be on a mission. Nick darted in and out of the people walking along the busy sidewalk.

One block turned into two, then three before the man suddenly disappeared. Where'd he go? Nick kept walking.

"Psst."

Nick glanced over his shoulder at the hissing sound.

The man he'd been pursuing stood inside the overhang of an abandoned store, the windows blocked out with black paper. The shop, like many in the current economy, was out of business. "Why are you following me?" His voice held a hard edge.

"I'm looking for someone. Thought you might know him." Nick worked hard at keeping his tone even.

"Why? I don't know *you*." He pushed back his shoulders.

Nick chose to ignore the man's defensive words and stance, and plodded forward. "Have you heard of River? I know he frequents these streets."

The man's mouth twitched. Either he was ignorant, or the mere mention of River's name made him nervous.

Better to set his mind at ease. "I'm looking for a friend of mine."

He gave Nick the once over. "Then why you asking about River?"

Nick tipped his chin in the air. "You do know him."

"What if I do? Doesn't make me a drug addict. You can't pin anything on me." His words shot out in a rush.

Nick raised his hands. "Relax, I'm not a cop. Only looking for a friend."

"By the looks of you, I don't think any friend of yours would hang out with a man like River Keaton." He pulled up his lip, as if the sight of Nick repulsed him.

Keaton. Nick filed River's last name in his mind. "Afraid so. Drugs can affect anyone. Are you going to give me River's whereabouts or should I move on?"

The man folded his arms tight across his chest. "Don't tell him who sent you—"

"I wouldn't dream of it." Nick leaned forward in anticipation of River's location.

"421 Riverside Avenue."

Riverside. River. The two must have a connection. "River is not his first name, is it?"

"I've said too much already. Now get out of here." The hippie clenched his fists and puffed out his chest.

Nick could take a hint. He didn't want to rile the man after he'd given him the address. He stuck his hand in his pocket and pulled out the twenty. "For your time."

"I don't want your money or anything that ties me to you." He pushed open the door of the shop and slunk inside. The dark windows concealed him.

Why wouldn't he take the cash? By his appearance, he could use it. But Nick understood loyalties ran deep. As much as he didn't agree with A.J.'s way of life, Nick genuinely cared.

And unless he was way off base, he had a hunch he'd find his friend hiding out at 421 Riverside Avenue.

He couldn't get there fast enough.

By the new composite roof, fresh coat of paint, and the white picket fence surrounding the home, no one would suspect a drug dealer lived inside. Nick eyed the house from his vantage point across the street. A.J.'s blue truck was nowhere in sight. He hadn't quite thought out how he'd approach the house. By instinct, he wanted to burst through the door and demand A.J. come with him, but he knew better than to make a scene.

The only clue that illegal activity might be going on behind closed doors was the fact that every window was covered with what appeared to be thick, heavy drapery.

Nick could stand there all afternoon staring at the house, or he could make his move and approach the door. His pulse raced. He had faced raging fires in his line of work, but nothing in his job made his heart beat as fast as now.

A childhood recollection crossed his mind.

A.J. had dared Nick to hold his breath under water. "Bet you can't hold it longer than I can," A.J. challenged.

"You're on!" Nick counted to three before they both dove into the deep end of the pool. He wasn't going to let A.J. beat him. After a while, Nick's head felt like it would explode from the pressure and he couldn't take it any longer. He pushed off the bottom and surfaced, gasping for air. He swam over to the side and hoisted himself out of the pool, expecting A.J. to be right behind, announcing he had won.

Nick shuddered at the memory of A.J.'s father diving into the pool and pulling out his friend's limp body. Nick panicked and sat frozen to the beach chair, but something snapped when he heard a deep voice shouting for him to call 9-1-1. Nick bolted inside the Lawsons' home and did as he was asked. Later as he sat beside Andrew's hospital bed, A.J.'s dad praised him for his quick response in seeking help, but Nick knew the truth. If it weren't for A.J.'s father, Andrew wouldn't be alive.

And through the years, Nick wouldn't have found the need to prove himself over and over again.

He stood on the threshold of River's small ranch-style house, shook off the memory, and pressed the doorbell.

33

After Nick rang the bell, he stepped back, and waited for River to come to the door. He glanced over his shoulder, feeling as though someone was watching him. Maybe River had a hidden camera. He rubbed his hands down the sides of his jeans.

The door creaked open. A young woman in her late teens or early twenties stood inside the threshold. Her oversized T-shirt came down to her mid-thighs, her shapely legs exposed. Was this River's daughter, perhaps? A.J.'s girlfriend had been under-age. A sickening feeling grabbed at his gut. Was this woman leading the same kind of life? She stared at Nick with lifeless eyes.

He'd have to be careful how he spoke to her. He didn't want to scare her or have the door shut in his face. "Is River here?"

She shook her head. "Just missed him. Come back later." She stepped back to close the door.

"Wait!" Panic laced Nick's voice and he inwardly chided himself. He'd have to remain calm if he didn't want to raise suspicions. He didn't want this woman to think he was a cop—or remember him at all. "Is Andrew here?"

"Andrew?"

"River's friend. Also known as A.J." Nick tucked his lip between his teeth and worried it for a few seconds.

The young woman smiled. "Yeah, he was here. Crashed on the front couch for hours. But he's gone now. Didn't want to stick around. Too bad. He was hot."

In a way, Nick was glad A.J. had left. Drugs and loose women were two vices he couldn't resist. *Was Jessica into drugs years ago?* Nick had a hard time picturing her that way. Besides, A.J. could charm the women even when he was clean and sober. "Do you know how long ago he left?"

She shrugged a shoulder. "Five, ten minutes, maybe."

Had he seen Nick out the window sitting in his Jeep? He'd been out there at least that long. Maybe A.J. had snuck out the back door. "Thanks." He lifted a hand and turned to leave.

"If he comes back, who should I say asked for him?" The young woman called from the doorway.

Nick wasn't about to give her any information. He acted like he didn't hear her question and rushed to his car. If A.J. hid his blue truck around the corner, maybe Nick could catch up to him. If only Nick knew which way he went.

After seeing what her words and actions had done, Jessica had to figure out a way to help her uncle see Evelyn again. From all he'd told her about their relationship, it was apparent they needed to talk. Jessica handed George his crutches. "I was being childish. What right did I have to ask you to forget Evelyn?"

"Can we discuss this later?" George hoisted himself out of her car and tucked the crutches underneath his arms. "Interesting apartment." He changed the subject and glanced up at the four-story structure. "I hope they have an elevator."

Jessica shut the car door and stepped beside George. "Maybe it's on the first floor." She'd broach the subject of Evelyn after they looked at the apartment.

"That would be even better. Did you ask Holly about the rent?"

"I didn't, but I'm sure Holly would recommend something affordable." She glanced at her watch. "We're right on time."

As they moved toward the main office, Jessica noticed the building needed a fresh coat of paint and the grounds could use some attention. She hoped the outside wasn't an indicator of what they'd find inside. She opened the door and allowed her uncle to pass through.

Stale air hit them the minute they walked in and approached the front desk. No one was there. A bell with a note that read, "Ring for assistance," sat on the counter.

George pressed the bell.

They heard giggles from the back room, and a minute later a young woman appeared, her heels clicking against the hardwood floor. She finger combed her jet-black hair and ran a hand down the skirt of her tight dress that showed off her curves. Her lips were pale, but her eyelids were colored a smoky blue. "Sorry to keep you waiting. My sister is getting married Saturday and she wanted me to try on my bridesmaid's dress one last time." She beamed and rested a hand on her hip. "It fits like a glove—"

"See you, Babe." A male voice called from the back room.

"See you tonight," she called over her shoulder.

"And that would be your sister?" asked George.

"No, silly." She shrugged a shoulder. "That's my brother."

It was none of George's business, or Jessica's, but the woman's story was sounding stranger by the moment. "He calls you Babe?" Jessica set her purse on the counter.

"That *is* my name. It's short for Babette, after my aunt."

"Right." George grinned and lifted an eyebrow. "I'm here to see an apartment."

She peered over the counter. "Say, are you George MacAllister? Our two o'clock appointment?" She must have noticed his missing limb.

"Yes, how'd you know?" George teased.

"Your sweet demeanor gave you away." Babette winked. She grabbed a key from a drawer and motioned for them to follow her down the hall, her hips swinging as she walked.

George hobbled after her and Jessica followed behind.

Babette looked at George over her shoulder and smiled. "A woman named Holly called earlier and asked for me to show you a first-floor room," she said as she led them down the corridor.

"I hope it's wheelchair accessible. Not that I use a chair all the time," said George.

That's what Jessica liked to hear. Maybe moving into this apartment would help her uncle get back to a more normal life.

"Here we are. Room 132." She put the key into the lock and opened the door. "It's a studio apartment. Go on in and check it out."

George walked in first. Besides the wider doorways for his wheelchair, the bathroom had plenty of space, the shower was easy to get into without a tub, and support bars were located in all the right places.

But the apartment was filthy.

Jessica noted a dead cockroach in the corner of the room and the musty smell threatened to gag her. "Will you be sending someone to clean before you rent it?" She wouldn't allow her uncle to move in as it was.

Babette settled her hand on her hip. "Yes, of course."

"I'll take it," said George. "How much for the rent?"

Babette cocked her head. "Didn't Holly tell you?"

"Tell me what?" asked George.

"She enrolled you in an assistance program for disabled adults. I'll have my manager go over all the details with you if you're interested in renting this room. Follow me and we'll get the paperwork started."

Leave it to Holly to figure out a way to help George. Jessica's cell phone vibrated in her pocket. She pulled it out and checked the screen. Melissa. So much had happened since the last time she'd spoken with her roommate. "Uncle George, why don't you go ahead to the office while I answer this call. I'll meet you there in a few minutes."

George nodded and followed the hotel receptionist out the room and down the corridor.

Jessica answered her phone. "Melissa! How are you?"

"Fine, now that it's been a couple of days without *you know who* coming to our door. Has he given up the search for Jacob?"

"Hardly." Jessica let out a breath. "Oh, Melissa, life is complicated."

"Details, please! Don't leave me guessing."

"I can't go into it at the moment, my uncle is waiting. But I think we found him an apartment. They need to clean it first. Right now it smells like old sneakers."

"Gross."

"That's what I say, but he seems to think it'll be okay."

"Maybe he's trying not to burden you any longer. Ever think of that?"

Jessica hadn't even considered that option. George wouldn't take the apartment so she and Jacob would go back home, would he? The idea of leaving town appealed to her knowing Andrew still roamed the streets of Santa Cruz. But even if her uncle did take the apartment there was still one more thing she wanted to do before going home to Fresno. "You'll never guess who else is in town?"

"Someone besides Jacob's birthfather?"

"Yes, Uncle George's first and only love. We ran into her today along West Cliff Drive. She's on vacation and renting a beach house."

"What did your uncle do when he saw her?"

"He turned his wheelchair around and wouldn't look at her. Sad, really. I know how much he loved her once, but she hurt him pretty bad. Ran off with a wealthy lawyer instead of marrying my uncle. I wonder if she's still married. Wish I could get the two of them back together."

Melissa sighed into the phone. "Sounds like you've softened your heart toward romance. Hey, wait a minute! Since when have you considered helping two people fall back in love? Have you met someone?"

Jessica leaned against the wall and looked out the window. Her uncle wouldn't have much of a view living in this apartment. Only a couple of trees stood next to a dumpster. "What are you talking about? I'm thinking of my uncle."

"Uh-huh. Before you left when I told you my co-worker was coming for Easter dinner, you rolled your eyes."

"And, your point?" Jessica rested her head against the window, thoughts of Nick filling her mind.

"Promise me you'll let me know when there's someone special in your life. I hear Santa Cruz is a beautiful place to live." Melissa's voice softened.

"Wouldn't you miss me?" Jessica matched her roommate's reflective tone.

"I know how much your uncle means to you. Family is important. I have my sister. And my parents are only a short drive away."

"Now you sound like you're trying to get rid of me."

"My life has changed in the past week, too." Melissa hesitated. "I think I've found the man I want to marry." Her roommate had dated a lot of men over the years they'd been roommates, but she'd never made such a bold statement. "Bryce and I have been friends for a long time and never considered dating until we spent time together on Easter."

"Really? Your coworker? Isn't there an unspoken rule about dating someone in the office?" Jessica pressed her lips together stopping herself from saying more.

"Yeah." Melissa giggled. "I better find another job fast. In fact, I'm thinking of doing exactly that." Her voice sobered. "I might need to move in with my sister until I find other work."

"You're not serious, are you?"

"Bryce and I are giving it time, but that's definitely the direction we're headed."

"Wow, I'm gone for a week and everything changes." Jessica sneezed. She had to get out of the apartment. Suddenly the air had become unbearable.

"Sorry I made the assumption you met someone. I guess since I found the man of my dreams I was hoping you had, too."

Should Jessica tell her about Nick? She really didn't see the point and doubted he'd ever want to see her again. She'd taken her fear out on him and said some things she regretted. But she could still feel his sweet kiss and strong hand in hers. And he was wonderful with Jacob. *If only.* "Well, actually—"

"You going to stand around all day talking with your roommate?" George's voice called from the doorway.

Jessica turned and faced her uncle. She noted George's teasing grin, and lifted her index finger to let him know she'd be another minute. "I'm happy for you, Melissa." A twinge of jealousy bubbled up, but she squelched it. "Say, I've got to run. We'll talk more later."

"Thanks, Jessica. Don't forget to call me back. I'm still your roommate, you know." Melissa's words calmed her anxious heart.

Jessica smiled. "You're the best."

"I know." Melissa laughed. "Bye now."

Jessica ended the call and tucked her phone in her pocket. "So, Uncle George, when are they going to let you move in?"

"There's one little problem." He scowled. "The apartment won't be ready until the first part of next week. Where am I going to live until then?"

34

Evelyn tossed clothes into her suitcase.

Patty leaned a hip against the doorjamb, her arms tightly folded across her chest. "You can't leave now that you've found George." Her friend's frustrated tone indicated she didn't agree with Evelyn's decision. "Give it time. You've rented the beach house for another week."

"I'll go crazy waiting for him to show up. He's made it quite clear he doesn't want to talk. You should've seen the way he turned his back on me." Evelyn picked up her shoes from the closet floor and jammed them into her suitcase. "I really made a mess of things years ago. And I've waited too long to make things right."

"My guess is that he still cares for you—"

"Where'd you get that idea?" A puff of air escaped Evelyn's mouth. "He couldn't wait for his niece to push him down the path."

"What do you mean 'push'?" Patty moved closer and sat on the edge of the bed.

"Didn't I tell you he was sitting in a wheelchair with a blanket covering his legs? His skin was slightly pale, but other than that he looked like he was on the mend." Evelyn moved to the closet and collected her robe off the hanger, bringing it to her chest. "He wouldn't even look at me. Must've been disappointed."

"Oh, please. You're beautiful. If anyone still has it, it's you, sister. Why, Horace was going on and on about how cute and fit you are. And my Ronald was nodding his head, agreeing with him."

"That's nice of you to say, but . . ." Evelyn stuffed her robe into her suitcase. "I'm not going to try and figure things out. I'm going home."

"Maybe George was embarrassed and didn't want you to see him sitting in a wheelchair. My Ronald, on the other hand, loves attention when he's sick, but if I remember correctly, George didn't like to be babied. Have you forgotten the time he burned his leg on the exhaust pipe of his motorcycle? He played it down, but you know it had to hurt."

Patty's words rang true, but they were adults for goodness sakes', and George had been through a life-altering illness. "Still, maybe he needs time. Now that I know he's alive and in Santa Cruz, I'll come back in a few months and try again. No use wasting my vacation sulking over what could have been."

"You're giving up just like that?" Patty leaned back on the bed and kicked up her feet. "Like I said, you've already pre-paid through next week and this beach house is simply adorable."

Evelyn closed her suitcase and zipped it shut. "I'll call the owner and ask her to give the remainder of my vacation days to you and Ronald. It's your anniversary soon, isn't it? It'll be my gift to you."

Patty sat up a little and leaned on her elbows. "Some present. We'll never be able to return the favor, but if you're positive you must leave, then Ron and I will gladly take it off your hands."

"Good." Evelyn set the suitcase on the floor and pulled it toward the front door.

Patty chased after her. "You forgot to show me what you bought today. You sounded excited on the phone."

Evelyn stopped in her tracks halfway down the hall at the mention of the heart-shaped necklace she'd removed from her neck after her run-in with George. She continued pulling her luggage to the front room. "It doesn't matter anymore."

"You're not making any sense." Patty shook her head. "What did you purchase?"

Evelyn gestured for Patty to follow her back down the hall to the bathroom. "I need to collect my toiletries."

"Are you going to show me or make me guess?" Patty followed close on Evelyn's heels.

Once in the bathroom, Evelyn took the box off the glass shelf and opened it. "A necklace. I purchased a necklace." She repeated and shoved it into Patty's hands.

Patty looked closely at the piece. "It's beautiful—classy and dainty. Why the change of heart? Oh, pardon the pun."

Evelyn's shoulders sagged. "When I was at the jewelry store, I saw a heart-shaped ring like the one George had offered when he proposed. Of course, I'd never buy myself an engagement ring, but I knew at that moment I wanted to buy a piece of jewelry that reminded me of George. That's when I saw the necklace." Her voice hitched. "I really thought God was going to bring us back together again. I feel so foolish."

Patty took the necklace out of the box and clasped it around Evelyn's neck. "In his heart, a man plans his course, but the Lord determines his steps."

Evelyn knew that verse from the book of Psalms. She'd read it many times.

"We don't know what God has planned. Keep your heart open." Patty wrapped her arms around Evelyn's shoulders and pulled her close in a sisterly embrace.

"Thank you." Evelyn released the breath she was holding.

Patty stepped back. "You sure you want to leave?"

Evelyn nodded.

"Okay," said Patty. "But remember, San Francisco is only an hour and a half away. Don't be a stranger, all right?"

"Give me a couple of months." Evelyn gathered her toothbrush, toothpaste, and small makeup case, and placed them into her tote bag.

"I'll call you and we'll do lunch." Patty smiled, attempting to lift her spirits.

"Remember you're always welcome to come visit me, too. My condo isn't big, but I have a guest room for visitors." Evelyn hooked her bag over her shoulder and moseyed to the kitchen. "I'll phone the owners and let them know what's going on. Then I'll be on my way."

Patty hung back while Evelyn made the call.

Since the beach rental was prepaid, it was no problem for her friend and her husband to stay through the week. "Everything's all set."

"I hate to see you leave this way." Patty walked Evelyn to the door.

"Don't worry about me. I'll be fine." She handed Patty the house key, then gathered her luggage. "Enjoy the sunsets out the side window. They're breathtaking." Her voice wobbled as she scooted out the front door.

"Do you need help?" asked Patty.

"No, I'm good." Evelyn opened her trunk and hoisted her suitcases inside.

"All right. Bye now."

The click of the door brought a welcome relief. Evelyn slid behind the wheel and drove away, finally allowing the tears to fall.

⸻

After a fifteen-minute search around Santa Cruz with no sign of a blue truck, Nick headed to the Branson home to speak with his good friend Aaron. Since his buddy told him he'd been laid off from his job and had a new baby on the way, Nick hadn't made the effort to spend time with him.

Nick pulled up to the curb and cut the engine. Normally he called ahead instead of showing up unannounced, but maybe it was better this way. Aaron wouldn't have time to put on a brave front. Nick rang the bell.

Ryan answered, his voice sounding breathless like he'd been running. "Hi, Uncle Nick. Come on in."

He stepped inside and shut the door. "Your dad home?"

"Nope. And my mom's in the shower."

"Didn't your parents ever teach you adults should only answer the door? What if I was a stranger?" Nick didn't mean to discipline the child, only scare him a little.

Ryan shrugged. "But I knew it was you. I saw your car—"

"Hey, Nick!" Jacob bounded into the front room.

"Nice to see you, Jacob." Nick ruffled the boy's hair. "Your mom here?" A knot gripped Nick's stomach, a mixture of hope and fear at the possibility of seeing Jessica again.

"Nope." Jacob shook his head. "She's with Uncle George looking at an apartment. I didn't want to go."

A twinge of guilt surfaced. "I understand." Nick smiled. "You'd rather hang out with your friend Ryan. I came to see my friend, too. Ryan, do you know when your dad will be home?"

"He went on an airplane, but mom said he's coming home tomorrow—"

"Ryan, who are you talking to?" Holly descended the stairs wearing jeans, a T-shirt, and a towel on her head. When she came in eye contact with Nick, a blush colored her cheeks. "Nick, hi. Give me a minute, okay?"

"Sure. No problem," said Nick. "Sorry to show up without calling first."

"Do you want to play with us?" asked Jacob.

The question warmed Nick's heart. His desire to become a husband and father had taken root long before Jessica and Jacob had come to town, but now the feeling was stronger than ever.

Before he could answer, he turned at the sound of small feet padding across the floor.

"Uncle Nick!" Sarah smiled and ran toward him, her ponytails bouncing with each step. "I'm watching Ariel."

Nick scooped her up, her chubby arms wrapping tightly around his neck. He had given Sarah *The Little Mermaid* DVD last Christmas. On several occasions, Holly had told him the movie was one of Sarah's favorites, but he thought she was only being kind. "Do you like that movie?"

"Uh-huh." Sarah grinned. "Ariel has a pretty voice."

Nick set the preschooler down.

"Come with us." Jacob tugged on Nick's shirt. "We're building a fort in Ryan's room."

"But I want Nick to watch the movie with me." Sarah grabbed Nick's hand.

"We asked him first." Ryan made a face at his sister.

Sarah stuck out her tongue.

Holly appeared, her wet hair pulled back in a sleek ponytail. "Okay, kids, behave yourselves and go back to what you were doing. I need to talk with Nick—alone."

Sarah was the first to leave, her shoulders hunched over and her movement slow.

"Come on." Ryan wrapped an arm around Jacob's shoulder. "We'll finish building our fort by ourselves."

Nick covered a laugh. It felt good to be loved.

"What brings you by?" asked Holly.

"Wanted to check in with Aaron. Is he doing okay?"

"Better than okay." Holly gestured for Nick to take a seat on the couch. "He has a job interview today for a company in Houston."

"Texas?" Selfishly, the thought of losing another close friend was more than Nick could take and yet he was glad for the excitement he heard in Holly's voice.

"Wow. Good for him."

"Nick, what happened between you and Jessica?"

The question and sudden change of subject caught him off guard. "What has she told you?" He didn't want to share Jessica's private information without knowing how much she'd already divulged. He'd rather not get in more hot water where Jessica was concerned.

"Not much," said Holly. "Only that the two of you have differences and that something is standing in your way."

Or someone. Nick leaned forward, his elbows resting on his knees. "That about sums it up." He didn't know where to begin, or if he should tell Holly anything more.

An awkward silence filled the room.

Holly bridged the gap. "If you'd rather talk with Aaron, he'll be home this weekend—"

"No. It'll be too late." Nick gripped the back of his neck and massaged his tense muscles. "Maybe a female's perspective is exactly what I need."

"I haven't seen you this distraught over a woman in a long time." Holly grabbed a pillow from the sofa and hugged it to her chest, a hint of a smile lighting her face. "I'm all ears."

Nick explained the situation as delicately as he could, layering the details so Holly could get the full picture. He kept checking the stairwell to make sure Jacob was out of earshot.

"What a mess." Holly tucked her legs beneath her. "What are the odds that your old friend would be Jacob's birthfather?"

"Yeah, I know."

"And wanted as an accessory to murder? It's overwhelming."

"I don't know if Jessica will ever trust me again."

"But you called the police. Shouldn't that count for something?"

"Yeah, but I gave them her name and she didn't like that."

"You know Jessica should be coming back any minute. Until you find Andrew and get Jacob's bear back, maybe you shouldn't be here when she arrives."

"I've searched everywhere. I'm running out of options."

"Do you think he might show up at your house again?"

"It's a possibility."

"Nick, much of what is going on is out of your control. You've done all you can. Maybe you should let God take care of the rest."

He'd already considered Holly's suggestion and had prayed about it in the wee hours of the morning, but he didn't have peace just sitting in his house and doing nothing. If he could make things right between Jessica and A.J. before A.J. was arrested and help his childhood friend come back to his faith, then maybe they could all move on with their lives—Nick included.

Holly continued. "You've tried to arrange a meeting between Jessica and Jacob's birthfather, you've called the police, and have searched for Andrew. I think you've gone beyond the call of duty." Holly's words were nice to hear, and yet it didn't change the situation. Jessica was angry with him, and A.J. was at large. *Lord, what do you want me to do?*

Do not be anxious about anything, but in every situation, by prayer and petition, with thanksgiving, present your requests to God. The words of Philippians 4:6 came to mind. He had prayed, but his anxiety remained. And from what he'd learned from a recent message at church, worry was a sin. "You know, you're right. It's time for me to let go. But before I do, will you do me a favor?"

"Name it."

"Would you mind keeping an eye on Jessica and her family? I feel responsible for kicking them to the curb, so to speak."

"Nick, it was Jessica's choice to leave. But yes, they can stay here as long as they need to."

"Thanks. I feel much better knowing they have a roof over their heads. A.J. will never find them here. Now I better go before Jessica comes back."

"Good idea." Holly walked Nick to the door.

"I'd like to say goodbye to the kids."

"Sarah, Ryan, Jacob," Holly called. "Nick's leaving."

The three practically tackled him to the floor, questions flying through the air as to why he had to go.

A car engine sounded outside. *Was it Jessica?*

Until he had the stuffed bear or Andrew was in jail, he'd rather not have a confrontation with her. Nick slipped out the back door, and rounded the corner of the yard. "What are *you* doing here?" Panic laced Nick's voice.

35

Jessica debated whether or not to tell her uncle they were headed to Evelyn's beach rental, but decided it was best to prepare him. "I promise we'll leave if you feel uncomfortable, but I hope you give Evelyn a chance. Did you see the way she looked at you? And I could tell she was hurt when you turned away."

"She was hurt? That's nothing compared to what she did to me all those years ago," said George.

"What happened to 'in all things God works for the good'?" Jessica hated to throw his words back at him, but wasn't he the one who defended Evelyn when they were watching the surfers at Steamer Lane? "It might be good for you to meet her husband and move on. And if she's single . . ." Jessica let her uncle fill in the blanks.

George let out a deep breath. "Now who's giving advice?"

"Hey, I learned from the best." Jessica smiled. "You've given me enough wise counsel to last a lifetime. Thought I'd share a thing or two." She stopped at a light and glanced at George.

The corners of his lips turned up. "Evelyn has aged well, don't you think?"

"She's adorable. I bet she was a real cutie when she was young." The light turned green and Jessica stepped on the accelerator.

"She was. Even now I'd be able to pick her out of a crowd." George tapped his fingers on his thighs. Must be anxious.

Jessica turned left on Mission Street. "Why didn't you talk with her earlier? I would've walked away and given you space."

"Didn't want her to see me in a wheelchair."

Jessica's suspicion was correct. "Uncle George! Remember what you told me when I didn't want to go to cousin Vicki's wedding seven months pregnant?"

"Using my words again, are you?" George stared straight ahead.

Jessica had him exactly where she wanted him. "When pride comes, then comes disgrace, but with humility comes wisdom—"

"I knew that was coming." George laughed.

Jessica joined him. The air coming through the window blew a lock of hair across her face and she tucked it behind her ear. "Evelyn seemed genuinely concerned about you. Said she'd been looking for you—and that has to count for something."

"You know what? It does." George agreed.

"That's the spirit." Jessica softened her tone. "Are you nervous?"

"A little. Never thought I'd ever see her again."

"Do you know what you want to say?"

"I have no idea. Think I'll let Evelyn do the talking," George said over the soft tunes coming from the radio. "Now it's your turn. You ought to give love a chance. Seems to me Nick genuinely cares for *you*."

George was doing it again. He'd turned the tables on her at Steamer Lane and now when the heat was on him. She didn't want to focus on what had happened between her and Nick. She'd blown it and overreacted. He'd only been trying to help. She owed him an apology, but didn't know where to begin. Maybe she'd be ready to face him in say, *forty years* like George and Evelyn. "Okay, I admit we did have a connection, but that's all it was. Nothing more. Nick and I have only known each other a week. There's no comparison between our relationship and you and Evelyn."

"I'm not comparing. Only making an observation." Her uncle's fatherly tone was like an embrace. As much as she appreciated him stepping into that role, now was not the time to figure things out between her and Nick.

According to her GPS, they were almost to Evelyn's vacation house. A nervous flutter danced in Jessica's stomach. It must be surreal for her uncle to be finally having a chance to speak with Evelyn again after all these years.

Jessica pulled to a stop in the bungalow's driveway. She looked at her uncle. "Ready?"

George's brows knit together. "Wish I had my prosthesis, but the crutches will do."

The admission brought a smile to Jessica's face. "I don't think it will matter to Evelyn."

His features relaxed. "You're probably right."

A couple minutes later they stood on the front stoop, anticipation bubbling inside. A woman answered the door, but it wasn't Evelyn.

"Can I help you?" She looked at Jessica, then her eyes moved to George. Her eyes widened. "George MacAllister?"

"Yes." George blinked. "Patty?"

"It's good to see you." She stepped forward and grabbed George in a tight embrace. "Wait till Ronald finds out we've finally connected." Her face sobered. "Oh, no. You just missed

Evelyn. She didn't think you'd come and is on her way home to San Francisco."

George swayed and Jessica steadied him. It was as if history was repeating itself. *Poor Uncle George.* How much could one man take?

———

Evelyn had made it up the coast to Davenport when she realized she'd forgotten to grab her towels and linens from the beach house. She had a full cabinet at home and could always call Patty and ask her to bring them when they met for lunch, but something inside made her turn around.

Now as she inched closer, she questioned her decision to leave in the first place. She'd made it out of fear instead of thinking it through rationally. Once the tears dried, she realized she wasn't quite ready to end her vacation. She'd planned to be gone at least two weeks and it felt good to get away from her daily routine.

And there was still a chance George might come and she didn't want to miss the opportunity to see him again and ask forgiveness.

What would she tell Patty? That she changed her mind? Hopefully her friend hadn't already called Ronald and made plans. But knowing Patty as she did, she'd understand completely and was probably waiting for her return at this very moment.

Evelyn's cell phone trilled. She glanced at the screen. Patty's ears must've been burning. Evelyn smiled. She fumbled through the glove compartment for her headset while trying to keep her eyes on the road. It wasn't there. After the fourth ring, the call disconnected. Wouldn't Patty be surprised when she showed up at the door?

"She's not picking up. I'm sorry. Are you sure you don't want me to leave a message and tell her you're here?" Patty handed George a glass of iced tea.

"No, that's all right." Lines etched George's forehead.

"Might be a good idea." Jessica hated the thought that her uncle wouldn't be able to finally put the past to rest. "Evelyn and her husband probably haven't gotten far."

"Husband? Edward died a year ago. This was Evelyn's first vacation on her own since his death—but she was ready. In fact, Ronald and I set her up on a blind date while she was here." Patty covered her mouth with a hand to hide her grin. "It didn't work. The next day all she talked about was finding you. We asked around and drove by your manufactured home. No one was home and the place looked like a storage locker. That neighbor of yours, Doris, is quite the character. She didn't know what happened to you and was concerned as well."

"Sold my unit a while back to some guy that saw my listing in the newspaper. Sad to think he's not taking care of the place. I should stop by and let Doris know I'm all right." George sipped his iced tea. "You say Evelyn's been talking about me?"

Jessica knew the thought pleased her uncle by the grin he was trying to hide.

"We've reminisced about old times and Evelyn shared how she hoped to make new memories. She really wanted to see you again. I saw the pain in her eyes when she told me she broke your heart."

It touched Jessica to know Evelyn cared for her uncle and wanted to make sure he was all right.

"Did she have a good marriage?" asked George.

"Yes, she did." Patty's face brightened. "She has a daughter and new grandbaby. And her son-in-law is wonderful, too."

"That's nice." George's tone was wistful.

Was he wondering what life would've been like if he'd married Evelyn? Jessica tapped his knee. "Tell Patty about your work in the Philippines."

"Doris told us that you'd bring her gifts—"

A knock sounded on the front door interrupting their conversation.

"Let me get that. I'll only be a minute." Patty moved to the entryway and squealed when she answered the door. "You came back!"

"I forgot my towels and linens. But truth is I wanted to wait for George." Evelyn's voice floated into the room.

"Come," said Patty. "He's here."

"Right now?" Evelyn's voice rose.

"Yes, right now." Jessica could see Patty gesturing, welcoming her in.

A grin spread across George's face. Jessica's as well. She had a feeling this reunion would be much different than the one along the path of West Cliff Drive.

Evelyn stepped inside, her movements slow and tentative.

"Go on. He won't bite." Jessica heard Patty's hushed tone and she glanced at George to see if he'd heard. It didn't seem to matter. George's eyes were glued on Evelyn and his face spoke volumes. He was still in love with his young sweetheart.

A blush colored Evelyn's cheeks and George cleared his throat.

Jessica gestured for Evelyn to take her place beside George on the couch.

Patty grabbed her purse from the counter. "I'll catch up with you two later." She motioned for Evelyn to call her and left.

"Uncle George, I'm going to Holly's to check on Jacob. I'll be back in a bit." As much as she wanted to watch the scene unfold, she respected her uncle too much to invade on his reunion with Evelyn. Lingering by the door, Jessica stole one more glance. The pair only had eyes for each other.

Evelyn took George's right hand between her own. "George, please forgive me for hurting you the way I did—"

"Eva, I forgave you a long time ago, but I've never been able to forget you." George reached up with his free hand and touched her cheek.

Jessica took her cue and slipped out the door. Was forgiving that simple? She didn't know if she could let go of the hurt so easily. She hadn't forgiven Andrew throughout the years and she certainly didn't give Nick a chance. The men had opposite personalities and values, and yet she'd lumped them together as if they were one and the same. Her heart now told her differently. Like her uncle, Nick was a good man—a man of character who'd only been trying to help her. Why had she questioned whether or not to trust him?

36

Nick would've been happy to see A.J. if it were any place other than the Branson's home with Jacob in such close proximity. He gritted his teeth. "How'd you know where to find me?"

"Wasn't hard. Followed you from River's house."

Nick pulled him over to the side of the garage where no one could see them. He had to get A.J. away from Jacob. "Let's go back to my place and talk this out—"

"No, I'm not waiting around anymore." He shrugged his arm away from Nick's grasp. "Either you're going in there and grabbing the boy or I'll do it myself." The man sounded crazed.

"Jacob's not here." Nick didn't like to lie, but under the circumstances, he didn't see any other way. He wasn't about to put the boy at risk.

"I don't believe you. I saw two boys Jacob's age through the window. One of them reminded me of the picture I saw at Jessica's apartment."

He knew what Jacob looked like? Nick's gut twisted.

A.J. made a move toward the back door.

Nick's senses heightened and he saw A.J. for the kind of man he was. Low. Selfish. Deceitful. He was capable of anything and Nick needed to play it smart. *God, please help me.* "Stop! You don't want to be reckless. Use your head."

A.J. turned to face Nick and pressed his thumb to his chest. "I say we do things my way from now on."

"You don't get it." Nick threw up his hands. "Do you want Jacob to hate you for taking him away from his mother, or do you want him to have an ounce of respect for you for doing what's right?"

"The police will find me if I stay in Santa Cruz, but if I snag Jacob now I'll have a better chance of getting away." Was A.J. high on something? He had definitely changed his tune.

"What happened to meeting Jacob and giving yourself up?"

A.J. stepped back, a cynical laugh escaping his lips. "You believed that nonsense?"

"It's better than accepting you've turned away from God and everything you've believed in since you were a kid."

"Whoa. Now you're getting religious on me—"

"A.J., please. Think it through. What you're about to do is wrong." A new thought zigzagged through Nick's mind. Maybe it was best to spell out the truth. "If you want to take the cowardly route, that's your decision. But if you want a relationship with Jacob, you're going to need to take the high road. Let me help you."

A.J. eyed him. "Are you messing with me?"

Nick shook his head. "I wouldn't do that."

"You got a plan?"

Plan? No, Nick didn't know what to do, but he'd learned from the last time to involve the police as soon as possible. "First, we get out of here. I don't want anyone to see us." Nick gestured for A.J. to go through the side gate near the driveway, but tugged on his sweatshirt when he saw Jessica going up the walk to the front door.

Nick held fast and whispered in A.J.'s ear. "Hold on. Wait till she's in the house." When Jessica stepped inside, Nick nudged him toward the street and his car. A.J. wasn't going to get away this time.

⸏⸎⸏

"Mom, we saw Nick." Jacob wrapped his arms around Jessica's middle, his cast hard against her back.

"Nick was here?" Her breath caught in her throat. "Was he looking for me?"

"No. He wanted to talk to Ryan's dad."

Disappointment flooded her. How could she have been so blind? Nick had been caring and kind, tender even, and she'd pushed him away. She let her anger toward Andrew get in the way of what could have been a meaningful relationship. With all that had happened between helping her uncle and running from Andrew, she'd stuffed down her feelings for the one man who'd not only given up his desire to tear down the cabin, but also put himself on the line for her.

Nick could be the man God intended for me.

"How long ago did he leave?" Jessica rushed toward the window and looked out.

"I don't know, I can't tell time." Jacob shrugged a shoulder, then ran up the stairs to Ryan's room.

"Jessica, is that you?" Holly called from the kitchen.

"Yeah, I'm back. Sorry it took me so long. George and I walked along West Cliff Drive and bumped into George's old girlfriend from long ago. We stopped by the apartment, and then I brought George to Evelyn's vacation rental." Jessica removed her sweater and hung it on the coat rack. "Oh, speaking of the apartment, it will be fine for my uncle once they clean it, but it won't be available until Monday. Do you think we could stay a little while longer?" Jessica turned toward Holly and her stomach clenched. "Holly, what's wrong?"

"You can't stay here." Holly's eyes were filled with fear.

"Please tell me what's going on."

"I hope you don't mind, but Nick told me about Andrew and the reason you left the cabin."

"I would've told you myself, but—"

"Please, don't feel like you owe me anything. I'm only telling you this because of what I just heard."

"What are you saying?"

"After Nick left I went outside to water the plants and I heard Nick talking to someone. I stayed close to the house and out of view to listen. It didn't take long to figure out it was Andrew. He said he was going to take Jacob." Holly's voice shook. "But Nick convinced him he had a plan. Said if he ever wanted a relationship with Jacob, he'd need to think things through."

Jessica's face paled. Had she let Andrew's hunt for Jacob go so long that he'd consider taking her son? "Until recently, Andrew's never wanted to be part of Jacob's life, but now that the police are going to arrest him, he's desperate."

Holly pressed her lips together and shook her head. "I don't think Andrew expected Nick to come out the back way."

"Thank God!" Jessica clutched her chest. "Why didn't Nick leave through the front door?"

"Because he didn't want to run into you. He couldn't face you. His decision was partly my suggestion, too. I've never seen him so heartbroken. What can I say, I'm protective of those I care about."

Jessica remembered something Aaron had said about Holly's personality being like a tiger.

"I've taken out my fears of my unstable childhood on Nick—and Andrew, for that matter. I've been running from relationships for so long that I couldn't see a good thing when it was right in front of me. And now it's too late."

"Nick wants you to trust him more than anything. I haven't seen him go out on a limb like this for a woman in a long time. He cares about you—and Jacob."

If Jessica was honest with herself, Nick had become more than a friend, he was her hero—a man who risked everything to help her move on with her life. Time to believe God had good things in store for her and her son.

Jessica's cell phone dinged signaling a text message. She pulled it from her pocket and glanced at the screen. *Get Jacob out of Holly's house and wait for my call. Nick.*

She was ready to follow Nick's lead. She typed a quick response, and then tucked her phone in her pocket. "I'm taking the next step and trusting God—and Nick. Jacob and I need to go."

Holly's shoulders relaxed. "Sounds like a plan."

Jessica pulled Holly into a quick embrace. "Thank you for letting us stay, but most of all for your friendship. I hope we'll remain friends for a long time."

"Me, too." Holly smiled.

"Now to separate our boys."

"It won't be easy."

Jessica followed Holly up the stairs to Ryan's room. Sarah and the boys were sprawled out on the floor playing with Legos, each building their own creation.

"Jacob, time to go," said Jessica.

Jacob's tongue was poking out in concentration. "Go where?"

Jessica leaned down and scooped up a handful of Legos and dropped them into the bucket. "Let's talk about it in the car. We haven't had a mommy and son date this whole week."

Suddenly, a sense of urgency rushed through her. If Andrew got away from Nick, he'd know exactly where to find them.

Trust, Jessica. It was as if God was speaking directly to her.

"Ryan and Sarah, help Jacob clean up," said Holly. "We have a couple of errands to run before Daddy comes home tomorrow." The kids obeyed without complaining and a few minutes later the floor was clean.

Jessica held Jacob's hand as they descended the stairs. "We'll need to grab our luggage and put it in the car."

"We're not coming back?" Jacob's brows puckered.

"We will before we go home to Fresno, but we won't be staying here tonight."

"Where will we sleep?" asked Jacob.

"I'm not sure yet." Jessica had an idea, but she needed to run it by Evelyn first. Sarah, Ryan, and Holly climbed down the stairs behind them.

"Mom, who was that man leaving with Nick?" asked Ryan. "I've never seen him before."

Jessica strained her ear to listen.

"What do you mean?" Holly darted the question.

"I saw them out my window."

Soon the time would come when Jessica would need to answer Jacob's tough questions about his birthfather. But she'd rather wait until she had time to think through what she wanted to say. For now, she'd take one minute at a time and enjoy her little boy and their relationship, as she knew it.

Ten minutes later, Jessica and Jacob said goodbye and climbed into her Honda Civic. The sun shone bright through the car window. "Want some ice cream?" Thoughts of carefree days drifted through her mind, but today she'd keep her cell phone close waiting for Nick's call.

Relief swept through Nick when he read Jessica's response. She was ready to do what was needed to get Andrew behind bars—including having him meet his son. If Nick's plan worked, A.J. would be in police custody within the hour.

Once home, Nick had suggested A.J. shower and shave so that he didn't scare Jacob. He was glad A.J. agreed and heard the running water. While he had a few minutes to himself, he pulled Officer Timothy O'Leary's business card from his wallet and punched the numbers into his cell phone. Nick wanted him to be privy to his plan without giving too much away—at least not yet.

"O'Leary here."

"This is Nick Fuller." Beads of sweat dotted his forehead. He wished A.J. had turned himself in to the police days ago and that it didn't have to come to this.

"Yes, Nick. What's the word?"

"I found Andrew Lawson, or rather he found me."

"That's great news." A scraping sound screeched in Nick's ear. Nick pictured Officer O'Leary jumping up from his chair. "Tell me his location and we'll come get him."

As much as he wanted to tell the officer they were at his house, the place where O'Leary had been less than twenty-four hours ago, Nick couldn't. "We don't plan on being here long, but I'll call you with our whereabouts as soon as possible."

"Be careful. For all you know, he could be armed."

His childhood friend was a drug addict and a womanizer, but Nick couldn't imagine him handling a weapon. Then again, he didn't think he'd consider kidnapping Jacob either. "I've known A.J. since we were kids—"

"All the more reason to watch yourself. He'll take advantage of you. Leave this to the police and stay put. Where are you?"

The shower continued to run behind the bathroom door. "I'll call you back once we're settled."

He disconnected the call, tucked his cell phone in his pocket, and paced the room until he heard the water stop.

37

Waiting for Nick's call had Jessica on edge. Her insides jittered as she stood at the counter of Marianne's ice cream shop, staring at the list of flavors. She leaned toward Jacob when it was her turn to order. "What kind would you like?"

"Bubblegum."

She wished she could make a decision that easily. "You sure?"

"Uh-huh." Jacob licked his lips and bounced up and down.

Jessica fished her wallet out of her purse and directed her words at the teenage girl behind the counter. "Two sugar cones, please. One with bubblegum, the other . . . chocolate." Her choice was solely an emotional decision. Chocolate calmed her nerves.

"One scoop or two?"

"Two, Mom." Jacob grinned, his puppy-dog eyes pleading.

Jessica shook her head. "Sorry, buddy. One scoop's enough."

The worker finished preparing their ice cream and rang up the order. Jessica and Jacob moved to the other side of the shop and chose a seat by the window.

She studied Jacob as he licked his cone. Ice cream surrounded his mouth and he hummed between bites, something she caught herself doing every now and then. He had manner-isms like hers, and yet there were times when his words and actions were foreign. Jacob was a smart boy, a good kid—and half Andrew's DNA.

Stepping into marriage because of the pregnancy would've been wrong and would've ended in disaster, but she hadn't given Andrew the chance to express regret for walking away. If she were honest with herself, she'd enjoyed keeping Jacob from Andrew this past week, hoping Andrew would realize his past mistakes and apologize for leaving her to raise their son alone.

Until today she'd never considered allowing Jacob to meet his father. Andrew had been out of their lives for so long and she'd come to terms with being a single parent. But he did want to see his son and was it her place to deny him? Jacob was his flesh and blood, and as long as they met in a controlled environment with Nick by her side, she was willing to allow Andrew the opportunity before he went to jail.

"Mommy, your cone is dripping." Jacob pointed, interrupt-ing her thoughts.

Like the ice cream, her once hardened heart was slowly beginning to soften. Jessica turned it around and licked the side. "Thanks, bud."

Her cell phone vibrated in her pocket, sending her pulse racing. She dug it out and glanced at the screen. She didn't recognize the number, but she answered it in case it was Nick.

"Jessi, everything all right? Thought you'd be back by now." George voiced his concern like an overprotective father.

"Jacob and I are spending some time together. We're at Marianne's. Do you need me to swing by?" If the soft jazz music playing in the background was any indication, it sounded as if Evelyn and her uncle were enjoying each other's company.

"No, no. Have fun with Jacob. Eva and I have some catching up to do. She's offered to make me dinner."

Jessica smiled at the lilt in George's voice. "Sounds romantic."

Jacob bit off the tip of his cone and sucked the ice cream out of the bottom.

"Why don't you give Nick a call? I'm sure he'd be willing to hang out with you and Jacob for a few hours. You might want to open up and let him know how you feel." Her uncle was anything but subtle. This was his third hint in less than twenty-four hours. Sixty minutes with Evelyn and suddenly he was the authority on love.

"Don't worry about Jacob and me. We'll grab some fish and chips somewhere." Jessica wouldn't dream of barging in on George and Evelyn's time together, but at some point she needed to ask Evelyn if the three of them could spend the night.

"Nick's got to eat. Call him." George's tone was adamant.

"Don't worry, Uncle George. Nick is a special guy and I won't let him get away." The idea sent chills down her spine. She considered telling her uncle about Nick's text, but decided against it. Uncle George didn't need to worry about what was going on in her life right now when he'd only just discovered love of his own.

"Good girl." George sounded pleased with her statement. "What was that?" His voice took on a distant tone. "Oh, wait . . . Eva says to swing by later for dessert. Says she has a special treat."

"What time?" Two desserts in one day? She'd have to get back to her running routine when she returned home.

"Between seven-thirty and eight."

"Okay, Uncle George. See you then." Jessica put her phone into her jeans pocket.

"Hey Mom, is that Nick's car?" Jacob gestured.

Her heart hammered in her chest and she glanced out the window. The Jeep was similar to Nick's, but definitely wasn't his. "No, honey. That's someone else's car." She popped the remainder of the cone into her mouth as her heart rate returned to normal.

Jacob licked his sticky fingers. "When are we going to see him?"

First her uncle, and now Jacob. She handed him a napkin. "I'm waiting for his call right now." The words slipped out before she had a chance to think it through.

"Yes!" Jacob pumped his fist.

As much as her insides danced knowing she'd see Nick again, she dreaded the upcoming meeting with Andrew, but it was too late to back out now.

"I recall you being a good dancer. Remember Patty and Ronald's wedding at the Cocoanut Grove?" Evelyn stood and swayed to the music.

"That was a long time ago," said George. "And I had two feet to stand on."

"Have you ever thought about a prosthetic? With your balance, I'm sure you'd be quite adept. And we could dance again." She winked.

Suddenly George's demeanor changed. Lines etched his forehead. Had she said something wrong? She stopped moving and sat beside George on the sofa. "Of course, I'm not as agile as I once was."

"Eva, from what I can see you're still light on your feet. Did you and Edward dance much?"

The question surprised her. Did he really want to know about her husband or was he making small talk? "We danced on occasion, but most of the time Edward worked long hours. We'd meet at functions, but once Amy came along, I was busy with my daughter."

"Patty told me you were a grandmother."

"Yes, can you believe it? Isabella's not quite four months old. It took Amy and Daniel years to conceive and now my poor daughter is suffering from postpartum depression. She called me this afternoon and told me she made an appointment to see her doctor. I'm glad she's getting the help she needs. If it's not one struggle, it's another."

"I understand. I thought my life was over when I became ill. My hearing isn't good in my right ear, and the lower part of my leg had to be amputated after gangrene set in. If it weren't for my niece and her boy, I don't know where I'd be—maybe living on the streets."

"You would've figured it out. The George MacAllister I remember doesn't let anything get in the way of his passion. You were a missionary for all these years, exactly like you said you'd be."

"Except you."

"Pardon?"

"I didn't fight for you." George clenched his fists. "Instead I expected you to put aside who you are for me."

"We were from two different worlds—"

"Still are."

"Maybe so, but I'm willing to see if we can bridge that gap. I suspect we're going to find we're not so diverse after all. I still enjoy bonfires, walks along the ocean, and Marianne's ice cream."

"And dancing?" George wrung his hands together.

"Yes, and dancing. But let's take it one step at a time." Evelyn smiled.

George's shoulders relaxed. "You don't mind hanging out with an older version of the man you used to know? A disabled one at that?"

"I don't mind at all. In fact, I'm thrilled. God called me to Santa Cruz for a vacation and He gave me you. I'm a fortunate woman."

George beamed. "You have a way with words, Eva."

A smile curved her lips. "Now, before I make you the best mango pork tenderloin you've ever tasted, I want to hear all about your missionary work. And don't leave out any details."

He reached over and gently took her hand in his. "As much as I want to tell you all about my life's work as a missionary, I'd like to look at you for a while. I can't believe God brought you back into my life."

Evelyn squeezed George's warm hand. "This time I'm staying right by your side."

After calling Jessica, Nick locked the front door to the house and he and A.J. climbed into his Jeep. "If this is going to work you need to promise me you won't do anything crazy." After the stunt A.J. tried to pull at Holly's house, Nick hoped he wasn't wasting his breath. Jacob and Jessica's safety was most important.

A.J. shot him a look. "Okay, okay. You don't need to treat me like a child."

"Don't I? Since when have you turned from your faith and into some kind of monster—someone who'd consider kidnapping his own son after not being part of his life?" Nick knew he was being harsh, but he had to get through to A.J. in order to wake him up to what he'd professed years ago. "I see your pain, but don't take it out on Jessica and Jacob, the two people whose forgiveness you need most of all." Nick softened his tone and started the engine.

A.J. ran his hand through his hair and looked out the side window. "Like that's ever going to happen."

"You'd be surprised. All things are possible when we put God first in our lives." Nick truly believed that statement and attempted to live by the motto, contrary to what others would say was a hero complex. But before this moment he thought he needed to prove himself, to work for God's approval, but now he understood God's grace and his desire to live for Him. Warmth filled his spirit.

A.J. expelled a weary breath. "Are you quoting Scripture at me?"

"No, but I can if you'd like." Nick smiled.

"Save it for someone else." A.J. toyed with the bow around the stuffed bear's neck. "Did you know I'm the one who bought Jacob this bear?"

Nick backed out of his driveway and pulled onto the bumpy road. "Is that right?"

"I left it along with the relinquishment papers. Some father I am."

"We all make mistakes. Trust takes a long time to build, but like I said, it's not impossible."

"Jessica will never trust me. She barely speaks to me." A.J. slunk down in the seat. "I've not only cut off my relationship with Jacob, but I provided the drugs that snuffed out my girl-friend and unborn child's life. There's no hope for me."

"There's always hope." Nick maneuvered his car toward the beach. "Remember all those Bible stories we heard as kids? Take David and Bathsheba. He was a man after God's own heart and he not only took another man's wife and got her pregnant, but also put her husband on the front lines during battle and had him killed. On top of that, the baby died because of what he'd done."

"I can relate." A.J. agreed.

"The difference between you and David is that he admitted his sin and turned back to God. I've been hoping and praying you'd do the same." What else could Nick say?

They rode the rest of the way to the meeting destination in silence.

38

Jessica sat on a towel at Cowell's Beach, looking over her shoulder every once in a while for Nick and Andrew to show up at the agreed meeting spot. Would she see them coming? Most likely, Jacob would be the first to spot them. He poured a shovelful of sand on the pile he was making a few yards away.

People were scattered across the beach, some wearing bathing suits, others in shorts and T-shirts, playing in the sand, relaxing, or having a picnic. Surfers rode long boards or were teaching others how to surf. A seagull flew overhead and landed not far from her, picking up a stray piece of debris left from previous beach goers.

"Do I have to wear this over my cast?" Jacob pointed to the plastic covering she'd purchased.

"Yes, honey." Jessica nodded. "It'll keep it dry and protect your arm."

"Nick is coming, right? He'll be able to fill the bucket with water."

"Yes. I'm sure Nick would be happy to do that for you." Jessica left out the fact that Andrew was coming, too. Nick had called immediately after she'd talked with George. When she'd sent Jacob to throw away their napkins at Marianne's she told

Nick she'd rather have him introduce Andrew as his friend and leave it at that.

Jacob returned to digging and Jessica leaned back, tilting her face toward the sun and allowing the warmth to penetrate deep into her soul. She thought about what she'd say to Andrew and still her mind was blank. What do you say to someone who seemed like a distant memory only to be forced back into your life? George had never stopped adoring Evelyn, a love Jessica and Andrew never had, but from her uncle's example she'd forgive and move on.

Wrapping her arms around bent knees, she pressed her toes into the sand. In the distance two male forms approached, one familiar with his muscular frame and sandy-colored hair, the other taller and thinner, wearing a red baseball cap and carrying something small and brown in his hands. *Jacob's bear.* Jessica sucked in a breath and let it out slowly. The time had come to see Andrew face-to-face.

Automatically, she straightened her posture and ran a hand through her hair, then reached into her purse and pulled out her lip gloss, as if it mattered at a time like this.

Jacob continued to play as if it was an ordinary day on vacation. She'd wait for the men to greet them and wouldn't draw Jacob's attention down the beach, but his head tipped up in the direction she'd been looking, and a grin spread across his face. He jumped up and pointed. "Mom, look! Nick is coming. And the man with him has my bear!"

"Yes, I see. He must have found it at Nick's house." Jessica swallowed the lump in her throat. She wasn't surprised Andrew had taken the bear and wouldn't hold it against him. In his mind, the stuffed animal was probably the second best thing to seeing his son in person.

Jacob waved his arms and jumped up and down. "Over here, Nick."

"I think he sees us."

"But I want to make sure." Jacob took off down the beach.

"Wait, no!" Jessica's voice disappeared with Jacob's retreating back.

———

Nick had planned to call Officer Timothy O'Leary the moment he pulled to a stop in the Cowell's Beach parking lot, but something held him back. Now as he and A.J. shuffled through the sand toward Jessica, he knew the reason—Jacob. Nick wanted to give A.J. as much time with the boy as possible before calling the police.

"He's running toward us."

The tenderness in A.J.'s voice soothed Nick's fear and confirmed his decision. "Jacob must've seen the bear. He's partial to it. Sleeps with it every night." He shaded his eyes to get a glimpse of Jacob racing toward them.

"Really?"

"Yes. Jessica came back looking for it after you'd left. Said Jacob was crying for his bear."

"Nick!" Jacob ran to him with a grin, his words coming out in a rush. "My mom said you'd be here. Want to build a sand castle with me? She won't let me get a bucket of water because of my cast, but you can."

"Slow down, partner." Nick bent down and rested his hands on the child's small shoulders. "I want to introduce you to my friend. Maybe he could help us build the sandcastle, too."

Jacob looked up at A.J. "Do you want to? Teddy could be the king of the castle."

"Hi Jacob, I'm Andrew. But my close friends call me A.J." He handed the stuffed animal to him.

"Where did you find him? Mom said she looked everywhere." Jacob clutched the bear to his chest.

"A.J. found him in the cabin," said Nick.

"He was hiding between the blanket and the sheet." A.J. adjusted his cap and tucked his trembling fingers into his jeans pockets, his nerves showing.

"Thanks." Jacob looked at A.J., took hold of Nick's hand, and tugged him forward. "Nick, come see the big pile of sand I made."

Nick ruffled the boy's hair. "You got it." He glanced at A.J. His smile had faded and lines formed between his brows. Was he jealous of his and Jacob's relationship? He would be if their roles were reversed.

With Jacob sandwiched between the men, the three walked the remaining distance to where Jessica kept watch on her beach towel. She would give anything to have been a fly on Nick's shoulder listening to the exchange of words that had just taken place. From her vantage point, Jacob didn't appear to be distraught in any way. Andrew must not have told him he was his father. Good. There'd come a time for that, but today was too soon.

Jacob gestured to the spot he'd been digging.

Nick leaned over and whispered something in his ear, then directed him toward the pile of sand.

Jacob nodded, gave her a small wave, and bounded to his sand toys. Andrew moved the few paces to Jessica's side.

"Nice to see you again, Jessica." Andrew lowered his head and drew lines in the sand with his foot, then looked up meeting her eyes. "Jacob is a nice little boy. You should be proud." His eyes were bloodshot. Was he on drugs now?

Her heart went out to him and she hoped he'd get the help he needed to turn his life around. "Thank you. It means a lot to hear you say that." Jessica hated the way her voice shook. "I'm sorry for keeping Jacob away from you. If I'd known you only wanted to meet him and not pursue custody—"

"Jessica, I've made some huge mistakes in my life—one of them was relinquishing my rights as Jacob's father." Andrew ran his hand through his hair. "I didn't mean to scare you, but if I told you the police were searching for me you never would've let me come close to Jacob."

"That night between us *was* a mistake and I take responsibility for my actions. But I have a beautiful little boy."

Andrew dug his hands in his jeans pockets. "Mind if I build a sandcastle with Jacob? I won't let on I'm his father."

As much as she wanted to believe him, a part of her didn't trust that he'd keep his word. Nick on the other hand had proven himself over and over again. "I don't know . . ." She hesitated. "As long as Nick's close by—"

"He's a good guy. I've known Nick since we were kids. It's clear that Jacob looks up to him. If I could choose a man to help raise my son, it would be Nick."

"Are you two talking about me? Did I hear my name?"

"Only saying good things." Andrew clapped Nick on the back and leaned in. "I'll leave you two alone while I hang out with Jacob. Don't worry. No funny stuff."

"We're counting on it." Nick's tone was firm.

Andrew walked the few yards to Jacob and sat down beside him. His back faced them and Jessica couldn't tell if he was talking to Jacob or not. A knot formed in the pit of her stomach remembering what Holly had told her. *Nick said Andrew was going to take Jacob.* He wouldn't dare grab her son at a crowded beach, would he?

"I'm not comfortable with this," Jessica whispered. "Are you going to call the police or shall I?"

"I alerted them a short time ago and told them I'd let them know of our location. I prayed the whole way here that A.J. would be the one to turn himself in."

"Do you really think he'd do that?"

"I don't know. Deep down he's loyal and I know he wants to make things right. I'm hoping a few minutes with Jacob will help him make that decision."

"How long should we give him?" Jessica fidgeted with the edge of the towel.

"As long as you want. Say the word and I'll make the call."

"Maybe I should join them—"

Nick grabbed her arm. "Give them some time alone."

"But I don't know what A.J. is telling him. What if—"

"They're only playing. Look."

Jacob set his bear on top of the sand pile and carved a path around it. He handed Andrew the bucket and pointed to the water. Andrew walked the few steps to the water's edge, dipped the bucket in the ocean when the tide rose, and poured it into Jacob's makeshift moat. He repeated the process until the water flowed over the sides. Jacob laughed and gave Andrew a high five. Her son was enjoying himself and she found herself relaxing.

Jessica never thought she'd see the day when Jacob and Andrew played together and yet that day was here. She couldn't describe the emotions warring inside, but in her heart she knew it was okay.

Nick took hold of her hand. "I'm proud of you."

"What for?"

"Putting aside your fears and giving A.J. a chance to spend time with his boy."

"I've finally forgiven him for walking out on Jacob and me. It feels good."

"I'm glad."

"You've spent more time with my son than Andrew. Jacob adores you."

"And what about his mom?" He bumped her shoulder.

Jessica couldn't stop the smile that tugged at her mouth. "She's crazy about you, too."

Twenty minutes later, Andrew moved toward them and knelt down in the sand. "Nick, I've really been thinking about what you said in the car. I'm scared, but I can't run any longer—from the police or from God. It's time to turn myself in."

Relief flooded through Jessica and her shoulders relaxed, the weight of Andrew's words giving her hope.

"Glad to hear it. You made the right decision," said Nick. He reached into his back pocket and handed Andrew his cell and Officer O'Leary's business card. "He's expecting a call."

Andrew punched in the numbers, gave his location, and handed the phone back to Nick.

"I knew you could do it," said Nick. "As kids when you got into mischief, you'd always come clean."

"That's not how I remember it. Guess you always brought out the best in me." Andrew sat beside Jessica and turned to watch Jacob. "Thank you." His voice sounded raspy. "I'll never forget this."

Jessica sighed. "Neither will I."

A few minutes later, a police car appeared at the top of the bluff.

Andrew stood, lifted a hand and called out. "'Bye, Jacob. It's time for me to go."

"'Bye." Jacob called back, grabbing his bear and waving it in the air. "Thanks for finding Teddy for me."

Jessica's throat constricted. Someday when Jacob was old enough to understand, she'd tell him that Andrew was his father, and that they built a sandcastle together at Cowell's Beach when he was six. She'd also tell Jacob that his father was sorry for leaving him the way he did and that he loved him.

For the first time, she believed it.

Epilogue

Six months later

In front of family and friends at Steamer Lane overlooking the Pacific, Uncle George stood next to the pastor, using his prosthesis and leaning slightly on his cane while he waited for Evelyn to approach. A broad smile lit his face. Jacob, the ring-bearer, held a small white pillow with the diamond ring attached by a ribbon. With Nick by her side, Jessica watched the scene unfold, and remembered a conversation she had with her uncle a few months back.

"No, I can't take it." George had lifted a hand and shook his head. "I gave the ring to you—"

"But you offered it to Evelyn first," Jessica argued. "She should have it."

"Maybe she'd like a new one."

"You're wrong, Uncle George. She lights up every time she sees it. I want her to have this ring. And like you said, by wearing it I might be holding someone back from pursuing *me*. It's time I move on." Jessica slipped the ring off her finger and set it in the palm of George's hand.

He tightened his grip around the precious stone. "You sure you don't already have someone in mind? You've been spending a lot of time in Santa Cruz."

"That's because you live in Nick's cabin." Jessica winked.

"And I thought you've been coming nearly every weekend to visit me." He teased back.

"Sorry to disappoint you." Jessica laughed. "By the way, when are you going to pop the question?"

"Next week. Evelyn is coming with me on a short-term mission trip to the Philippines."

"I'm happy for you, Uncle George. You've finally reconnected with your one true love." Jessica sighed. "It's so romantic."

"Now don't get sappy on me." George had rolled his eyes, and then looked at the heart-shaped diamond in his hand. "But seriously, thank you for the ring, Jessi. It means a lot to me."

Evelyn walked past and stood between George and her daughter Amy, pulling Jessica from her recollection. George's bride wore a satin, floor-length dress, and had *Sampaguita*, the national flower of the Philippines, in her hair. She was simply elegant.

Nick reached for Jessica's hand as the ceremony began.

"Dearly Beloved, we are gathered here in the sight of God and in the presence of these witnesses, to join George MacAllister and Evelyn Sweeney in holy matrimony . . ."

Jessica's thoughts strayed to Andrew. He was locked up in the San Diego county jail awaiting trial. On several occasions, Jacob had asked about the guy who found his bear and whether or not they were ever going to see him again. Jessica didn't know if father and son would ever have a relationship, but the idea didn't scare her anymore. Her heart was no longer hardened toward Andrew, and she found peace about the future—whatever that may be.

Twenty minutes later while the bride and groom had their pictures taken, Jessica walked up the beach with Nick and Jacob, collecting shells and throwing rocks into the ocean.

Jacob caught up to her. "Mommy, look what Nick found. He told me to give it to you." He held out his hand. A heart-shaped stone filled his small palm.

Jessica turned her gaze toward Nick.

He smiled and pulled her close, kissing her lips and whispering the words she longed to hear. "I love you, with all my heart. And I love Jacob, too. I want you both to always be a part of my life."

Dare she hope he meant what she thought he did? Jessica's eyes widened and she sucked in a breath. "Nick, what are you saying?"

"I'd like us to become a family." While holding her hands, he bent down on one knee and continued. "Jessica MacAllister, will you marry me?"

She glanced at Jacob.

He stood beside them with a grin on his face. "Mommy, you're supposed to say 'yes.'" Leave it to her son to set her straight.

Jessica tilted her head back and laughed, then pulled Nick to his feet and wrapped her arms around his neck. "Yes, yes. A hundred times yes."

He placed his mouth against hers, gently at first before deepening the kiss. *Beloved. Cherished. Treasured.* The words swirled in her mind in Nick's embrace. She loved this man with every ounce of her being.

"Eww. Gross." Jacob covered his eyes.

"Get used to it, buddy." Nick grinned and gave her another tender kiss. "There's going to be a lot more where that came from."

Discussion Questions

1. The story begins with a surprise phone call from the absentee father of Jessica's son, Jacob. Have you ever received a phone call that took you by surprise? How did you handle it? Do you relate to Jessica's desire to run away from the situation?

2. It has taken a year for Evelyn to remove her husband's clothes from the closet after a year of grieving. When her mind takes a new direction and she thinks about her first love, how does that make her feel?

3. What was Nick's reaction to seeing his childhood friend on television? Why would he consider helping A. J.?

4. Jessica's uncle George has had a life-altering illness. He's devastated and withdrawn. Have you, or anyone you know, experienced this? How does having a relationship with God help someone cope?

5. Evelyn chooses to take a vacation even though her daughter is having a difficult time with postpartum depression. As a parent, when do you think it's okay to put your needs above your children's?

6. Jessica wears the diamond ring her uncle gave her to ward off men and keep unwanted questions at bay. Has there ever been a time in your life when you didn't want people asking you personal questions? What did you do to avoid them?

7. Nick, a fireman, blames himself for the toddler's death in the Santa Cruz Apartment fire, thinking he could've prevented it from happening. How does pride factor in? How does that shape his view of himself?

8. Jessica has a big decision to make in whether to allow Andrew, someone who had rejected her and her son, back into her life. Do you think she made the right

one? Why or why not? What would you have done in her situation?

9. What was the biggest reason Evelyn wanted to find George again? Is there someone in your life you need to search for to ask forgiveness?

10. Besides a romantic interest, Nick shows Jessica he can be trusted. How does his consistency and example help Jessica grow spiritually? Is there someone in your life who's done the same for you?

Want to learn more about author
Sherry Kyle and check out other great
fiction from Abingdon Press?

Sign up for our fiction newsletter at
www.AbingdonPress.com
to read interviews with your favorite authors, find tips
for starting a reading group, and stay posted on what
new titles are on the horizon. It's a place to connect
with other fiction readers or post a
comment about this book.

Be sure to visit Sherry online!

www.sherrykyle.com